THE FATEFUL DAY

Previous Titles in this series by Rosemary Rowe

THE GERMANICUS MOSAIC
MURDER IN THE FORUM
A PATTERN OF BLOOD
THE CHARIOTS OF CALYX
THE LEGATUS MYSTERY
THE GHOSTS OF GLEVUM
ENEMIES OF THE EMPIRE
A ROMAN RANSOM
A COIN FOR THE FERRYMAN
DEATH AT POMPEIA'S WEDDING *
REQUIEM FOR A SLAVE *
THE VESTAL VANISHES *
A WHISPERING OF SPIES *
DARK OMENS *

* *available from Severn House*

THE FATEFUL DAY

A Libertus Mystery

Rosemary Rowe

Severn House Large Print
London & New York

This first large print edition published 2015
in Great Britain and the USA by
SEVERN HOUSE PUBLISHERS LTD of
19 Cedar Road, Sutton, Surrey, England, SM2 5DA.
First world regular print edition published 2014 by
Severn House Publishers Ltd., London and New York.

British Library Cataloguing in Publication Data

Rowe, Rosemary, 1942- author.
  The fateful day. – (A Libertus mystery)
  1. Libertus (Fictitious character : Rowe)–Fiction.
  2. Romans–Great Britain–Fiction. 3. Slaves–Fiction.
  4. Great Britain–History–Roman period, 55 B.C.-449
  A.D.–Fiction. 5. Detective and mystery stories. 6. Large
  type books.
  I. Title II. Series
  823.9'2-dc23

ISBN-13: 9780727897947

Severn House Publishers support the Forest Stewardship Council™
[FSC™], the leading international forest certification organisation. All
our titles that are printed on FSC certified paper carry the FSC logo.

Typeset by Palimpsest Book Production Ltd.,
Falkirk, Stirlingshire, Scotland.
Printed and bound in Great Britain by
T J International, Padstow, Cornwall.

To Lily, both Dianas, and Violet

Foreword

The story is set in Glevum (Roman Gloucester, a prosperous 'republic' and a *colonia* for retired soldiery) during spring AD192, a time when the Empire was rocked by an almost unimaginable series of events. The cruel, capricious and half-crazed Emperor Commodus had been assassinated at the turn of the year and the soldierly and austere Helvius Pertinax – a previous governor of Britannia and the supposed friend of the fictional Marcus in this story – installed in his place to popular acclaim.

Contemporary writers give differing accounts of the new Emperor's short rule. Some – especially those who had enjoyed the flamboyant hospitality of his predecessor – describe him as mean to the point of cheeseparing; but others suggest that faced with empty coffers he was simply *a* prudent manager who eschewed excess. This is the version favoured in this tale.

Austerity did not win Pertinax popularity. In particular, he refused to pay the whacking bonuses that Commodus had always paid to the Praetorian Guard – the powerful military elite who acted as personal bodyguard to the Emperor – claiming, with truth, that there were insufficient funds remaining in the Imperial Purse. (One is irresistibly reminded of the story of the incoming treasury official in our own times, finding the note saying, 'There is no money left.')

Refusing the praetorians their bribe was dangerous: they had already engineered the downfall of earlier Emperors who had refused to pay them for their loyalty. There was an alleged attempt to oust Pertinax early on, while he was out of the city: but if there was indeed a plot, it failed. (This event is not mentioned in the narrative, as some ancient accounts don't allude to it at all, and in any case it is unlikely that rumours would have reached Britannia, since there was no execution of those responsible. It is said that Pertinax attempted to win the loyalty of the conspirators by appealing to their honour.)

Indeed, the new Emperor had a reputation for being merciful: freeing those financially ruined by his predecessor, some of whom had been sold as slaves, pardoning those exiled on some trumped-up charge who had seen their assets forfeited to finance Commodus's notorious, increasingly extravagant and lascivious lifestyle – though enemies said he charged a fee for this and so turned a small profit for himself. He even attempted to reform the currency by halting the recent decrease in precious metal in the coins.

In late March, the praetorians lost patience with all this and demanded payment. Pertinax faced them and attempted to explain that he did not have the funds. He was no orator, but (according to one contemporary account) it seemed that rational argument might win the day, until one disaffected soldier threw a spear at him – at which point all the other guards joined in and killed him on the spot. (This version of events is plausible, since the punishment for treason in the ranks was decimation of the regiment – executing one in ten of them – and this would have been a likely outcome this time, if Pertinax had lived. By killing him outright, they avoided this and gained the initiative themselves.) Pertinax – mindful of the safety of his young family – had never given his son Imperial titles or nominated him as successor, but had promoted his father-in-law to the Prefecture of Rome. Titus was therefore generally expected to succeed, especially as he undertook to pay the guard their bribe.

However (as outlined in the novel) another claimant, Didius, made his presence known, offering to pay the guard a larger sum. Titus responded with a larger offer still, and Rome was witness to the unedifying spectacle of the rivals publicly trying to outbid each other for the role of Emperor. Finally Didius made an offer which his rival could not match, and was duly proclaimed by the praetorians – an early form of military takeover. (It was not to last, however – there was genuinely no money with which to pay the guard. From the outset there were counterclaims and – as the commandant in the novel predicts – there followed a period of armed unrest which amounts to civil war, though this is outside of the scope of this story.)

This, then, is the extraordinary background to this tale. It is frankly doubtful that the news would have arrived in Glevum as quickly as the story suggests – in early spring the mountain passes are still difficult – but claims were made that news of Commodus's death had reached every part of the Empire 'within half a moon', and for the purposes of the narrative the same thing is taken to be the case here.

The Britannia to which these tidings caused such shock was the most far-flung and northerly of all Roman provinces, but still occupied by Roman legions, criss-crossed by Roman roads, subject to Roman laws, and administered by a provincial governor (indeed on the death of Pertinax, Clodius Albinus was one claimant to the Imperial throne). Latin was the language of the educated, people were adopting Roman dress and habits, and citizenship, with the precious social and legal rights which it conferred, was the aspiration of almost everyone, though – as the narrative suggests – there still were small groups of dissidents who refused to yield, especially in the forest of what is now modern Wales.

These rebellious Celtic bands were often associated with Druid practices – perhaps as an act of additional defiance against Rome, since the religion was officially proscribed. (Unlike Christianity, Druidism had been outlawed for some time, because of the cult of the severed human head, and adherence to the sect was technically a capital offence.) Stories were circulated of its gruesome practices: the sacred groves adorned with severed heads of enemies, the wicker man-shapes filled with human forms and torched, and the use of living human entrails as a divination tool. This suppression of the cult served to drive it underground and secrecy soon added myth to mystery. However, at this date, there is no record of any incidents occurring as far east as this story would suggest.

4

Glevum (modern Gloucester) was an important town. Its historic status as a colonia for retired legionaries gave it special privileges: all freemen born within its walls were citizens by right. Most inhabitants of Glevum, however, were not citizens at all. Many were freemen born outside the walls, scratching a precarious living from a trade. Hundreds more were slaves – what Aristotle once described as 'vocal tools' – mere chattels of their masters, to be bought and sold, with no more rights or status than any other domestic animal. Some slaves led pitiable lives, but others were highly regarded by their owners, and might be treated well. A slave in a kindly household, with a comfortable home, might have a more enviable lot than many a poor freeman struggling to eke out an existence in a squalid hut.

Power, of course, was vested almost entirely in men. Although individual women might inherit large estates, and many wielded considerable influence within the house, they were excluded from public office, and a woman (of any age) was deemed a child in law, while the killing of an errant or unfaithful wife – though not encouraged – was legally defensible. Marriage and motherhood were the only realistic goals for well-bred women, although tradesmen's wives and daughters often worked beside their men, and in the poorest households everybody toiled. It was, however, a superstitious age so there was a market for female soothsayers and 'wisewomen' (often skilled in herbal remedies), who, if successful, were accorded unusual respect, regarded with suspicious awe, and even – as suggested in the text – regularly consulted by the credulous.

In the same way there were important rituals surrounding any death. It was believed that if these were not properly observed, unquiet spirits might return to walk the earth – especially those of murder victims considered 'innocent'. Infants, however, were not regarded as having souls as yet, and so could be interred without remark, while slaves were often buried without any rites at all, unless the deceased had been a member of the Funeral Guild, which (for a regular subscription) would see that the proper rituals were observed – all matters integral to the narrative.

The rest of the Romano-British background to this book has been derived from a variety of (sometimes contradictory) pictorial and written sources, as well as artefacts. However, although I have done my best to create an accurate picture, this remains a work of fiction, and there is no claim to total academic authenticity. Pertinax, Didius Julianus and events in Rome are historically attested, as is the existence and basic geography of Glevum. The rest is the product of my imagination.

Relata refero. Ne Iupiter quidem omnibus placet. I only tell you what I heard. Jove himself can't please everybody.

One

Perhaps it was my own fault that I got involved in this affair. It was none of my business who was calling at my patron's country house. But since I knew that Marcus was away – gone to Rome, in fact, and likely to be gone for several moons – when I saw the expensive private carriage standing at the gate, I thought it only fair to warn the occupants. Marcus had left only a few slaves to run the place – his wife and son had moved back to the town-house in Corinium while he was gone: she was expecting a second baby soon, so it was risky to go with him, and this way she'd be closer to a midwife if need be. So, I was only trying to be helpful, or so I told myself. Of course, there were still gatekeepers and slaves to pass on this kind of news, but to be honest – given the magnificence of the equipage – I was hoping that there might be a few *quadrans* in it for my having taken the trouble to explain.

As it turned out, I could not have been more wrong. I have wished a thousand times since that I'd not happened by.

It was mere chance that I was in the area at all. It was only because I'd gone out on my newly acquired mule to look in at some additional new farm fields that my patron had bought, quite close to his existing property but further down the lane.

The land had been allowed to run down dreadfully for years – the previous owner being short of funds – but Marcus was now full of plans for it and since I'd been instrumental in the purchase of the place, he'd left me to supervise the work.

'I'll speak to the commander of the garrison and you can send me a message with the imperial post from time to time,' he told me loftily, the day before he went. 'Let me know how things are getting on. I've left orders for the land-slaves to grub up all the ruined crops and try planting a few grapevines in their place. Other farms round Glevum have had good results with them, but I'm afraid my slave-master is rather sceptical and thinks the plants won't prosper in the cold. Far too damp out here, he told me openly. He will do as I've instructed him, of course, but his heart's not in the task and I think he would be gratified to find that he was right – so I need a trusted pair of eyes to keep a watch on things.' He put a ringed hand on my shoulder with a smile. 'And naturally, I thought of you, Libertus, my old friend. You only live a mile or two along the lane, and there's no one else that I would trust as much.'

This was intended to be flattering, of course, but it was not quite the honour which he seemed to think it was. The round trip was considerably more than 'a mile or two' and the task necessitated my going out there almost every day in addition to attempting to ply my trade in town. I have a mosaic workshop to maintain, and every hour it took me to ride out to the farm and back was an hour of laying pavements which was lost

8

to me – and it also meant that I was obliged to hurry home each day in order to get out there before the daylight failed. Besides, the land slave-master was a new man, whom I didn't know, and I did not think my presence would impress him very much.

But one does not argue with a powerful patron like Marcus Septimus Aurelius, especially when he's a personal friend and favourite of the brand-new Emperor. So there I was, in the encroaching dusk, spurring on my skinny mule as fast as possible, when I saw this carriage at my patron's villa gate.

I could hardly have missed it, even in the dusk. It was extremely large – a handsome covered travelling coach with heavy leather springs and it was facing towards me, its four fine horses stamping and snorting in the cool evening air of spring. The fancy oil-lamps at the corners had not yet been lit, but all the same I could see how elaborate the conveyance was: the shafts and wheels were painted red, its wooden panels gilded, its side-posts decorated with elaborate ivory figurines, and it was completely blocking up the lane. I was obliged to stop.

I shambled my faithful Arlina to a stop, looked up at the driver and was about to speak, but before I could say anything at all, the shutters at a window-space were dropped, the curtain was thrust back and a florid, frowning face leaned out and looked at me.

'What are you doing, gawping, you stupid piece of scum?' The voice was every bit as unpleasant as the words. 'Get that wretched animal off the

9

track at once. It is late and we are wanting to depart and you are in our way!'

The injustice of this outburst was almost breathtaking – it was not my poor animal that was blocking the road – but of course it was not prudent to protest as much; a man of such obvious wealth and status was not someone to cross. No doubt there was a broad patrician stripe around the toga that I had glimpsed. So I fixed an obliging, foolish smile upon my face and said, with careful courtesy, 'I merely stopped to warn you, citizen, that if you hoped to find His Excellence Marcus Septimus Aurelius at home, you will be disappointed. He has gone to Rome – to congratulate his long-time friend and patron, Pertinax, on his elevation to the Imperial purple.'

Actually, that wasn't quite the case – Marcus had gone to see the Emperor, it is true, but more to warn him of the dangers of the role than to congratulate him on his rise to power. Pertinax, he'd told me, was too honest for the job: it would never occur to him, for instance, to offer bribes to the Praetorian Guard as Commodus had done, and therefore (since the praetorians were officially responsible for protecting the Imperial Person) his life might quickly be in jeopardy if they felt that they could replace him with someone who would pay what they believed to be their due. However, that was not something that I wished to share with this unpleasant visitor.

The florid face set in a scornful scowl. 'Gone to seek preferment in the Imperial Court?' He gave a furious snort. 'Why in Dis was I not informed of that? I've made a wasted journey,

10

and at this time of night. Someone will pay for this. You, if you're not careful. Get out of my way, you son of Celtic swine, or I'll have my horses trample over you.' And before I could answer he had slammed the shutter down and thumped the carriage as a signal to depart.

I just had time to swerve the mule aside before the driver raised his whip. The horses moved away and a moment later the whole heavy vehicle was trundling down the lane, gaining speed until it disappeared in clouds of dust – much of which settled on Arlina and myself.

I was distinctly shaken. Another instant and there would have been an accident – to the horses and carriage as much as to myself – and it was obvious that the driver of the coach had feared the same. I had glimpsed his face as he urged the horses on – white, set and terrified – but determined too: there'd been no hesitation in obeying the command. Florid-face was clearly not an owner to thwart or disobey.

I shook my head and turned Arlina round, abandoning my visit to the fields for the night. I would go first thing tomorrow, I promised inwardly – before I even set off for my workshop in the town. That wasn't what I'd promised Marcus that I'd do, but it might even be presented as a clever move: the land-steward would not expect me at that hour. My visits up till now had been, perhaps, far too predictable. Besides, although the little incident had happened very fast, it had caused me a delay and I could persuade myself that it was getting too dark to proceed. Mostly, however, it had given me a fright.

So I was not sorry to get home to my round-house and my wife, and the delicious stew she had prepared for me. The pair of red-haired slaves who had come back from town with me, but had already preceded me indoors, were waiting with warmed water to rinse my hands and feet and the kitchen slave had put a pot of spiced, honeyed mead to warm. Relaxing in the pleasures of my simple home, I soon forgot the horrid little incident. Or tried to, anyway.

I thought of sharing it with Gwellia, my wife, but she had learned from the slaves that I had earned a lucrative contract for a pavement at the baths, and I decided that it was a shame to spoil her joy by dwelling on the threat and the rudeness of the carriage passenger. I simply mentioned that I'd seen a visitor, apparently hoping to find Marcus in.

She looked up from kneading flour into a dough. 'I wonder who that was.'

I shook my head. 'I've no idea,' I said. 'Nobody that I have ever seen before. Somebody wealthy by the look of him. Great big carriage blocking up the road – a proper *carpentum*, with four horses pulling it. Shutters and oil lamps and leather springs, besides. Could have come a long way with a vehicle like that.'

She punched the bread-dough with an expert fist. 'Well, wherever it came from, it won't go far tonight. I suppose they were hoping to stop at Marcus's. I wonder where they'll find accommodation now?' She stretched the dough, then punched it down again and set it by the fire to rise a bit before she sealed the pot with clay

12

and placed it in the embers to bake overnight. 'If they were known to your patron – and as wealthy as you say – I'm a bit surprised the servants didn't let them in. I know that there are hardly any slaves left in the house, but they could have offered a traveller some sort of hospitality, I'm sure.'

'I think I prevented him from asking at the gate,' I said, wondering why I hadn't thought of that myself. I suppose the sudden fright had addled my poor brain. 'He was sitting in the carriage when I came along the lane, and so was his driver – and they didn't seem to know that Marcus wasn't there. When I told them so, he got quite cross and drove away at once.'

'So he hadn't sent his slave in to enquire?' Gwellia had started on the morning's oatcakes now.

'If he'd sent in an attendant, he'd have waited for him to come back to the carriage, wouldn't he?' I said. 'I didn't see a servant, come to think of it – apart from the driver, and that hardly counts. Though I suppose there must have been one.'

'In the coach, perhaps? It's an odd place to seat a mere attendant, but men like that don't drive around the roads without an escort as a rule.'

'Mmm!' was all I murmured in reply. Trust Gwellia to see the obvious.

I watched her for a little, going about her evening tasks. She was a pretty woman, even now, although her hair was grey. And sharp-witted too. It was not the first time that she'd thought of things I should have seen myself.

'Perhaps I should tell Marcus about that visitor,' I said at last. 'Especially if no one in the house had seen him come. It does seem an odd encounter. I wonder who he was.'

'That's what I said half an hour ago.' She grinned across at me. 'But you didn't ask him and now we'll never know. I don't suppose it matters, anyway. Whoever it was has come and gone and there's an end of it.' She had set the cakes and bread to cook by now, so I raked the ashes over them and lit a slow taper in a jar to keep a flame alight.

'I'm sure you're right, as usual,' I told her tenderly, as I blew the candle out and pulled her down beside me on the bed of reeds.

We could not guess how wrong she'd prove to be.

Two

I awoke even earlier than I'd intended to, though feeling less than rested after a night of troubled dreams in which I was being pursued by speeding chariots. Gwellia was still sleeping, though I could hear Kurso (our little kitchen slave) rattling the water-bucket as he came back from the spring. I shook myself awake and went out to speak to him.

He looked up from pouring water into the shallow irrigation channel that ran round my kitchen crops.' 'You're up early, master.' He stared at me, obviously surprised to find me standing there wearing just the tunic that I'd been sleeping in – though I had managed to strap my ancient sandals on my feet. Then he recalled himself. 'Do you want a drink?' He gestured to the little ewer beside him on the wall. 'Filling the jug up was the next job on my list. I can do it now and get some more water later for the plants and animals.'

I shook my head and picked the ewer up. 'I'll go and get some from the spring myself, and breakfast on a little of Gwellia's new bread,' I said, causing him to look even more startled than before. 'You make sure Arlina has been fed and watered while I've gone – I want to set off early to look in at my patron's fields and perhaps call in at the villa afterwards if there is time enough.

I saw a strange carriage outside there yesterday, and I'm curious to find out who the caller was and whether he managed to make contact with the household there.' I smiled at Kurso's earnest little face. 'Tell the others that I'll be coming back, ready to go back into town as usual – my errand shouldn't take me very long.'

In fact, I was able to tell them for myself. By the time that I got back from the spring, the whole of my little household was awake and the slaves were clustering round to help me have my meal and pull my working tunic over what I wore. 'And put a cloak on, husband, for Minerva's sake!' Gwellia said crossly, handing me the warmest one I had. 'It will be a wonder if you haven't caught a cold, walking round at dawn without one at this time of year! It's a chilly morning.'

It was crisp, certainly – and I was grateful for the cloak. The ride out to the fields was quite a bracing one. But not a very useful one, it seemed.

'Far too chilly to be planting vines,' the chief land-slave told me, hastening over to meet me at the wall when he saw me arriving on my mule. 'Too early in the season for this corner of the world. And I'd tell the master just the same if he was here. Them plants are tender. He'll lose the lot of them, if you ask me.'

'He told me he'd looked into it, and other people had achieved success with them,' I said, by way of offering a half-rebuke.

The overseer laughed. 'Looked into it? He's bought an amanuensis-slave at great expense and had him in the villa scribbling away for half a moon, copying out some borrowed treatise on how to care for vines – and now of course, he thinks he knows exactly what to do. Never mind that the author is talking about areas around Rome! It's nonsense trying to apply it here – although of course I'll have to do as I'm told.'

'And I would like to watch you for a bit.'

'I'm sure you would, citizen. But—' he gestured to the land-slaves in the field beyond, who, having selected shovels, rakes and hoes, were mostly leaning on their implements and watching us while they awaited their instructions for the day '—we won't be starting yet! Not until the day's warmed up as much as possible. It will be an hour or more before the sun is high enough – and I'm leaving the seedlings in the warmest barn till then. No point asking for disaster, is there, citizen? In the meantime we'll just go on breaking up the soil. You want to wait and supervise till we start to plant?' He beamed at me, the picture of innocence and helpfulness.

Of course the enquiry was barbed, but he had made his point. I am not a wealthy landowner like his owner is. I am a working man and have my own affairs to see to in the town. He knew quite well that his polite suggestion was impossible, and he no doubt resented being answerable to somebody like me.

I shook my head. 'I'm sure that won't be necessary,' I replied, as though I had considered his proposal and rejected it. 'I'll look in tonight and see how you are getting on.' And, without so much as getting off my mule, I turned around and trotted off the way that I had come. But he

17

was not deceived. I'm almost sure I heard derisive laughter behind me as I went.

So I was not in the best of tempers as I approached the villa gates. Having been so short a time out at the fields, I had decided that I did have time to call.

I tied Arlina to a tree nearby and knocked on the gate, but I was not prepared for the reception I received. Or rather, lack of it. My continued rapping brought no response at all. There was no sign of the usual burly gatekeeper, not even his enquiring eye at the peephole of his cell beside the gates. Even my tapping directly on his wall produced not the slightest movement from within. Either the fellow was asleep, or he'd slipped off for a meal. Or possibly a morning visit to the slaves' latrine! But meanwhile the gate was unattended. That wasn't good enough, I thought grimly. Marcus would hear of it, when I next sent word to him!

I knocked again, a good deal louder now, shouting as I did so – strongly enough for my voice to carry to anyone on duty in the front court of the house – 'Greetings of the morning. Open up the gate. It is Libertus here. I'm on my patron's business and I have some information to impart.'

Still there was no answer. That was curious. I got down from Arlina and thundered on the gate. 'I tell you, it's Libertus. The gatekeeper's not here. Somebody come out and let me . . .' I broke off as the gates creaked open at my touch – almost as though they'd not been fastened properly: latched, perhaps, but certainly not bolted as they

18

should have been – especially if there was nobody on watch. Even more curious! Ever since Marcus's child was kidnapped and held to ransom years ago, he had been fanatical about security. I pushed the gates again. They opened slightly wider and I slid a cautious head into the gap and looked around.

At first sight everything appeared to be exactly as it should – the villa looked quite peaceful in the morning light, standing at the far end of the entrance court, with its new wing and private gardens to the left and the walled storage yards and orchards to the right. Too peaceful, perhaps. There did not seem to be a single slave about. I knew that Marcus had left only a very few of his household servants – as distinct from the land-slaves who tended the estate. And he wouldn't have people keeping the hypocaust alight, so there would be none of the usual slaves scuttling around with fuel from the orchards to stoke the fires for that, but surely there would be someone working at this hour – sweeping the steps, or taking shutters down, or raking leaves from round the entrance court? It had not been done today. There were a lot of leaves – a brisk little breeze was blowing them in spirals as I watched. But there was no sign of human movement anywhere.

And it was oddly silent, too. I called again and listened carefully. No distant answering voices. No hurrying footsteps coming from within. No clatter from the store-yard behind the inner wall. A faint, insistent tapping was the only sound – and even that, on consideration, was not coming from the house. It seemed to emanate from

19

somewhere at my side – apparently from the little cell beside the gate, where the absent gate-keeper had his sleeping-bench and stool. I frowned. Where could everyone have gone, and what could the gate guard have left behind that made that knocking sound – irregular but repeated and scarcely audible?

I was increasingly uneasy, but extremely curious by now and, though the door to the keeper's porch was closed, I pushed it gently open. And was appalled and horrified by what I found.

The tapping sound was caused by the inhabitant himself. He was suspended by his own belt from a ceiling hook. The stool on which he had been standing had been kicked away and he was swinging gently in the draught which blew in through the stone bars of the window-space. He was extremely dead. At first I was inclined to guess at suicide but I quickly realised that it was nothing of the sort. As he rotated slowly in the air, his hands came into view – firmly secured behind his back with a short length of chain.

I sat down on the sleeping bench and tried to take this in. There could be no mistake – it was the gatekeeper all right. I'd have known him anywhere, even without the uniform tunic – a great bear of a fellow with a mane of tawny hair and the muscles of an ox. He'd been a wrestler in a travelling show when Marcus purchased him. It must have taken someone of enormous strength to subdue a man like that, overcome his struggles and hoist him up on the hook. Or, more likely, several someones working as a team.

He had never been a handsome man in life, but

in death he was entirely hideous. His face was purple and contorted horribly, his tongue protruding like that of an ox-head on a plate, while his bulging, bloodshot eyes stared sightlessly at me. The air was foetid with a smell like a latrine, and I could see what caused the tapping: one sandal seemed to have dislodged itself (during his final struggles, probably) and now dangled from its straps, just low enough to lightly touch the corner of the table as he swayed.

Noticing the sandals drew attention to the feet. They – and the lower legs – seemed blotched with pooling blood. That was so astonishing I took a closer look – indeed, my first impression was correct. This was not bruising, it was simply that the blood had gathered there. I shook my head, bewildered. I'd seen enough of bodies to be fairly sure that such a thing took quite a time to manifest itself – which suggested that the man had been here many hours. Could this be connected in some way with that carriage I had seen?

But that could not be right. Marcus's land-slaves must have been here at the villa overnight. Surely they would have known if somebody had killed the gatekeeper – and I couldn't believe that it would occasion no remark. Wouldn't that be the first thing that the overseer said to me, instead of calmly discussing the proper time of day for planting vines?

Perhaps I was wrong in my estimation of the time of death. I reached out a reluctant hand and touched the lifeless thigh. It was cold – which in itself was not a proof of anything, since the body had been hanging in a very chilly draught. But it was also stiff – so stiff that when I tried to move the knee, it would not budge at all. I would have needed to apply such force I would have snapped the joint. That kind of rigid stiffness did not occur for many hours – another indication that the victim had been dead since yesterday.

My mind went back again to the florid visitor of the night before. It was tempting to suppose that he was guilty of this death. But I shook my head. From what I'd seen of that aggressive citizen, he was middle-aged and over-fed and not especially fit. He would be no match for this burly gatekeeper (who – it occurred to me – was generally armed, though there was now no sign of his cudgel anywhere). And the driver of the carriage could not have done this, I was sure. He was thin and wiry, but he was very slight. He would have lasted no longer than an instant in a struggle with this strong, athletic guard, never mind managing to hang him from the hook. One might as well suggest that a cat could kill and lift a bull.

In fact, the more I thought about events, the more it seemed to me that the likely explanation was the very opposite: that the carriage I'd seen was standing idling in the lane precisely because the occupants (like me) had not succeeded in getting a response – which suggested that the gatekeeper was already dead by then. It was not what I secretly wanted to suppose, but it made sense of things – including the citizen's furious response that he'd had a wasted journey, his angry departure, and even his willingness to take my word that Marcus wasn't there. It also fitted well enough with my observations of the corpse.

But in that case, what about the other servants in the house? Had they not realised there was something wrong? Even if someone (or those several someones) had got in through the gates – perhaps admitted by the gatekeeper himself – and murdered him without raising the alarm, surely the other servants in the house would finally have come out here to look for him, if only to bring him something for a meal? I thought back to the silence I had noted in the court.

I glanced up at the dead man, still swinging from his noose, and decided that I wanted witnesses. In any case he was too high and heavy to manage on my own. If I could find the servants, they could come and help. If not . . .? I didn't know exactly what I would do, in that case.

But there must be servants, surely? The land-slaves had been here until shortly after dawn, and did not seem to have noticed anything amiss. Perhaps the indoor staff had only found this body later on, when someone came to call him to break his morning fast. I shook my head. If so, would they not have checked the gates and raised some sort of immediate alarm – by sending to my roundhouse, for instance? It was not far away and Marcus's servants all knew where I lived.

Or was it possible that they – or some of them, at least – had strung him up themselves? That would explain why nobody had told the land-slaves anything. And it was vaguely plausible.

23

The man had been chosen for his brute strength and bullying qualities – once, when he thought that he was unobserved, I'd seen him bullying a page. No doubt he had made other enemies among the staff, especially now that his owner was away.

So, suppose that they had killed him, carefully leaving the outer gate unlocked to suggest that this was the work of an intruder? There were certain to be callers – like myself – who could 'discover' this and be relied upon as impartial witnesses. I brightened. Perhaps the remaining servants were all busy, even now, sending for the slaves' guild to provide the funeral and collecting wood to build a pyre on the estate.

That was a possible explanation and once I'd thought of it, I felt a good deal better about going in search of them.

Assuming that there was anybody to be found. Otherwise . . .?

I shook my head. That was something I would face if I was forced to it.

I left the body swaying there, and – with some trepidation – set off for the house.

Three

I was further encouraged, when I reached the villa door, to find that it was bolted on the inner side – as one might expect if there were no slaves on duty in the interior. If it too had pushed open at my touch, I think I would have fled, but when my gentle tapping brought no response at all, I convinced myself that my theory had been right and that I would find the servants gathered at the outbuildings beyond, making preparations for their colleague's funeral. The slaves had their sleeping quarters in a separate barn-like building at the rear, so if that was really where they were, of course they could not hear a caller thumping at the door.

My next thought was to go round and find out. There was another entrance to the villa from the back – in fact, off the farm track that ran through the estate. There was even another gatehouse with its own man on guard. However, that was a consid-erable distance, even on a mule, because the road wound all the way round the estate. Perhaps I'd take Arlina and ride there, all the same. It wasn't easy to reach the slave-barn otherwise from here because the entrance court was screened off from the remainder of the grounds, partly by the villa building itself, and then by a high wall which ran all the way across from either wing to meet up with the garden and orchard walls each side. This arrangement was intended to offer some privacy by providing a framing feature for the gardens at the front while cutting off the inner courts from casual visitors.

However, just as I was about to go out and clamber on my mule, I remembered that there was one unobtrusive gateway at the left-hand end – screened from view and very small indeed – so that the gatekeeper could go and visit the latrine, and the slaves who stoked the hypocaust could carry through the fuel without needing either to walk the long way round or to traipse through the villa every time. When it was not in use this gate was generally bolted from within (as part of Marcus's insistence on security) so it was likely that I'd find that it was barred today. But it was probably worth the short stroll over to find out.

In fact, I found it had been left upon the latch, so I pushed it open and walked through, calling as I did so, 'Is anybody there?' There was no reply. I was in an inner courtyard used for storage purposes, a place that I had been in only once before. I was alongside the long, blank side wall of the villa here, right outside of the handsome guest quarters, but none of them had window-spaces looking out this way: they were all designed to command a view of the pleasant inner garden court, not this unprepossessing area, which was reserved for tradesmen and slaves.

I picked my way across the little court with care, skirting around the heaps of stockpiled wood, and taking care not to step in any of the huge amphorae in the ground. This was where the household generally kept its stock of oil and grain. There was a heavy outdoor hand-quern for grinding any home-grown corn and rye to household flour, and the subterranean storage pots not only kept these staples dry but also safe from rats and other thieving animals. However, with the owner and his wife away, several amphorae were clearly not in use. They were empty and currently without their fitted lids, making them open to the sky and therefore traps for the unwary passer-by. Presumably they were in the process of being cleaned and aired.

But there was no one cleaning anything today. I left the court and made my way out through the further arch towards the kitchen block. This small stone building was set back on its own a little way apart from the remainder of the house – as these things always are in case there is a fire – and with its own convenient access to the storage area. I was vainly hoping that there, at least, I might find slaves at work – the kitchen is always a very busy place – but that too was as empty as the court had been.

I stuck my head around the kitchen door. There were signs of recent activity in here: bunches of cut herbs were standing on the bench, together with a half-empty barrel of dried beans and a basket full of leeks. A single crust of bread and a small end of cheese suggested that these items had been the ingredients of a meal not long ago. A mortar and pestle had clearly been in use – some half-ground substance was still lying in the bowl – and someone had evidently been shelling nuts as well. Apart from that, there was no sign of life. The usual array of pots and implements were neatly stacked for use and half a pig had been suspended to smoke above the cooking-fire – though it wasn't doing so. The flames had been permitted to go out. Some time ago, as far as I could judge.

This was extremely odd. No one permits the cooking-fire to die. I picked up a handful of ashes from the grate, and ran them through my fingers – which only confirmed what I already knew. They were completely cold. I lifted a cloth from a baking iron nearby, and found unleavened bread dough neatly shaped into a loaf but it had not been set to cook. In fact the handsome domed 'clay' bread-oven on the farther wall – an unusual luxury for a private house – had not yet been swept out and relaid with fresh twigs. The bake-stone on the bottom wasn't even warm. (It was called a 'clay oven', as Marcus's chief cook had once explained to me, because once it was hot and the fire inside was raked away, whatever was baking was inserted in the space and the opening sealed with clay to maximise the heat.) But there was no heat today.

I shook my head. Even a depleted staff would have to eat and – by tradition – cook-slaves do not attend the dead for fear that ill luck might attach to them and somehow be passed on in what they served. So where was everyone?

The slave quarters perhaps? That had been my guess at first. The building was just a little further to the rear and I hurried over there, though my hopes of finding anybody there were dwindling rapidly, especially as I heard no noise as I approached. No whisper of voices, no sound of a lament. It was fairly evident that there was no one there.

The door was slightly open – as it generally was – and I stooped down and went inside. I'd been before and knew what I would find: a long, low building, divided into two – one half for females and the other for males – with the chief steward's private curtained sleeping-room positioned in between, beside the door. The lesser slaves had only a small sleeping-space apiece, marked by a straw mattress, each with a blanket over it and a little chest beside it for a change of clothes and anything else they happened to possess. I tried the lid of one at random. It wasn't locked – few slaves have anything that's actually their own, and if they get tips they tend to hide them somewhere else – and I found only a neatly folded tunic and a hoarded piece of twine.

The room was clean and ordered, too, with everything in place. There was no sign of any struggle, nothing overturned – none of the elements which might suggest a panic or a raid. Certainly no sign of any funeral. Or of any servants, come to that. I shivered.

With that in mind I went out to the gatehouse at the rear, fearing that I'd find a replica of what was in the front, but the place was empty and the gate was duly barred. The whole back court-yard was as silent as a ghost.

No sooner had I thought of ghosts than I wished that I had not. The spirits of murdered are said to walk abroad and haunt the area where they were killed, putting a curse on everything until they are avenged. There is a villa near Glevum where a killing once took place, and which has been famously ill-omened ever since. The family that owned it all met dreadful fates: one brother had been forced to flee abroad, a second to sell himself to slavery, while the third one hanged himself. Such is the power of a vengeful ghost, they say. I only hoped that the gatekeeper's spirit was not lurking here!

I listened. The sound of my own footsteps seemed unnaturally loud and when I heard a sudden creaking of a gate I felt the few hairs on my neck stand up and bristle like so many hedgehog spines.

I retraced my steps, but it was only the gateway to the inner court, which was open and swinging in a little gust of wind. It was unusual for that gate to be unlatched. It led into the garden courtyard and the house itself. My mouth was dry, but having come this far I controlled my fears and forced myself to go inside to check.

Once again, there was nothing obvious amiss. The peristyle garden looked as pleasant as it always did. The central fountain was not playing, which was unusual, but not all that surprising since the owner was away. Otherwise everything looked much as when I saw it last: the garden quartered by four little walkways meeting at the fount, each section with its own array of flowers, bushes and sweet-smelling herbs, and interspersed with arbours and little statues of the gods.

There was a covered walkway round the whole perimeter, of course – a sort of outdoor corridor connecting all the rooms – with the atrium and other public reception areas at the further end and various bedrooms, guest accommodation and the like, stretching back towards me on either side. There was no sign of human movement – which, paradoxically, encouraged me this time. A single walk around, I told myself. Most of the rooms had windows made of horn, so it was impossible to look inside them from the court, but I would quickly reconnoitre and see what I could see.

Not that I expected to discover anything. By this time I was reconciled to finding the place deserted, and I was already planning the message I would send to Marcus later on. The first thing I'd do when I got into town was go and see the garrison commander and arrange a courier.

I walked along the covered path, my footsteps scrunching on the gravelled ground. I did not want to venture into my patron's room, but I did try a door to what I knew was a sleeping-room for guests – indeed I had stayed there once myself when I was ill. I pushed the door, which opened at my touch – and there was the neat bedroom complete with bed and stool, just as it had been when I was sleeping there.

I tiptoed out again and went on with my patrol. Over to the corner of the court, through the side entrance, and so into the main reception rooms – the atrium, the study, the *triclinium*. They were all strangely empty – Marcus had clearly sent away most of his better furniture and expensive ornaments – but they were clean and ordered. Everywhere, the outer shutters had been taken down and the rooms were light enough for me to need no lamps. The floors were swept, and nearby

31

in the servants' waiting room someone had placed the usual scatter of clean rushes on the floor so that hurried footsteps did not ring so much. But there was no one, dead or living, to be seen. It was as though some magician had come and put a strong enchantment on everybody here, causing them to simply fade away like smoke.

I was standing, thoughtful, in the small reception room, gazing in the direction of the entrance court. The windows in these public rooms were made of stylish glass rather than being simply shuttered spaces like my own. This let a lot of light in, and kept out the cold and draughts but it did make it quite difficult to see the world outside. Could one make out the gatehouse through the blue distortion of the pane? Could someone standing here have witnessed what occurred?

My thoughts were interrupted by a movement in the court – a shadow so swift and immediately gone that I was almost doubtful of my eyes. And there it was again. I cursed the glass that turned it to a blur. But I had seen something, and I was almost certain what it was: a person, or people, moving swiftly in the court – not walking boldly to the entrance as one might expect an honest visitor to do, but skulking like shadows, unwilling to be seen.

Moments before, I had been looking for signs of human life, but now that I had glimpsed them, I was petrified. I stood stock-still – I don't believe I could have moved a muscle if I tried – and listened carefully, but for several moments I could near no sound at all.

Then it began. A creak – that inner gate again. A footstep on the gravel of the path, so soft I would have missed it if I hadn't strained my ears. Another. And another. Getting closer now. Then the sound of muffled sandals in the corridor outside. By this time my heart was beating so hard against my chest that it was almost all that I was conscious of. I braced myself, unable even to turn round to face the door, fearful of making the slightest scuffling. No one could have known that I was here, I told myself. No one could have seen me through the window glass. So it wasn't me that they were looking for. If I could hold my breath – which I was doing anyway – so they couldn't even hear me breathe, perhaps they'd go away and wouldn't know that I was here.

It was a faint hope, as I was all too well aware. The footsteps had paused outside this very room. I kept on holding my breath, concentrating hard, but suddenly the door flew open and before I'd even had the time to whirl around, a hand fell on my shoulder and a voice said loudly, 'There you are, at last. I wondered where you'd got to! What are you doing here?'

Four

Almost faint with apprehension and alarm, I forced myself to turn and face this newcomer, only to find that I was staring at my own adopted son. Relief undid me. My old knees crumpled and I sat down heavily on the mosaic floor, my legs deprived abruptly of the strength to hold me up.

'Father!' Junio had come and was bending over me. His face was all concern. 'Are you all right?'

I nodded, reaching out a hand for him to help me to my feet. 'You almost gave me a heart attack, that's all. What are you doing here?'

'Looking for you,' he said, ignoring my hands and coming round behind me to lift me by the elbows and haul me to my feet. 'We got concerned when you were gone so long, and set off for the prospective vineyard field to search for you.'

With his help I found myself unsteadily upright. 'And they told you that they'd seen me, I suppose?'

He was still holding both my arms to support me, but he said, 'We never got that far. When we reached the villa we saw the mule outside and guessed that you had come here. We didn't realise there was no one else about. We hammered at the gate, but it was open anyway and when no one answered we decided to come in.' He looked around. 'What's happened, by the way?

Has there been some sort of change of plan? Where have the servants gone?'

'You didn't look inside the gatehouse, then?' I said, freeing myself and readjusting my tunic round my knees.

He shook his head. 'When there was no answer, there did not seem to be much point. As I said, the gate was open so we didn't really need the man to let us in. We assumed that he was busy bringing you inside . . .' He broke off, looking anxiously at me. 'Why, Father? What made you ask that question? Don't shake your head like that. What happened at the gatehouse? Something did! I see it in your face.'

'The gatekeeper!' I muttered, still too shaken to give a full account. 'I looked in and found him . . .'

'If that brute treated you disrespectfully, just let us know!' he said. 'We'll go and talk to him. He may be big but there are two of us. He won't try that again!'

'Two of you?' I murmured stupidly, though of course he had been talking in the plural all the time. I should have worked out that he hadn't come alone.

'Minimus came with me, naturally,' he said. 'You might have needed help – if you had fallen off the mule or something of the kind. In fact, you look as if you need some help right now. You're still looking shaken. I think we should find somewhere for you to sit down.'

I shook my head. 'Marcus seems to have put most of his furniture in store. We'll probably find it stacked up in a barn, unless he's sent it over to Corinium for his wife. But I'll be all right now, the more so since you and Minimus are here.'

He grinned. 'Maximus was disappointed to be left behind. We three had all been waiting to accompany you to town, but Mother insisted that one of us should stay, just in case you came home by some different route. You might have ridden back across the fields, she thought, if the land-slaves were not working where you thought they were. Then you'd have wanted someone to come and fetch us back. But you'd been so long that we were quite alarmed for you.' He raised an eyebrow at me. 'And something's shaken you. Was it something to do with this gatekeeper of yours? Where is he, if he isn't at his post? Should I go and talk to him?'

'It would do no good,' I told him. 'He couldn't answer you. Someone has strung him from the ceiling by his belt and he is very dead.'

'Dead?' Horror and disbelief were dawning in his face.

I nodded. 'It's not a pleasant sight. Let's just hope that Minimus does not stumble on it unprepared. Where is he anyway?'

'He went to the back courtyard looking for the slaves – we couldn't see any.'

'I don't think there are any others here to find, alive or dead.'

He wrinkled his nose in mock perplexity. 'So what's happened, do you think? Has Marcus left for good and put them up for auction at the nearest sale?'

I shook my head. 'I know no more than you.

It's a mystery to me. I should have thought that if he'd done that he would have let me know. And if he had decided to sell them on a whim, wouldn't he have sent his land-slaves to the market, too? But they are out there working in the fields and do not seem to be aware that anything is wrong! I spoke to them this morning.'

Junio frowned. 'Minimus had the feeling that something was amiss, ever since the moment that we found the gate ajar. He swore that when he worked here Marcus would never have permitted that. He thought it was just slackness by the staff because their owner was away – but it made him very nervous all the same. He was quite concerned at coming to the house at all.'

'But came in any case.'

He gave me a wry grin. 'We were fairly sure that you were in the house, and it was you we'd come to find.' This brave concern for my welfare was rather humbling, but before I could say anything my son was rushing on. 'Of course, we went to the front door first, but nobody was there either. However, Minimus knew about a servant's side-gate in the wall, so we hurried round that way, trying not to make ourselves conspicu-ous. He thought there might be trouble if someone spotted us. He had no right these days to be going that way at all – and nor had I, of course, though as a citizen I might have got away with it.'

'You need not have worried,' I put in. 'There was nobody about. Though I suppose you didn't know that.'

'We were soon aware of it. In fact, we could

not find a trace of any living soul until I spotted fresh footsteps on the gravel near the gate. So I went in that direction, and there you were, indeed!'

'Though you almost made me die of shock,' I said. 'I was sure that a murderer was bursting in on me.'

'I was a bit alarmed about what I might find, myself,' he said. 'That's why I sent young Minimus the other way, in the direction of the servants' block. He used to know most of the slave-force in the household here, so they are likely to be friendly to him if he does find anyone. They might even talk to him and explain to us why everybody else has disappeared.' He looked around again. 'It is odd, isn't it? The place is positively eerie.'

'I might have believed your theory about the slave-market,' I said, 'if it wasn't for the presence of that grisly corpse.'

'Dear gods!' Junio exclaimed. 'The gatekeeper! I have just realised the force of what you said. "Someone" strung him up, you said – presumably meaning that he didn't do it himself? I was somehow supposing that he'd taken his own life – perhaps out of despair or something because the household was being broken up. But you don't think so?'

'Nor would you, if you had seen him,' I replied. 'His hands are chained behind his back. He could not have arranged the noose around his neck.'

Junio was goggling at me. 'No wonder you were talking about murderers,' he said. 'That does seem proof that something criminal's afoot. Yet the land-slaves have gone off to work as usual, apparently thinking that it was an ordinary day?'

I nodded. 'I don't imagine that they knew there'd been a murder here – and that is something which I can't understand. I know they don't all sleep in the same slave quarters as the domestic staff. There are so many of them now that Marcus has converted a barn on the estate for them just opposite the rear entrance to the house. But the overseer comes in, and still they get food from the kitchens and all that sort of thing. So how could this have happened without their knowing it?'

'Unless the killer is a member of the household, possibly? Took the food across to them and managed to convince them that things were just as usual. In that case, is it possible he's still somewhere about?' He glanced uncomfortably round the room. 'I don't like this, Father. Let's get out of here ourselv—' He broke off suddenly and looked into my eyes. 'Dear gods!' I saw the horror dawning on his face, just as I felt it rising in my own. 'Are you thinking what I'm thinking?'

'Minimus!' I said.

He nodded. 'I have sent him off searching the back court on his own! Come on!' He was already leading the way towards the door. 'We'd better go and find him before someone else does.'

I hastened after Junio as fast as my old legs would carry me – through the vestibule, into the peristyle garden and out towards the back. This time we did not stop to skirt the rooms but hurried directly down the central path.

Past the fountain, through the inner gate and

out into the courtyard where the slave quarters stood. I led the way inside and looked around. 'Minimus?' I shouted.

But it was already clear that nobody was here.

The room was exactly as I'd seen it earlier – neat and ordered and empty as the skies. I glanced at Junio, who was staring at the rows of tidy sleeping-spaces on the floor – obviously surprised to find the place so undisturbed. 'No one left here in hurry,' he observed. 'But there's no sign of Minimus.'

'Perhaps he's in the courtyard – in one of the other outbuildings, maybe?'

We hurried out again, scouring the empty stables, the barns, the storage sheds, and still calling Minimus at every step. I even went back into the inner yard and checked the open amphorae in the ground. But there was no sign of him and no answer to our shouts. The echoes mocked us, bouncing off the walls.

I was about to suggest to Junio that we go back into the house, in case the boy had followed him inside and we had somehow missed him as we left, but I was suddenly conscious of a distant sound behind the right-hand boundary wall. I glanced at Junio and raised a warning finger to my lips. It was ridiculous. A moment earlier we had been shouting loudly for a slave! But it suddenly seemed vital that we did not make a noise.

There was a little gateway that led out of the court into the orchard which adjoined the house. When I looked at that gate earlier the bolt had been secured, but I could see from where I stood that it had been opened since. I gestured to Junio, who followed the direction of my pointing finger with his eyes.

He saw the bolt and nodded. He repeated my finger-to-the-lips routine, held up a hand to indicate I should stay where I was and started to inch silently towards the gate. He had been born to servitude and had acquired the knack – which as a slave myself I'd never quite achieved – of moving absolutely silently. I could only watch him and admire his stealth, though my heart was in my mouth as he placed one noiseless hand upon the latch and the other on the gatepost. Then with a sudden motion he released the catch, pushed the gate wide open and burst into the orchard in a single lunge.

Nothing happened. No one set upon him. No one cried out in surprise. From where I was standing I saw him hesitate and crane his neck in all directions to look around the field. I was about to go and join him but he shook his head at me.

'I think there's something moving over there,' he mouthed, pointing with a tapping motion at the farther wall. He peered a little longer and then came back to me and murmured, too softly to be overheard by listeners-in, 'There's certainly something, though I can't see what it is. You stay here. I'll go and have a look.'

I was about to protest but he shook his head again. 'One of us had better stay here in case Minimus turns up,' he insisted with a firmness that wasn't usual for him. 'Besides I'm better at moving quietly – and if there is any problem and

I don't come back, it's better if one of us can go and call for help. Stay where you are, and make sure you are out of sight behind the wall.' And before I could reply he was through the gate again and had disappeared from view among the orchard trees.

I'm not accustomed to my former slave dictating what I do and I was inclined to bridle inwardly – but I did as I was bid. I knew that his assertiveness was born of care for me, and it had to be admitted that he was no doubt right: I am not as young and agile as I used to be. If there was any danger he was better placed to flee, or even to put up a struggle and defend himself. But I did not enjoy the moments that I spent listening to the silence, cowering by the wall and wondering what Junio was doing on the other side of it.

After several moments there was another rustling – this time coming very close to me – and I could hear someone breathing heavily. I was half inclined to make a lumbering run for it and try to get into the slave quarters and hide, when Junio came bursting through the gate again.

'That's the second time today that you've half frightened me to death . . .' I was beginning, with a chuckle of relief. Then I saw the expression on his face.

'You've found something! Tell me it isn't Minimus!'

He shook his head as if attempting to dispel a dreadful dream. 'Oh, I've found Minimus all right and he is still alive – but I couldn't bring him back. He wasn't well enough. There's something in the orchard. You'd better come and see.'

Five

Before I could say anything at all he was leading the way back through the still half-open gate into the orchard field. I followed him, but as I glanced around I could not see anything particularly out of place. The trees – apples, walnuts, damson, sloes and pears – had just begun to sprout their new spring buds, but otherwise the branches were quite bare, making it possible to see through the tangled trellis of their twigs right to the other corner of the field, but I could see nothing unusual at all, except what looked a random pile of coloured cloth against the further wall.

Even that was not especially surprising, given that the master and the mistress were away. Most of the cloth that I could see was roughly the distinctive scarlet shade of the house uniform of Marcus's house-slaves – except for a much smaller heap of greenish-brown a little to one side – so this was presumably drying laundry I was looking at. The diminished household that had been left behind were hardly likely to take their tunics into Glevum to be cleaned or dyed: the fullers gave no credit and the dyers even less. That small amount of laundry would be done at home, just as Gwellia always personally dyed and washed our own – except of course for togas, which required the whitening that only a profes-sional fuller could provide.

So if a lot of odd items were being dyed to match and the result was not especially critical – which at a quick glance appeared to be the case – then what could be more natural than to spread it out to dry on the long grass beneath the trees, particularly on a windy, bright spring morning like today?

'There's Minimus. Can you see him? I think he's being sick.' Junio broke across my thoughts, indicating the direction with a thumb.

It was then I realised that the green-brown heap was Minimus – or rather his slave-tunic, which was all that I could see. He was crouching up against the high stone wall, his head bowed away from us and his shoulders heaving slightly as I watched. I hurried towards him, down one of the grassy strips between the trees – and as I grew nearer I got a clearer view – and then looked more carefully at the other pile of cloth.

What I was seeing stopped me in my tracks. There was no question now of what had happened to the missing slaves. I had been right in thinking I could see their uniforms – what I hadn't realised was that the owners were still wearing them. The whole household of servants, what was left of them, were lying two deep in a sort of ragged line, some on their fronts and others on their backs, some with their feet towards me, others facing the other way. It was not a tidy pile. Many of them overlapped their neighbour in some way – a leg here over someone else's shoulder there – and the variation in the famous crimson shade was occasioned not by the recent application of a dye, but by the streams of blood which had soaked into them, and which now had dried in random patches of a darker hue.

It was not hard to see where all this blood had issued from. The heads were missing. Every one of them had clearly been hacked off at the neck. Some of the bodies had been cruelly stabbed as well (several in the back, I noticed), but some corpses appeared to bear no other mark. There must have been a dozen or so in all – surely the whole of the small staff that Marcus left behind: male and female, young and old, kitchen slaves and pages, even the amanuensis and the steward (easily distinguishable by their longer robes) all jumbled together in this macabre equality of death.

I turned to Minimus, still retching in the grass. He knelt up to greet me, ashen-faced and with an effort at a sickly smile. 'Master! I'm sorry. I should have come to you . . .'

I held up a hand to silence him. 'I'm not surprised this has affected you. It would take a man without a heart not to react to this . . .'

He gulped. 'That boy there – the second smallest one – I knew him, I am sure. I helped to train him when he first arrived. He was going to be page, but in the end they made him kitchen-boy. His name's Pauvrissimus. I recognise him from that scar there on his arm where he tripped and fell into the brazier one day.' He seemed to feel that he was showing disrespect, so he put one still-shaking hand against the wall and pulled himself upright. 'And that big, hulking one beside him, I am almost sure, is the second-ranking cook who used to do the baking for the house.'

I nodded. I had forgotten that these people would be personally known to my red-headed slave. 'I'm sorry you had to find this on your own,' I said. 'What made you come into the orchard anyway?'

'I'd already done as the young master said – looked into the slave quarters and all the other outbuildings and sheds. But there wasn't anyone . . .' he tailed off incoherently, gazing at me with a supplicating look upon his face.

I tried to help him. 'So you decided to come and have a look round the estate?'

Another anguished glance. 'Well, not exactly that. You see, I noticed that the egg basket was gone . . .'

I found that I was staring at him. So was Junio. 'The egg basket?' I echoed.

He nodded. 'The basket that's used for collecting the eggs. It hangs on the wall inside the servants' sleeping-room – at least, that's where it was kept when I belonged to Marcus.' It was the first long utterance he had managed since we'd found him here.

'It was clever of you to have noticed it was gone,' I said gently. 'I certainly hadn't noticed it myself.' Although, now he mentioned it, I had a recollection of an empty hook beside the door and a faint mark on the wall where something had once hung.

Minimus was still gasping, but I'd encouraged him. 'Pauvrissimus used to take it out to get the eggs first thing in the morning.' He glanced at the headless corpses, and glanced away again. 'Well, I thought that's what he'd done. You

46

wouldn't take the basket if you weren't collecting eggs. And, since there wasn't any poultry in the yard, I thought they must have been let out underneath the trees to scratch for worms and things – that's what they always used to do when I was here – though it's a bit early in the season. I know the chickens that you keep at home aren't really laying yet. But Marcus breeds several varieties of hens, as well as ducks and geese – on purpose to get eggs as long as possible. So I came into the orchard . . .' He shook his head again. 'Poor Pauvrissimus! Who did this awful thing? And what's happened to their heads?'

'I don't know,' I told him. 'But I'm anxious to find out. I'll discover who did this to your friend, I promise you. And if you can bear to look again at the other bodies, it is even possible that you can help.'

'Me?' Minimus turned a chalk-white face to me. 'If it will help to catch the killer, I'd do a great deal more than that.'

'Then look at them and tell me – you know that Marcus only left a tiny indoor staff behind, just enough to keep the villa open while he was away. Apart from the steward and the amanuensis, whom I recognise myself, do you think that this is all of them?'

Minimus swallowed hard and forced himself to look at the pile of headless bodies that used to be his friends. 'It is hard to tell exactly who is who – and there's certain to be some people who were purchased when I'd left – but most of them I'm fairly certain of. That little boy beside Pauvrissimus was a trainee page, I think, here to open the door

47

and deal with visitors. That one there's the general messenger, and that's the girl that used to mend the linen and do general sewing work. That couple with the cook will be the other kitchen slaves – someone has to feed the household and the land-slaves too – and that fat lad with them is the boy who fetches fuel to feed the cooking stoves and things.' He considered for a moment. 'The other general slaves I'm not really sure about. There'd be three or four to clean the villa, I suppose. It looks as though His Excellence has ordered an effort to do that while he's away – someone has been scrubbing out the storage vats, I see, and there'll be all the household cutlery and ornaments to clean, so he'll have left sufficient staff to do it properly. I didn't have a lot of contact with the more menial staff, so I would not necessarily know them anyway, especially now there is no face to recognise.' He wrinkled up his nose. 'The only thing I can't see is a gatekeeper . . . I know that there were changes after I had gone, but there's no one left who looks the build for that.'

I found myself exchanging glances with my son. There was a little silence.

'Ah, the gatekeeper,' Junio said, at last. 'My father's already found him, so he's accounted for. It seems that he was in his cell, but dead, when we came in. That is why he didn't answer us.'

Minimus was frowning. 'But there should be two of them. One for the back gate as well as for the front.'

I glanced across at Junio, who raised his brows at me, 'Even when the master is away?' I asked my little slave.

He shrugged. 'I don't think Marcus would have gone and left the back gate unguarded, or permanently locked. All the land-slaves have to come and go that way – if only to deliver crops or tend the animals.'

I stared at him. Of course, the lad was right. In fact, while the owner of the villa was in Rome and few visitors of rank were liable to call, the rear entrance was probably the most important and frequented one. Marcus's gatekeepers were invariably selected for their strength and their ability to frighten off unwelcome visitors, so one would expect to find some muscular he-bear of a slave, just like the keeper of the other gate. I knew that my patron had bought a new one, fairly recently. Yet Minimus was right again – there was no obvious candidate among the dead.

Junio was obviously thinking the same thing. 'So there is someone missing?' he observed to me. 'Or we assume there is. It may be that his body is lying somewhere else – if he let in the killers inadvertently. But then, you'd think, the land-slaves would have known.'

I nodded. 'I think I'd better go and have another word with them. They would know who was on duty at the rear gate – yesterday, I think it must have been. And perhaps they can explain how this could happen here while they remain oblivious of it.'

'And I shall come with you,' Junio declared. 'Even if you're riding on the mule and I'm obliged to walk. It isn't wise for anyone to go down there alone in case the killer is still somewhere roaming the estate. Minimus can run back home and tell them what's occurred and reassure them that you are safe and well. Mother will be really worrying by now.'

I nodded. 'Very well. I'm tempted to think that one of us should stay to keep a watch on these.' I gestured to the headless bodies on the ground. 'But nothing that we do will help these people now. And if the killer's still about it might be dangerous for us. So we'll go back through the villa and do as you suggest.'

We retraced our steps in silence, all of us listening, wary and alert, fearing to hear noises or stumble on some new atrocity. By common consent we skirted round the house, taking the route out through the storage yard, and by and by we found ourselves at the front gate again.

Junio glanced at me, then at the gatehouse cell. I nodded. He motioned to the slave-boy not to follow him, then pushed the door open and went inside. He came out looking shaken.

'Still there, then?' I enquired.

He made a little gesture of horrified assent. 'I see what you mean about the chains around the hands,' he said. 'It's obviously murder and not a suicide. Just another one to add to our criminal's account.'

'But there's Arlina, anyway,' I murmured with relief, rushing through the gate to fondle my old mule. 'At least she's safe and well. I was beginning to fear that someone would have stolen her.' I undid the rope that tethered her. 'I'll get on and ride. I'll be all right alone. You two go back together. It's more dangerous on foot.'

Minimus looked beseechingly at me as I hoisted

myself up onto the saddle on Arlina's bony back. 'Master, it's not my place to interrupt, but may I speak to you?'

I smiled. 'It seems you're speaking! What is it you want?'

'If you're going to find the killer of Pauvrissimus,' he said, 'please take me with you, master. You can even take me to sit up on the mule. I am small enough for both of us to ride, and we'll get there much more quickly than if someone has to walk.'

I glanced at Junio. 'The boy has already had a fearful shock today. Perhaps it would be better . . .' I was about to say, 'for him to go straight home', but Junio interrupted.

'If anyone is going to travel on the lane alone, it should be me,' he said. 'But if I think you two have gone too long, I shall bring Maximus and come and look for you. And I'll bring the wood-axe with me, just in case!' He waited till Minimus had climbed up ahead of me, then he smacked Arlina's rump and turned away in the direction of our homes.

I found myself bumping down the lane again towards the prospective vineyard where the land-slaves were.

Six

The chief land-slave saw us coming down the lane. He abandoned his view-point position on a high point of the field and called out in surprise, 'Why citizen, I see you're here again! But be assured, we've not been idle while you were away. We've started digging the trenches for the vines. I'll show you, if you wish!' The undertone of mocking half-contempt was, as usual, barely concealed by the outward courtesy. 'Come down to the enclosure gate and I will let you in.'

I ignored this invitation. I dismounted where I was and went directly over to the boundary wall, leaving Minimus to tether up the mule. 'Never mind the vines,' I shouted back. 'I've more important things than vineyards to discuss with you.'

He must have realised that something was afoot because the carefully adopted fake-attentive smile faded from his lean, tanned features instantly. He positively scurried across the field to meet me where I was and when he spoke his manner was quite different from before. 'Why, whatever is it, citizen?' For the first time in our acquaintance he looked straight into my eyes. 'Has something happened to the master while he's been overseas?' He saw that I was beginning to shake my head, denying this, and before I could say anything, he'd made another guess. 'Or has the mistress

perished giving birth to the new child? It's something serious, I can see that from your face.'

'It's not what happened to your owners, it's
what has happened here.' I had to hold my hand
up, even then, to silence him before he started
to interrupt again. 'But before you ask me questions, there's one I have for you. Think carefully
before you answer it – much may depend on
what you tell me now. Did anything strike you
as unusual last night when you went back home
to the main estate again?'

He was frowning. 'But we didn't! Surely you
must have been aware of that?'

'Didn't what?' I was as perplexed as he appeared
to be. He was still staring at me in bewilderment,
so I said, to make it clearer, 'What was it that
you didn't do?'

'Go back to the main estate last night!' he said,
as if this were the strangest notion in the world.
'Even since that message was delivered two days
or more ago, none of us land-slaves has been
back at all.'

'Message? What message?' I was beginning to
sound like Echo in the myth. 'I didn't know there
had been any message to the house.'

He gave me a sly grin. 'Then you're not as
much in the master's confidence as I supposed
you were. Oh, indeed there was a message,
citizen. A whole great scroll of it. We had strict
instructions. There's a disused farmhouse here
and we were to sleep in that till they had finished
in the villa – even the animals were moved down
here meanwhile.'

I nodded. Obviously the cleaning operations

53

had been Marcus's idea – that was only what one might expect. But moving all the land-slaves out was rather radical, and had obviously led to the slaughter of the indoor staff. 'So you aren't even using the courtyard barns down there?' I persisted. I was remembering the empty stalls and stock enclosures at the rear of the villa. I should have realised that it was unusual, but I had been too anxious about the missing slaves to really take in the significance.

'Not at the moment, citizen.'

'But why not? Isn't that what you generally do? Even if this great cleaning spree is taking place, you wouldn't hinder it. And the outbuildings at the villa are in much better repair.'

'We weren't wanted at the main estate, tending the creatures and getting in the way, and this arrangement made things more convenient. Or so the master thought, apparently – though, of course, in fact, it made a lot of extra work for us.'

I waved away this piece of grumbling. 'Convenient for what?'

He was edging towards that former mocking air again. 'For seeing to the animals, citizen, of course. Even during this season there is lots of work to do, especially when you're caring for the new kids and lambs and calves.' He gazed at me and seemed to realise that I really was bemused. 'There are empty barns and stables here that are quite usable. Plus, there is a chicken coop or two, and quite a nice enclosure for the goats – the whole place was a working farm till recently. You're right, of course. Several of the buildings were in a dreadful state. But I've had such labour as I could afford doing their best to mend them while we moved the stock – and I'm glad to say that everything's a little better now.' He stopped and looked at me triumphantly.

He was obviously seeking to be as helpful as possible, but I still had no idea what this was all about. However, a suspicion had begun to dawn on me. 'Never mind the arrangements for the animals. Who was it decided that you should stay up here?'

He took a small step backwards in surprise. 'It was the master's orders. I thought I'd told you that.' He had adopted a weary, patient tone, as if talking to a failing intellect. 'He sent this message several days ago saying that on his travels he had found a house in Gaul and all the precious objects in the villa here were to be packed up and crated and sent over to him there.'

I boggled at him. 'So he's closing down the villa?'

'Not immediately, citizen, I think. I understand he hopes to come here now and then, if only to see this vineyard that he wants so much. But in the end, perhaps. It would not affect his role as magistrate – he still has a smart apartment in the town.'

'Of course,' I murmured. 'And a fine house in Corinium as well. But he's devoted to this villa. And I know he planned to pass it to his son when he's of age. Why would he part with it?'

He acknowledged this information with a little bow. 'Perhaps he thinks that this new place he's found would make a sort of halfway house where

55

he can stay if he is travelling more frequently to and fro from Rome, and obviously that's something that he intends to do.' He gave me a knowing grin. 'Not surprising now his friend's the Emperor. But I thought you would have known all this in any case. Marcus always seems to tell you everything.'

I looked thoughtfully at him. In principle, the thing was not impossible. My patron was given to sudden whims like this, very often not thought through in any detail – as witness the very vineyards we were looking at, or his one-time enthusiasm for those neatly matching pairs of slaves. And it would certainly explain the missing items from the house. I could see why the overseer had not questioned it.

But it did not explain what had happened to the slaves. I shook my head. 'You are right. I hadn't heard,' I told him, soberly. 'And I'm not sure that I believe it now. You are quite sure that the message was from Marcus Septimus?'

He stared at me as though I were insane. 'I'm absolutely certain, citizen. I saw the scroll myself.'

'And you could read it?' I enquired, genuinely impressed. One does not expect land-slaves, even senior ones like this, to be literate at all. Such skills are not required in the fields and few owners go to the expense of teaching them, though occasional bright individuals do contrive to teach themselves by studying known inscriptions on public monuments, learning to decipher the letters bit by bit.

But the overseer was not one of these exceptions, it appeared.

He looked at me, abashed. 'Well, not exactly, citizen. I can make out a word or two of course, but it takes me quite a time. The steward read it to us and handed it around to let us look at it. It's what he always does. He would not have made it up, I'm sure.' He brightened. 'Anyway, I recognised the seal. It was the master's, I am positive of that. And the message even listed all the things that had to go . . . which stools and statues and which ornaments. Who else but His Excellence could know details like that . . .?' He saw my face and trailed off in dismay. 'Oh, I suppose the steward would. You really think the letter was a fake? So . . . there's been some kind of robbery? Is that what you believe?'

I nodded. 'Among several other crimes!' I said. 'And robbery is perhaps the least of them.'

He made a doubtful face. 'Well, I can't believe the steward was involved in it,' he said. 'Though I suppose that things look rather bad for him. But I'm sure the message said exactly what he claimed. He was as irritated as the rest of us at all the extra work that was required. And I can't believe it was a forgery. The steward's been with Marcus Septimus for years. How could he be deceived? Wouldn't he know the handwriting and seal? But if you doubt him – and you obviously do – why don't you go and ask him to produce the scroll?'

'I'm very much afraid—' I had begun to say, but he was rushing on.

'That it will have been sent back with another message written crosswise – as a palimpsest? I know that sometimes happens, but not this time,

I don't think. I'm sure that he's still got the scroll exactly as it came. He was using it as an inventory of items to be sent. And he can hardly refuse you if you ask for it – he'll know you are in our master's confidence – and then you can read and judge it for yourself.' He stopped and gave me a sudden, startled look. 'Oh, dear gods! He's not gone missing too? Is that why you've come down here to ask me this? You said that much depended on what I had to say. You think he's guilty of arranging this?'

I shook my head. 'I don't know what to think. But the steward isn't missing. He is there all right. And so are the others. Or what is left of them.'

'What is left of them?' All the swagger left him suddenly, and the swarthy face was white beneath the tan. 'You can't mean that they're dead. The household slaves? Surely not all of them.'

'I think so, though I don't know exactly how many indoor slaves there were,' I said. 'But there were a dozen bodies in the orchard, by my reckoning.'

He did a calculation on his hands. 'I make it fourteen with the gatekeepers,' he said.

'They were not included,' I replied.

'Then that would be the whole of the domestic staff.' He gulped, seeming suddenly to realise the dreadful force of this. 'All twelve of them? Dear Jupiter! What happened? Was there poison in something they ate? It must have been some kind of accident.' He looked into my face again, saw the truth and said with disbelief, 'Not intruders, surely? There are armed men always watching

58

at the villa gates! No one could get in and simply murder everyone.'

There was no kind way to tell him, so I did not try to mask the brutal facts. 'But someone did. This was no accident, I fear. All the heads were missing – hacked off the neck.' I gestured to Minimus, who – having tethered up the mule – was now waiting patiently a little further on. 'And these were certainly the bodies of the indoor staff. My own slave used to work at the villa and he recognised a few.'

The chief land-slave gawped at me. 'So it was obviously murder?'

'Of the most callous kind,' I said. 'Some of them were clearly stabbed as well – so they might have been dead or dying before the final blow.'

He had stopped talking now, and was digesting this. 'And the gatekeepers weren't with them? What does that suggest? I suppose they could be killers – they are strong enough, especially combined. Though I wouldn't for a moment have thought that of them.' He shook his head. 'And I'm absolutely certain they could not have sent the scroll. Neither of them ever learned to read a single word, let alone write one, which is the harder skill.'

'The guard from the front gate is accounted for!' I said. 'He wasn't with the others. He was hanging in his cell. Not by his own hand, if I am any judge.' I explained what I had seen. 'And it's possible we'll find the body of the other one somewhere.'

My listener was as shaken as Minimus had been. 'You think it's an attack against the household then? And these . . .?' He nodded towards his land-slaves, still working in the field, who were occasionally glancing towards us as they dug, but were oblivious – as yet – of what awaited them at home. 'You think that they'll be next?'

He sounded so concerned about his men that I was rather touched. I wanted to reassure him a little, if I could. I shook my head. 'I doubt it very much,' I said, although in fact I wasn't sure of this at all. 'Someone's taken trouble to have you moved away.'

He nodded. 'Probably because we're generally fit and muscular. Working outside on the land all day every day for years, does build you up a bit.' He said it with some pride. 'We'd be a great deal more difficult to overcome than that soft-handed lot who only work indoors, to say nothing of the fact that there are far more of us. Especially at the moment, with the master gone away. It does not take many to look after the house, but – as I said before – this is a very busy season on the farm. The crops and animals need tending just the same and there are almost as many land-slaves as there ever were. Marcus had more sense than to dispose of most of us.'

I looked around the field. There must have been thirty or forty men at work. 'So this is all of them?'

'Dear gods! Of course it's not!' He looked at me appalled. 'I'd forgotten that. I have sent another half a dozen up there to the estate.' He raised an apologetic brow at me. 'I know that my instructions did not allow for that, but I had to do something useful with them and I thought there'd be no harm. Just some of the youngest and the oldest who couldn't dig all day. I sent them to do slightly lighter jobs – pruning, mending hedges and that sort of thing – though they're not working near the villa, I made sure of that.' He gazed into my face. 'You think that something awful might have befallen them, as well?'

'I doubt it,' I told him. 'I think all this happened yesterday. But perhaps we should go up there and see, in any case.' He was looking so stricken that I was moved to add, 'If they were working nearer to the villa at the time, it is possible that they have useful information to impart – for instance, if any tradesmen or visitors arrived, at the back gate in particular. As it happened, I saw somebody myself, some sort of patrician in a travelling coach. But I think the slaughter had already taken place, because I know the caller got no answer at the gate.'

My efforts to divert his thoughts had been successful, it appeared. He frowned. 'Who was that, I wonder. Someone from abroad? All Marcus's acquaintances know that he's away.' He raised a brow at me. 'Maybe the owner of that house in Gaul?'

'If indeed the house in Gaul exists,' I murmured inwardly. Aloud I said, 'That is certainly a possibility. In any case I must discover who that caller was, and exactly what happened when his slave knocked at the gate. If the answer is nothing, then at least we'd have a time before which all this horror must have taken place.'

He looked at me keenly. 'I think you're right. I'd better come and take a look myself. I could tell you, at least, if all the household is accounted for. And I'd be glad to know if I've lost any of my land-slaves in this dreadful incident.'

'But you saw them all this morning and they were accounted for.'

'You are assuming, citizen, that these murderous men have not come back. It may be that we land-slaves are scheduled to be next.' He gestured at the labourers still digging in the field. 'Would it be acceptable to leave this lot, do you think? I know that Marcus forbids it generally, but in the circumstances . . .'

I nodded. 'I think he would agree. Are you going to tell them what happened at the house?'

He screwed his face into a horrible grimace. 'I don't think so, citizen. Or at least, not yet. They can have a little longer to enjoy their ignorance. I'll wait until I've seen these horrors for myself before I tell them what has happened to their fellow slaves. Time enough to give them nightmares then. In the meantime, I'll just tell them that you've come to call for me, and we can leave your own slave here to keep an eye on things.'

I looked at little Minimus. 'And that would be enough?'

'They wouldn't question it, if I instructed them – though it might occasion giggles, I'm afraid. But they know the boy is acting as your eyes and ears, and that's sufficient to ensure that they keep working while we are away.'

'But I'm just a humble tradesman!' I protested

62

with a smile. 'My rank would hardly count for anything.'

He shrugged. A little uncomfortably, I thought. 'You have a sort of reputation as a spy, snooping round for Marcus while he is away, and determined to find something to report.' He gave me a sheepish smile. 'My fault, citizen. I fear I haven't talked of you with very much respect.'

I looked him in the eye. 'And I, in turn, have underestimated you. You've shown a real concern about your men which I applaud. I was once a slave myself. So shall we, like warring generals with a common enemy, forget our differences and declare a kind of truce?'

He looked away. I saw him hesitate. 'You? A slave? I'd not imagined that!'

I nodded. 'Seized by pirates and sold into slavery. My master bequeathed me freedom when he died, together with the rank of citizen. That, after all, is how I gained my name: Libertus, "the freed one", as no doubt you know. You may call me that in future, when we two are alone.' I grasped his forearm and shook it heartily, as the Romans do. 'And you must tell me what they call you, too.'

'I would not dare be so familiar as to call you by your name,' he protested, colouring, and extracting himself from the handshake with embarrassment. 'But I am Georgicus. You can imagine why.'

I could. The word means 'agricultural', and it rather suited him. I noted, though, that he had not responded well to my suggestion that we might forget our differences. 'Well, Georgicus,'

I said, trying to pretend that I did not feel rebuffed, 'give your slaves their orders and I'll do the same with mine, and we'll go down to the villa and decide what's to be done.'

Seven

Minimus was almost beside himself with pride at being put 'in charge' and for the first time since we'd found Pauvrissimus, I saw a fleeting smile. We left my small slave standing where Georgicus had been, preening like a young patrician at his new-found role and staring round the field with a proprietary air – though any of his temporary charges could have lifted him one-handed if they had chosen to. However, his borrowed authority seemed to be enough and they turned back to their tasks without a word.

So we left him to it. We had urgent business of our own. In fact, in the interests of getting to the villa as fast as possible, I suggested to Georgicus that he could ride with me, sitting in front as Minimus had done, though it would have been a tight fit for us and a heavier burden for poor Arlina than I'd generally have liked. But the chief land-slave brushed the thought aside.

'It will be faster for us, citizen, if I run beside the mule,' he said, and as if to prove the point he set off at a trot – so fast that, by the time I'd climbed onto the creature's back, it took me minutes to catch up with him. Indeed, he was very nearly at the villa gates before I shambled up beside him on my mount

He raised his head to greet me but he did not slacken pace. 'Ah, Citizen Libertus! I am glad you've caught me up. I was not looking forward to going in there alone.'

I shouted my agreement. 'Better if we keep together while we're there, I think. It will take me a moment to tie this creature up, so I'll go on ahead and wait for you outside.'

I did not have to wait. I had no sooner tethered up the mule than Georgicus came loping smoothly down the lane. He had been running by this time for better than a mile, but he seemed scarcely out of breath. No wonder that he boasted of how fit the land-slaves were. Without my mule, I could never have kept pace. But I refused to be abashed. Considering what awaited us within the walls, and the fact that the killer (or killers) might still be nearby, there was a certain consolation in having someone with me who had strength and stamina.

He padded up beside me. 'No sign of my other land-slaves anywhere about,' he said. 'I suppose you noticed that?'

I hadn't, but I didn't tell him that. 'They should have been in sight?'

'There should have been several working in the fields back there – though not close to the villa, as I said before. But I could not see them where they should have been.' He raised a brow at me. 'Another little mystery, citizen, for you to solve.' The tone was courteous but there was something in the eyes which hinted a little at ridicule.

I affected not to notice. 'Then in we go!' I said, with a pretence at heartiness, and pushed the gates open as I had done before. 'We'll start with the gatehouse, I suggest.'

But Georgicus, behind me, had halted in his tracks. 'Dear gods and all the spirits of the underworld! This is how you found the gates? Unbolted and unbarred?' He saw my nod and made a little grimace of astonishment. 'Of course – you told me you'd got in without the assistance of the gatekeeper. But I'd not imagined this. Not even really latched! You did not tell me that.' He pursed his lips. 'Marcus would have had somebody flayed for less!'

'I know!' I murmured. 'It seems whoever came here simply pulled them shut, so a casual passer-by would not see anything amiss.'

'And that tells you something, does it, citizen?' It was a challenge, though perfectly polite.

'Unfortunately not. Except that they had the leisure to do so as they left. Obviously they could not bolt them from outside. Although,' I added, as a thought occurred to me, 'it might give us grounds to hope that they have not come back. If they were here now, they would doubtless have relocked them from within.'

But he was hardly listening. He was bending over, examining the gates. 'These bars and bolts aren't damaged. You see what that must mean? They did not force an entry. Someone let them in.'

I nodded. 'I had come to that conclusion, anyway,' I said. 'I think they came here, as the letter said they would, and loaded up their wagons with items from the house. No doubt assisted by the steward and the domestic staff.'

He raised an eyebrow at me. 'By Mercury, they must be clever – if you're right! And no doubt dangerous. Be careful, citizen before you get involved.'

There was that curious timbre in his voice again. Was he mocking me? I glanced at him sharply. 'And what about yourself? Aren't you planning to be "involved" in this, as well?'

He shrugged. 'I have no option. I'm a slave of Marcus's and in the absence of the household steward, I suppose I'm senior now. It is my duty to discover what's happened to my owner's property, including the murdered servants. They were valuable things. But it's not the same for you. No one could blame you if you simply left me here and went and reported this to the authorities.'

'I'm involved already,' I told him. 'I've promised Minimus I'll find out who it was that killed Pauvrissimus, and I have a duty to my patron too. So it looks as if we're working together over this, my friend.'

'Friend?' He sketched an imitation bow. 'I'm honoured that you think to call me so. But I am hardly that. We are of different ranks. I know my place, I hope. However, it is my duty to help you if I can, though no doubt you are quite capable of solving this yourself. My master has often boasted of your skills with problems of this kind. You can provide the intellect, perhaps, and I'll provide the brawn.'

There was that touch of mockery again. 'There's nothing the matter with your intellect,' I murmured guardedly, pulling the gates closed behind us as I spoke, 'you're obviously observant. You noticed instantly that the locks had not been forced.' It sounded patronising, so I added hurriedly, 'So come into the gatehouse cell and tell me what you think.'

This time I stood back and let him lead the way inside while I watched him carefully. It had not escaped me that he might know more about this than he would have me think. He would have unquestioned access to the house and grounds and there was something in his manner which I found disquieting.

But perhaps I was wrong to be suspicious. His reactions in the gatehouse seemed genuine enough. There was already a faint, unpleasant odour in the air and I saw Georgicus hesitate as he caught a whiff of it and when he pressed on to the interior his shock appeared unfeigned.

'Dear gods!' He whirled to face me. 'I think you're right about him being dead a day. You said you found him hanging. This is exactly as he was when you first got here earlier?'

I nodded. It hadn't occurred to me that it might be otherwise, until Georgicus turned to me and said, 'Well, it seems my missing land-slaves haven't been here, anyway. I wondered if they might have wandered up here after all, since we didn't get our usual warm meal yesterday. The first day we were down there, they sent us a stew to heat, but last night there was no sign of anyone. There were some grumblings, as you might expect, but we had sufficient bread and cheese in any case, and since we had the hens there, we ate some eggs as well.'

'The kitchens sent no food down, and you didn't question that?'

He raised an eyebrow at me. 'Citizen, we're

land-slaves. It's not our place to ask. We'd been warned that it might happen, because even the kitchen staff were being asked to help to load the carts. So, though we didn't like it, we were stuck with it. We're always the last ones to be fed in any case, and we'd had our strict instructions and we adhered to them. Mind you, I am not saying that I would not have come and made a fuss if nothing had arrived for us today. That's why I wondered if my missing slaves had been here – but obviously not.'

'Surely, they would have come and told you what they'd found.' I glanced up at the corpse.

'I suspect they would have cut him down first and taken him away – if only to prevent his spirit haunting them.'

'Taken him – where to?' I was surprised at that.

He nodded. 'There's a hut out in the courtyard where dead slaves are always laid until someone can make contact with the Guild of Slaves who will arrange a decent funeral for them. The master sees to that. He pays the subscription dues for all of us. I thought you would have known that, citizen.'

'I had forgotten,' I told him truthfully. 'Though Marcus did tell me that he always paid the dues, so no one's ghost would have to walk the earth because their body has no proper resting place.' I sounded sanctimonious, even to myself.

Georgicus glanced at the gently swaying body on the rope. 'That would not apply to suicides, of course. But this is not a suicide, you think?'

'I am sure of it,' I told him 'You will see the hands are chained.' I was childishly pleased to

70

have the chance to point out something he had not observed himself.

He had to go around the back to check that I was right. He examined the arrangement silently a moment, and then said, 'So someone strung him up. Yet gatekeepers like this are valuable things. I wonder that the robbers did not take him too, and sell him on.'

I shook my head. 'When they had finished in the villa and took the stuff away, I think they simply disposed of any servants who could inform on them.'

'So if the staff had consisted solely of illiterate deaf-mutes, perhaps they would have lived?' He raised that brow again. For a man who was looking at a colleague's corpse, I thought, he seemed remarkably unmoved. 'I suppose you may be right,' he said at last.

'But . . .?' I prompted. 'You do not sound convinced. You see some flaw in my theory, I presume.'

He shrugged his powerful shoulders. 'We all believed the movement of the goods was done at Marcus's command. And slaves are merely objects, anyway, in law, simply part of the chattels belonging to the house.' His tone was cynical. 'If the villa was to be vacated and the furniture removed, no slave would think it strange if they were taken off and sold. I would not have questioned it if I were sold myself, vineyard or no vineyard. And most of this household were quite expensive slaves. So why did the thieves not take them to the slave-market, at least, and make a little extra profit on the side?'

I shook my head. 'I think they thought they couldn't take the risk. The slaves were sure to talk about their former home. To their new masters or to tradesmen calling at the house.'

'And who listens to a slave?'

'No one at first, perhaps, but that would change when Marcus got back home. He'd be shouting in the forum that his slaves and goods were gone – and people would start listening then, I'm sure. Once it was clear that the letter was a fraud, there'd be an outcry in the town, and the slave could doubtless describe the culprits perfectly. They could not be permitted to survive.'

'You think these thieves are local people, then, if such a description could lead to their arrest?' Georgicus sounded frankly sceptical. 'I would doubt that. If Marcus ever catches up with them, they would be lucky if their death was merciful.'

'Yet they have to be people who know Marcus, don't you think?' I pointed out. 'And fairly well at that. Well enough not only to know he is away, but also to be familiar with the contents of the house. Otherwise this robbery could not have arranged.'

He thought for a moment. 'You're right. Though it only requires one person to have that knowledge, I suppose. The same might not be true of all of them.' That concession to my viewpoint earned me a half-smile. 'And I suppose we are agreed that there were several of these men? That no one person could have done all this alone?'

I nodded. 'Five or six of them at least. And very likely armed.' I thought of the beheaded corpses in the orchard. 'Swords and daggers, at the very least. And clubs as well, I shouldn't be surprised.'

'So how in the name of all the gods did they get in?' He furrowed his weather-beaten brow again and nodded at the corpse. 'There were keepers at the gates! Large men with weapons, like this unfortunate. I can see that he would let in people that he thought had come to work – carters and wagoners and that sort of thing – but he would never have admitted a gang of men with swords. Not without a struggle anyway. But look at him. There is no sign of wounds. He doesn't even look as if he's fought with anyone. And the household staff were to load the carts themselves. It isn't as if they needed extra men for that.' He shook his head again. 'So perhaps the carters did it and then let the others in. Though how many carters do you think there must have been to overcome a household full of slaves? And they must have had weapons. Yet, that must be the solution. The gates have not been forced.'

I let him work all through it before I intervened. 'But, Georgicus,' I said patiently, though not unwilling to demonstrate he hadn't thought it fully out, 'no one sends wagon-loads of treasure on the road without a guard. The servants – including the gatekeepers, of course – would have expected Marcus to arrange an escort for the trip. So the arrival of armed guards would not come as a surprise. In fact, it's just what you'd anticipate.'

He made a reluctant gesture of acknowledgement. 'So the gatekeepers would let them in! And once inside . . . I see!' He gave me a long, appraising look, as though reassessing my abilities. Then with a grimace he shook his head. 'By Dis, these men were clever. I like this less and less.'

'You'll like it less still when you see what's lying in the orchard field,' I said. 'Come and I'll show you.' And I began to lead the way around the back.

Eight

The pile of sorry corpses made my throat go dry again and this time even Georgicus looked shocked. 'Dear Ceres! You are quite right! All of them are dead. Who would have thought those people would do anything like this?' The words seemed shaken from him.

I glanced at him, wondering exactly what he meant. 'Those people?' I echoed. Did he know more about them than he was willing to admit?

'Surely this is the handiwork of our robbers, isn't it? I thought we had agreed in principle on that.' He was staring at the bodies with a stricken look, but his tone was businesslike.

I decided to reply in kind. 'Do you think that this accounts for all the household staff?'

He nodded, bitterly. 'I'm pretty sure of it, although of course as outdoor slaves we didn't really mix with them. Indoor servants regard themselves as much more highly trained and most think it is below them to have much to do with us. But we were all the possessions of the same owner, after all, and with the steward dead I suppose I'm now responsible for everything. I'll have my land-slaves build a pyre for these unfortunates and I'd better get a message to the Funeral Guild as well.' He looked at the head-less corpses of his colleagues and shook his head. 'I don't suppose the master would object if we arranged one big cremation in a field out here?'

'I'm sure that Marcus would insist on it.' I meant it. 'With so many bodies, it would prove expensive otherwise.'

He gazed around as if searching for a site. 'Up at the other property, perhaps? Not the vineyard field, but a fallow one that hasn't been brought under proper cultivation yet? Then the funeral urns could all be buried in the master's land without too much disruption to the crops. You're in his confidence, what would you suggest? It would take too long to send word to him to ask him for advice.'

'But of course his wife is in Corinium,' I said, 'That is only a half-day's ride away. If you're concerned, I am confident that she will give consent.'

The land-slave captain shook his head. 'Send her a message? But I don't know who—'

I cut him off. 'I shall be going to Glevum later on, myself. The garrison commander is a friend of Marcus's and he has the swiftest couriers available. I mean to ask him to send a messenger to my patron anyway – your owner should know what's happened here as soon as possible – and I'm sure a rider can be sent to Julia as well. And I'll speak to the Slaves' Guild for you while I am in the town.'

He did not thank me, just gave a sober nod and looked down at the bloodied bodies of people he had known. 'Then, with your permission, citizen, I'll get back to my work. I'll send a land-slave up here to start on the lament. It seems to be the least that we can do. And having someone here might put a stop to these flies!' He flapped away a pair of lazy, bloated ones which had settled on the dead cook's severed neck. 'Perhaps we could find something with which to cover up the dead?' For the first time there was genuine emotion in his voice – it actually seemed liable to break.

'I think there are some blankets in the slave quarters,' I said.

But before I'd even managed to complete the words, he was halfway across the orchard with that loping run of his. A moment later I heard a mighty shout. 'Got them!' and he was running back again.

It did not take an instant to cover up the slaves and once we had done so I, too, felt more at ease. 'Now, then . . .' I began, as we left the orchard and walked back into the enclosure where the slave quarters were. I was about to suggest that I would wait until he'd sent his promised mourner back, preferably with Minimus, so that once the lamentation had begun I could set off on my mission to the town. But before I'd manage to complete the words, I was interrupted by a frenzied rattling at the main gates at the rear.

I froze, feeling a prickle of cold sweat run down my neck. Who would be coming to the back entrance of the villa now? A carter with deliveries, possibly – but what would they be bringing while Marcus was away, and would they dare to rattle on the gates like that? Yet if wasn't that, who was it? Could it be the armed intruders coming back again?

I looked at Georgicus and he looked at me. 'Tradesman with deliveries?' he murmured.

'At this time of day, I suppose that's possible. On the other hand . . .' I cast around for something with which to arm myself, but could think of nothing better than the kitchen knives I'd noticed earlier. 'Wait here!' I called to Georgicus. I dashed in through the arch towards the house, burst into the kitchen block, picked up the biggest blade that I could find and thrust it through my belt – to the side where it would not dig into me but was still easy to get to, underneath my cloak. I picked up the pestle for good measure, too. It wasn't very heavy but it would make a cosh, of sorts.

I hurried back. At first sight I couldn't see Georgicus anywhere, though the rattling at the gate was even louder now. I was still not altogether sure of him and glanced around in panic. Then I saw him. His thoughts must have been turning the same way as my own, because he'd knelt beside the gatehouse to remove the heavy timber that was used to bar the gate. As I watched, he slid it from its frame, where, when the gates were sealed, it lay crosswise across the aperture as an additional security to the bolts. It was long and stout and sturdy. He got up, carrying it loosely in one hand, weighing it against the other as though it were a club. I could scarcely have lifted it with both.

'Undo the bolts,' he told me, gesturing for me to join him at the gates 'If that is just a tradesman delivering to the villa, well and good. But if it isn't . . .' He mimed the act of hoisting the piece

78

of wood above his head and smashing it down on top of someone's skull. 'If it is our murderous friends again they are doubtless armed with swords. But we'll take someone with us, or my name's not Georgicus.'

I nodded. I was just a little thoughtful about being the person to unbolt the gate when he was standing behind me with his makeshift weapon raised. However, I bent and put my free hand to the lower bolt. It was surprisingly difficult to move as it was vibrating with the violent rattling of the gate, which now seemed even more peremptory than before. Even when I put down my cosh and used both hands I couldn't pull it back.

'All right!' I shouted to whoever was outside. 'Give me a moment to undo the bolt.' The rattling ceased abruptly, but there was no reply. That was alarming. One might have expected a cart-driver to have shouted back. I called again. 'Who is it anyway?' But once again there was no response at all.

As I straightened up I noticed a knot-hole in the wood-strut of the gate, just a little above my shoulder height – hollowed out by some imaginative guard, no doubt, to give a view of anybody in the lane outside. I was about to bend over and apply to my eye to it when I realised that Georgicus had stepped up very close to me and was hovering, his hulk of wood upraised.

'Go on! Have a look!' he murmured in my ear.

More nervous now than ever, I did as I was told. It wasn't possible to keep one eye on Georgicus as I would have liked, so I had to commit myself to peering through the hole – and found to my astonishment that there was nothing to be seen. I wriggled round to adjust my vantage point, but there did not appear to be anyone at the gate, or in the small portion of the lane that I could see. That was somehow more worrying than a brace of swordsmen with their weapons drawn.

I turned to Georgicus. My mouth was suddenly too dry for speech. I shrugged my shoulders at him, and spread my hands apart to indicate that there was no one there. 'Nothing!' I managed. I drew out my blade.

'May be a trap,' he whispered. 'Be careful, citizen.'

Better to face danger head on than wait for it, I thought. I clenched my knife more tightly and – keeping it firmly levelled at what I hoped would be chest-height to any incomer – I pulled the bolts back with my other hand. They moved easily enough now that the rattling had stopped but, though I tried to do it silently, the metal squeaked loudly.

Georgicus came back to stand beside me with his baulk of wood upraised. He gave me a curt nod, and – realising finally that I was not at risk from him – with a sudden movement I thrust the gates apart.

I was half expecting killers, dangerous and armed. What I found, when I had lowered my eyes sufficiently, was an extremely frightened little boy – a sort of infant land-slave, from the ragged tunic that he wore. I hadn't seen him through the knot-hole because he was so small.

I was so relieved that I could hardly speak, just stood there staring at him stupidly.

He might have been perhaps as much as five or six years old, though he was so under-developed that it was hard to tell. His dirty, tousled carrot-coloured curls reached scarcely to my hips. He was as thin as he was tiny, and his legs were bare, though an enormous pair of cut-down peasant 'boots' reached almost to his knees. (These rough bags of cow-skin were far too big for him and had clearly been formed on someone else's feet.) His skinny face was filthy, streaked with mud and tears, and his red-rimmed eyes were staring in terror at my knife.

I heard the thud behind me as Georgicus let fall his makeshift club. 'Tenuis! What in the name of all the gods . . .'

The child's gaze never faltered from the blade. 'Captain! Overseer Georgicus! You can see it's only me. Don't let the citizen stab me with his knife.'

I pulled myself together, turned the blade aside, and stood back to let the child come in. 'One of your land-slaves?' I said to Georgicus, trying to sound as if I hadn't been afraid. 'He seems to know who I am, since he calls me citizen.'

'All my land-slaves know who you are, citizen. And he's mine all right. But as to land-slave, I am not so sure, though that is what they call him. The smallest one we've got,' Georgicus said. 'Come on in then, Tenuis.'

The apparition unwillingly obeyed.

'Came as part of a job lot that the master bought last year,' his overseer said, putting a hand on one shoulder to usher him inside. 'I was at the slave market with him at the time. There were four half-decent land-slaves at an attractive price. I only wanted them, but the dealer insisted that we took this one as well. Though it is a puzzle what to do with him.' He put a finger underneath the small boy's chin and tilted up the face. 'Not pretty enough to be a household page, and far too small and puny to be useful otherwise. No good for proper land-work, because he isn't strong enough to dig, but he can fetch eggs and carry firewood and that sort of thing. When he keeps his mind on it, which he obviously can't. He was sent to look for kindling this morning in the woods, not come wandering to the villa of his own accord.' He squeezed the chin quite roughly before he let it go.

The child recognised that he had been rebuked. 'I know you told us not to come up to the house,' – his voice was terrified – 'but the others sent me here.'

'The others?' I echoed. 'You mean the land-slaves who were supposed to be working in the fields? We didn't see them as we came along.'

Tenuis nodded eagerly. 'Exactly. They saw you though, captain. You were running up the lane. They decided you must be coming up here to the house, but of course they didn't dare to leave their posts themselves. So they sent me to find you. Then if anyone was punished . . .'

'It would be you,' I said, moving to close the heavy gates again.

Tenuis seemed unaware of any irony. He turned towards me. 'Exactly, citizen. But they weren't expecting any trouble of that kind. I'm younger than they are and I can run in and out without the house staff taking much account.'

'You were trying to avoid the house staff then?' Georgicus raised an eyebrow and jerked his head towards the orchard wall. I knew exactly what he was signalling – that Tenuis, at least, had no idea of what had happened there.

I nodded to show I'd understood and murmured to the boy, 'Go on with your account.'

Tenuis needed no encouragement. 'I didn't care about the steward, anyway, today, 'cause I had a proper errand. I was sent to find you, captain.' He turned to Georgicus. 'They want to know if it's all right to go back to their tasks and leave the wood-pile unattended for a time. Nobody has come for it, though they've been waiting hours.' He dropped his glance and muttered to his feet. 'At least that's what they say. I think there's really something else that they're not telling me. There was an awful lot of whispering that I couldn't hear.'

But Georgicus was not listening. He had crouched down to gaze intently into the slave-boy's face. He turned the lad towards him, holding both the skinny shoulders as he said, 'What wood-pile is this?'

Nine

Tenuis looked at him with startled eyes. 'Why, captain, the wood-piles that you told them to build up yesterday. You know, all the dead boughs and fallen branches from the wood . . .' He saw the expression on the overseer's face and trailed off into silence. 'At least, they said you told them . . .'

'I did no such thing. I did give them instructions, but my orders were specifically for jobs to do elsewhere: pruning and weeding and working in the fields. Surely you heard me. I make these announcements in front of everyone!'

Tenuis shook his head. 'But . . . wasn't that countermanded afterwards?'

Georgicus let go of the boy, stood up and frowned at me. 'Did our intruders contrive this, do you think? Just to make sure that there was nobody about to see them come and go?'

I had been busy bolting up the gates and struggling to put back the heavy wooden bar. 'It's possible,' I said addressing Georgicus over the head of the boy, who had his back to me. 'But your land-slaves wouldn't take orders from a stranger, do you think? Especially not if they contradicted yours.'

Tenuis whirled around to stare at me with startled eyes. 'Strangers? Intruders? What . . .? Oh!' He clapped a startled hand across his mouth. 'Has there been some sort of problem overnight? Is

84

that why the back gate was all locked and barred with no gatekeeper on duty to let anybody in?'

Georgicus turned impatiently to him. 'Never mind that now. Though we do have a problem, certainly. I'll tell you in good time. Meantime, you can tell me about my land-slaves and who it is that they've been talking to. The citizen is right. I had given them orders for the day. Who told them otherwise?'

The boy shrugged skinny shoulders. 'I don't really know. I thought that it was you. If not, it must have been the chief steward, I suppose.'

I would have come to that conclusion in his place, I thought. The chief steward was officially in charge of everyone, including the land-slaves, while the master was away. He would have authority to over-rule any orders which Georgicus gave – though to do so without informing him would be discourteous at best.

The captain of the land-slaves clearly thought so, too. 'Did they just receive a message? Or did the steward come himself?'

Tenuis shrugged. 'I wasn't there when the new instructions came. The others were all over working in the fields, but I was out there in the forest anyway, picking up kindling, like you told me to. Then they came rushing over, saying that they had this urgent job. I didn't ask who gave them orders to do that. They wouldn't have answered me in any case, but they certainly did not seem to think they'd disobeyed.'

The story was so startling that I joined in as well. 'Urgent? What made a simple wood-pile so urgent all at once?'

Tenuis looked at me distrustfully. 'I don't know, citizen. You'd better ask the steward about that. Something about a provisional contract that the master had agreed, where the conditions had unexpectedly been met. The slaves were to pull all the big dead branches and logs that they could find into the clearing in the middle of the wood. That much I can tell you because I saw them doing it. There was a lot of private grumbling, in fact, because it had to be done as fast as possible and it was very energetic work'

Georgicus exchanged another glance with me. 'I'm sure it was. No doubt it kept them fully occupied for several hours.'

A nod. 'And they weren't slacking either, captain, they worked right through till dusk. They had to take the leaves and little twigs off every branch – which took a lot of time – and then they were to sort the wood according to its size, different kinds of wood in different piles, ready to take away and sell. And if they hadn't finished by the time that it got dark, they were to carry on this morning until someone came for it so that the master's profit was as large as possible. Then they were to help to load it on the carts – that was supposed to be about an hour after dawn today. But nothing's happened.'

'And nothing's likely to!' Georgicus snorted.

The slave-boy stared at him. 'What do you mean?' His eyes were very wide. 'You think all this was nonsense? You don't believe the steward really ordered this at all. And you didn't either? Is that possible?'

'Listen!' Georgicus had grasped the youngster

86

by the elbows now. 'I always give out my instructions for the day first thing in the morning. Everyone knows that. So even if people mistakenly supposed that those instructions yesterday had somehow come from me, don't you think I would have mentioned it today, instead of giving everybody other jobs to do? And the chief steward would have sent me word last night if he had countermanded what I'd ordered my labour force to do – especially if he wanted them to go on doing it. But you were there. You know no message came.'

A shake of tousled curls. 'But it was supposed to be a secret. That's what we were told. In case the other slaves were jealous of us having earned a tip, and thought they should've been relieved of other jobs so they could come and help. Only there wasn't enough profit for everyone to share.'

'A tip?' Georgicus shot a disbelieving glance to heaven. 'For collecting fallen timber in the wood? You believed that? When did you ever know the master give a land-slave anything? Much less a gratuity for just doing what he's told?'

An embarrassed shuffle of the enormous boots. 'We thought that things were different this time, captain. It might be the last time we ever worked for him. And it was a rush, you see. The master had arranged a contract for the wood with whoever it was he bought that villa from in Gaul. But only if there was enough room left over on the ship after all the household goods were loaded on. And it turned out unexpectedly there was. But of course the ship is due to sail for Gaul

87

today, if the wind allows. So if we got the timber on the carts and it reached the docks in time, there would be an *as* or two for everyone out of the profits as a small reward. But we weren't to breathe a word to anyone who hadn't been involved.'

Georgicus shook his head. 'Especially not to me?'

'It was a secret, as I said before. And of course, we thought you knew about it anyway.' He gazed at his overseer with eyes that brimmed with tears.

'But they told you, of all people – although you weren't involved, I think?'

'I couldn't help but know about it, captain. I was there when they came over to the forest to start to the pile.' The voice was tremulous. 'Though, anyway, I was a little bit involved. I brought a branch of pine-wood for the wood-pile, just in case.' The tears were spilling over and running down his cheeks, but his arms were still imprisoned and he could not dry his face. 'But now it seems there wasn't any tip in any case.'

'You really believed that, didn't you, you poor little idiot!' Georgicus released him, stood up and spoke to me. 'Citizen, it's clear that Tenuis is telling us the truth, as he understands it. And it's true that the steward might have over-ridden me if he thought he was serving the master's interests. But it's preposterous. Who on earth would want to pay a contract price for bits of fallen wood, which anyone could go into the forest and collect up for themselves? Let alone pay extra to the land-slaves doing it?'

Tenuis had been listening. 'That's just what one

of the older land-slaves said,' he blurted, through his tears. 'But one of the new men told us that he'd known such things before. His previous owner traded wood with buyers overseas, he said, because timbers from Britannia are good for different things. And then somebody said that . . . oh . . .' He trailed off in embarrassment.

'Said what?' Georgicus urged.

But the boy had turned unwilling, suddenly. 'Nothing!' He shook his head.

'Tenuis!' The overseer's voice was dangerous. 'What did the fellow say? Tell us before I have to beat it out of you!' I don't believe he flogged his land-slaves very much, but he looked as if he meant it this time, certainly.

The slave-boy looked down at his ugly boots and gulped. 'He said . . . that the master does have sudden fads, sometimes, and perhaps if we were wise we shouldn't query it. It wasn't me. I didn't say it – he did. But everyone agreed. It's not up to us to question anything, they said. We're only land-slaves, we just do as we are told.'

It was so nearly what Georgicus had said to me himself, it almost made me smile. But the overseer was not amused at all.

'Then – not content with speaking so disrespectfully about His Excellence – they disobeyed my orders and sent you here today? When I had specifically told everybody they were not to come up to the house?'

A nod.

'So why, when you did come running, did you go round to the back? Surely the front gate is much the quickest route.'

89

Tenuis turned scarlet and looked about to cry again. 'I've never been through that front gate in my life,' he muttered tearfully. 'I didn't even try. The gatekeeper would have given me a clout around the ear. Though I was beginning to think that I'd have to brave him after all when I came round here and hammered and there was no reply.'

It was my turn to raise a brow at Georgicus. Another death that Tenuis didn't know about. 'We didn't hear a knock,' I murmured to the slave.

'Oh, I knocked,' the boy said eagerly. 'Perhaps not loud enough. I was afraid those people might still be loading up the carts. And then I heard you calling, captain, and realised you were here. So I started rattling for you to let me in. I didn't want to have to dodge those wagoners again . . .' He tailed off into silence.

Georgicus glanced at me. He stooped again and took the boy more roughly by the arms. This time he shook him as he looked into his eyes. 'Again?' he echoed. 'You mean that you have seen them? You'd been up here before?'

Tenuis turned scarlet and tried to look away. 'I didn't say that,' he muttered. 'I didn't see anything. I don't know what I'm saying. I wasn't here at all.'

'Little liar!' Georgicus exclaimed, yanking the child upwards by his arms until his boots fell off. He put him down again. 'You saw these people. It's obvious you did. You must have come here yesterday, though I had explicitly forbidden it. And the place was full of strangers. Isn't that the case?'

The boy refused to meet his overseer's gaze. 'It was only for a minute.' He sat down and started to pull his dreadful footbags on. 'It hardly counted as coming here at all. I didn't have a chance to notice anything.' His voice was quavering with fright, but his face was mutinous and there was clearly something he wasn't telling us.

'If you did see someone, it might be fortunate,' I put in, as gently as I could. I have often found that kindness loosens tongues where fear does not.

Tenuis looked up doubtfully at me. 'I didn't see intruders. There were just the men with carts. The ones we were expecting. Or perhaps you didn't know – the master wrote and told us that they were going to come.'

I shook my head. 'They were intruders all the same. The master did not send them. You have been deceived. They were not honest carters, they were thieves – and murderers.'

'Murderers?' The boy was horrified.

'It rather looks like it. Several of the household slaves have been found dead. You can see it's serious. So you won't be punished if you just tell us the truth.' I saw that he was hesitating still. 'And nor will anybody else.'

Tenuis looked at Georgicus, who gave the slave-boy a reluctant nod.

The slave-boy put his boot on and scrambled to his feet. 'Well then, I did come to the villa. Not for very long.' A sniff. 'I only came to see the kitchen slaves.'

I should have guessed. The boy was skinny to

91

the point of being partly starved. 'Because they give you food?'

'Occasionally,' Tenuis said, unwillingly.

Georgicus reacted sharply. 'What for? You have your slave-ration like anybody else!'

'But I'm only little, captain. Sometimes the bigger land-boys bully me and take away my lunch. The cook once saw it happen – he came into the orchard when we were working there – and ever since then all the kitchen slaves have been very good to me. If someone takes my food away I come and tap the door, and they generally find a stale crust or something else that I can have. Something that would otherwise have gone out to the pigs – not stealing anything. But I'm grateful just for that. I sometimes think I'd die of hunger otherwise.'

Georgicus was frowning. 'Who is it takes your lunch? Tell me the culprit and I'll see that he is flogged.'

The slave-boy shook his head. 'I don't know, captain,' he said, then added, with more truth, 'and if I did, I wouldn't tell. They would only beat me and hold me in the well. They say that I don't deserve the meal because I am no use. But I get awfully hungry, that's why I came up here even though I knew that I was disobeying you. I'd made up a story to tell the gatekeeper, pretending I had a message about sending down some scraps. But I didn't see him anyway . . .' He trailed off. 'Great gods! It isn't him that's dead? Is that why there wasn't anyone today to open up the gate?'

I thought of the sorry pile of headless corpses

92

that we'd left lying in the orchard. 'We don't know what's become of him,' I said. 'He wasn't at his post when we arrived today. Nor yesterday, from what you say of him. So how did you get in?'

He made a comic face. 'The gate was wide open. I was quite surprised, but the court was full of carts, so I suppose that there was lots of movement in and out. They must have been nearly ready to depart. There were a lot of people rushing round with lists, and coming and going into the house with packed-up goods. They were all so busy that they didn't notice me. So I did a silly thing. I made a dash for it and rolled underneath the nearest cart, thinking I could wiggle over to the arch one wagon at a time and get into the kitchen that way. But when I popped my head out, I realised there were escort guards as well, standing by the wall and watching everything.'

'Escort guards? With weapons?' Georgicus looked at me. 'We thought there must have been. But that did not surprise you?'

It seemed to be the question which surprised the child most. He shrugged. 'Not really, captain. Of course there'd be an escort for the master's goods – and he'd taken his own usual bodyguards with him. And that's clearly what they were. Ugly-looking creatures with clubs and swords and things, all dressed in some sort of livery. Some of them were huge. I hadn't seen them from the gate – the wall had hidden them. But when I did, I realised that I'd have to give it up. They were keeping a close watch on everything going on, and if I wasn't very careful they would notice me. I backed off hastily and was just about to shuffle myself round and creep back to the lane, when I saw the little kitchen-boy come out through the arch. He was carrying a jug, obviously going to get something from the storage yard. He—'

I interrupted him. 'Was this Pauvrissimus, by any chance?'

He looked at me, amazed. 'That's right, citizen? How do you know his name?'

'He was a friend to my own slave, Minimus, who was once a servant here. But go on with your tale. You saw Pauvrissimus . . .?'

He nodded. 'He bent down to tie his sandal strap and saw me hiding underneath the cart, though – thank Juno – no one else had done. He put his finger to his lips and gestured to the side wall of the court, obviously meaning I should come round there and he would bring some food. But then the chief steward saw him and shouted at him for taking such at time, so he got up and hurried to the storage courtyard with his jug and when he came back he didn't look my way again.'

'So you went to the orchard?' I glanced at Georgicus.

Tenuis looked puzzled. Then he shook his head. 'Not the side wall that way, citizen. The other one – beyond the storage yard. It's high, but there's a field the other side and a gate a little further down so you can get there from the lane. I knew that's what Pauvrissimus had meant.'

'And I suppose he could find a reason to back get into the yard,' I mused. 'So that is what you did?'

94

He nodded. 'I managed to sneak out again went round into the field, over to where I thought the storage court might be. The wall is high. You can't see over it, especially if you're me. But after a while, I heard a whistle from the court the other side. I tried to whistle back, though I can't do it very well, and a moment later a crust of bread came flying through the air. I picked it up and ate it. And that's all I know.'

That explained the cut loaf on the bench, I thought. It had not been cleared away. So it could not have been long afterwards that everyone was killed. 'You were lucky no one saw you!' I told him. 'Luckier than you know.'

'No one except Pauvrissimus, though I expect he told the cook.' For the first time I saw Tenuis give a shadow of a smile. 'He couldn't have smuggled that bread out to me otherwise. All the same, I'm afraid he got a beating over it. I had just started on the bread when I heard a lot of shouting and then a muffled squeal – probably the steward catching up with him.'

'A squeal?' That confirmed what I'd been thinking. 'Oh, dear gods!' I exchanged a startled glance with Georgicus, who had clearly come to much the same conclusion for himself.

Tenuis misinterpreted my expression of dismay. 'I couldn't help him, citizen. I would only make it worse, so I went back to the woods and tried to help the others with collecting up the pile. But I'll thank him when I see him. He took a risk for me. I just hope he didn't get into too much trouble for my sake.'

I turned to Georgicus. 'I think it's time we told

95

him. We'll show him what we found – and then we'll go and get your other land-slaves from the wood.'

The overseer nodded, grimly. 'I'll send somebody in with you to tell the Funeral Guild. Then I suppose we ought to find the missing heads. Some of the male land-slaves can institute a search. In the meantime I'll have some women start on a lament. And there'll have to be a pyre. There are quite a lot of corpses to be burnt. So there may be a use for that wood-pile after all.'

I shook my head at him. This was not the way I'd meant to break the news to Tenuis. But it was too late. The poor little lad had been listening to all this, and his white face told me that he'd understood exactly what had happened to his friend.

'Funeral? Heads? Corpses? Oh, dear Juno . . .' It was a strangled sob. Blank as a sleepwalker, he took a stumbling step.

I darted forward and was just in time to catch him in my arms before he fell crashing to the paving in a faint.

Ten

It took us some moments – and half a bucket of water from the well – to bring him round again. When he did revive, the poor child looked like someone who had brushed with death himself.

'It's true?' he whispered, sitting up and shaking his damp locks. 'I didn't dream it? Pauvrissimus is dead? Someone chopped his head off?' He sounded as if he could not believe what he was saying, even now.

I reached out a hand to help him to his feet. 'Among a lot of others, I'm afraid. If it is any comfort, I've promised my own slave that I'll find out who the killers are, and see that they are made to pay for this – and for stealing everything of value from the house.'

He looked doubtfully at me. 'If robbers did this, I suppose there is some chance. The master would want them punished for theft, if nothing else, so the authorities would have to help you, wouldn't they? Though they mightn't care too much about the death of a few slaves.'

'Oh, I rather think so. They were his possessions, too,' I pointed out.

He bit his little lip. 'I still can't quite believe those men with carts were bad men – thieves and murderers. The steward didn't think so. He even let them in.'

'And now the steward's dead,' Georgicus said and sobered him again.

'But why did they want to kill all the master's slaves – especially the little ones, like Pauvrissimus? He couldn't possibly have done them any harm.'

'Because he saw them. We think they killed the witnesses – anyone who might describe them afterwards. It wasn't a question of how big they were,' Georgicus said.

Tenuis was young but life had made him sharp. 'So if those guards had seen me, I'd be dead as well?' He turned as pale as chalk and I thought for a minute he was going to faint again but all that happened was that his eyes filled up with tears, two of which spilled over and trickled down his cheeks. He was too stunned even to attempt to wipe them off.

'It makes you a valuable witness, from our point of view,' I said heartily. 'You saw them, but nobody saw you – so they won't be looking for you and you should be quite safe.'

I meant to be supportive, but the boy looked terrified. 'But what about when His Excellence comes back? I don't know anything. Don't let them question me. I didn't really look. It's no good asking me. I can't remember anything at all.' He buried his head in both his hands and sobbed like the little boy he was.

I understood his terror. It is commonplace for courts to torture slaves to make sure that they're not withholding evidence. I put a friendly arm around his heaving back. 'We won't let them hurt you,' I said, trying to sound as sure of that as possible. 'And no one knows that you were here – apart from us.'

'Or do they?' Georgicus put in sharply.' 'Have you been talking to anybody else? Any of the other land-slaves?'

The child refused to meet his eyes. 'Of course not, captain. I wasn't supposed to come here yesterday. I didn't say a word. I was afraid that somebody would ask me where I'd been, but the others were too busy fetching wood to notice whether I was there or not. Most of them don't talk to me, in any case.'

'Then don't say anything to anybody now,' his overseer warned.

'But you can talk to us,' I told him. 'If you think of anything at all that would help us find these men – what they looked like, the colour of their hair, even how tall they were, perhaps – you must let us know at once. In the meantime, stay close to Georgicus. He'll take good care of you. Go with him now and show him where this famous wood-pile is. I'm going to go to Glevum and call the Slaves' Guild out to deal with the bodies, but in the meantime we need one of the senior land-slaves to start up the lament.'

Tenuis nodded. He ran a scruffy tunic-sleeve across his nose, then squared his skinny little shoulders and lifted his small chin. 'Can I see Pauvrissimus before we go?'

I glanced at Georgicus. 'Better not, I think. But when the Guild have prepared the bodies for the funeral and laid him on the bier, you can walk beside him to the pyre – which will obviously be on the property somewhere – and help lament him then. I think that your slave-captain would agree to that?'

Georgicus nodded brusquely. 'I suppose that all we land-slaves will have to be involved. That's all that's left of the household, isn't it? Jove knows how I'm supposed to get the grapevines planted now – or what the mistress is going to say when news is brought to her! It will bring her to her child-bed before her time, I think. You're sure that it is possible for you to contact her?'

'There'll almost certainly be a courier from the garrison riding to Corinium anyway,' I said. 'There are messages between them almost every day. And if there's any problem, I'll hire a private messenger and tell him that the recipient will pay.' That is not unusual, in fact, since it ensures that your message actually arrives and the rider doesn't simply take the money and abscond. 'I'm sure that Julia will agree to your proposals for the funeral. It's obviously sensible to have the pyre out there on the fallow field – it involves the least expense.'

Georgicus looked doubtful.

I wondered what it was that troubled him. Perhaps he thought that mentioning expense seemed rather disrespectful to the dead. It couldn't be concern about the sum involved, because the guild would be paying for the funeral in any case.

'And being cremated in the fields they knew is the best way of showing proper respect towards the dead,' I added hastily.

But it wasn't money that was causing him anxiety. 'Should we wait for permission from the mistress, do you think?' he said. 'I suppose she'll get an answer back to you as quickly as she can. In fact, if she sends a verbal message it could come straight to me. But I wonder if we should begin on the preparations, anyway. With so many corpses, there is a lot to do. We'll need a massive pyre.' Then a thought seemed to strike him, and he added suddenly, 'Though it occurs to me that, while the master is away, I was told that I was answerable to you. So I can reasonably act on your authority.'

I wasn't sure I altogether welcomed this. I didn't want Marcus holding me responsible if there were any problems. But it was obvious that Georgicus was right. We couldn't leave the dead slaves lying where they were. 'Then, I suggest that you start working on the pyre and I'll send the Funeral Guild as quickly as I can. I'll get word to Julia, explaining what has happened, and tell her what we've done. Now, since I don't think there is anything else we can do here without your slaves, we'll leave this back gate bolted and go out through the front. That's where my mule is tethered, anyway.'

Georgicus picked up the wooden bar again and slotted it back so it secured the gate. 'I wonder where that gatekeeper has got to!' he remarked, shaking the gate to make sure it held fast.

'I expect he'll turn up somewhere – dead, more than likely,' I said, leading the way across the court into the storage yard.

'There's the other one to deal with sometime, too.' The overseer was following closely, with Tenuis straggling a little way behind. 'But I'll come back for that – get a couple of land-slaves over here to cut him down.'

I glanced at Tenuis to see how he was taking this but after what he'd learned about his friend, gatekeepers obviously did not concern him very much. His wide-eyed expression was all about our route. 'Are you going out to take me with you through the front?' he said, in wonderment. 'I've never been out that way in my life!' He spoke as if that were a score of years at least.

I managed not to smile. 'It will be all right today. Just stay with us.' I led the way out through the little gate and so out to the front enclosure of the house. Tenuis glanced around in awe, taking in the gravelled drive, the handsome statues, garden beds and trees. Obviously his duties had never included sweeping leaves or weeding here!

We hurried him past the little cell beside the gate, but his goggle-eyed admiration for the fountain we'd just passed preserved him from any interest in the gatekeeper's abode, where – just visible from this angle through the half-open door – the corpse of the unhappy occupant was still dangling from its hook. Fortunately Tenuis did not glance that way.

Georgicus pulled the gates ajar and closed them after us, so that they looked very much as they had when I arrived – though of course they still could not be bolted properly. In the meantime, I untied my mule. She was munching grasses by the verge and seemed reluctant to abandon them, but with hauling and coaxing I got her to the path and with Georgicus's assistance I climbed onto her back.

102

'When you get back to the vineyard, send my attendant home,' I told the land-slave captain, reaching into the branches overhead to break off a supple length to serve me as a switch. Without it Arlina would stand stolidly all day.

'Home? I thought you were taking him to Glevum,' Georgicus replied.

'Tell him he can help my wife this afternoon, instead. I probably shan't go to my workshop now. In any case, I'll let my son take care of any business today. I'll just call at my roundhouse and reassure him that I'm alive and well, and leave him to make his own way into town. I'll have to hurry if I'm going to pay a visit to the garrison. And if I mean to call in at the Funeral Guild as well, in time for them to get here before dark, I really don't have time to wait for Minimus to come,' I said, peeling the unwanted leaves and twiglets off my switch.

Georgicus frowned. 'But that means you will be without an attendant for the day, citizen. Would it not be better for me to fetch your servant here? I'll find a land-slave to take over from him in the vineyard now. I think I know exactly where this clearing is, and I can have someone down there in no time at all. Your slave is only acting as a symbol, anyway.'

I shook my head. 'If I'm to catch a courier from the Imperial post today, I must be in Glevum before the noonday trumpet sounds. The commander of the garrison is a friend of Marcus's. When he knows what's happened here I'm sure there'll be no problem about those messages. But it is already later than I realised – look at those shadows – and it will take some time to get to Glevum, even with a mule. The forest paths are still treacherous with mud. Better if I go as soon as possible.'

Georgicus waved a hand at Tenuis. 'Then why don't you take him with you for the day? He's not much use to me. But he could mind your mule for you. Or even take the message to the Funeral Guild and come back here with them.'

Tenuis looked rather terrified at this. 'I don't know Glevum, captain. I would just get lost. They would not believe me, either, if I asked them to come. I'd have to have a proper message written down.'

Georgicus looked a little sheepish. The boy was right. He was so young that he was an unlikely messenger, and of course the slave-captain – like most land-slaves – could not really read or write.

'I'll see to that,' I offered quickly. 'I have a writing tablet at my workshop, and a seal. You can give that to the guild. That should be enough authority. And as for getting lost, I'll deliver you to the proper place myself. But it will save me time if I don't have to go inside and talk to them.' I turned to Georgicus. 'A good idea, slave-captain. The guild will bring him back to you. And it will not slow me down. Arlina is accustomed to carrying two of us, and Tenuis is even smaller than my slave. Lift the boy up and he can ride with me.'

'I'll go and get my land-slaves started with that pyre and that lament, and send your slave back home as soon as possible,' Georgicus said. He scooped the boy up as though he were a sack and lifted him to sit in front of me, where Minimus had been, though Tenuis was so light and skinny that he seemed no weight at all. I dug my heels in, flicked my switch and Arlina shambled off.

I turned my head to see Georgicus staring after us, looking, I thought, a little bit relieved. He watched me for a moment, raised one hand in farewell, then turned and set off running down the lane with that distinctive loping gait of his.

Eleven

I tried hard to talk to Tenuis, as Arlina began shambling down the track. I hoped to gain his confidence, now we were alone, and learn a little more about the men that he had seen at the villa, but it was no use. The boy was obviously unused to being on an animal – I think it was the first time that he'd ever been hoisted up so high – and he was far too terrified to speak. This was going to be a tedious journey into town, I thought.

But we'd hardly turned the corner when I heard a voice.

'Father!' It was Junio coming towards us, the promised wood-axe in his hand, and Maximus, my other red-haired slave-boy, at his heels. 'There you are! Mother and I were getting quite concerned . . .'

'We were going to come and save you,' Maximus added. 'I've got a weapon too.' He proudly showed me the wooden hammer he was carrying – an old one that I used for hammering stakes into the ground. 'It's just a pity Minimus isn't here. He can use a slingshot wonderfully.'

It was rather touching, given that Junio had seen the corpses in the orchard earlier, and knew what he might be facing if the murderers had come back. But Maximus was an unlikely warrior. Despite his name, he was the smaller of my slaves

– the top of his head reached scarcely to my chest – and it was all he could do to hold the hammer high with both his hands. But there was no mistaking his sincerity or the look of grim determination on his face.

I repressed a tiny grin. 'Thank you, Maximus, but that won't be necessary now,' I said, as gravely as I could. I turned to Junio. 'I think I know what happened at the villa, now, though it's a rather a long tale.' Very briefly, I outlined what I'd learned of yesterday's events.

Junio whistled. 'So that's why most of the furniture has gone. The household was first tricked into assisting with the robbery, and then killed because they might identify the thieves. So no one is alive who saw anything at all?'

'Only this little fellow.' I nodded down at Tenuis, who was still sitting on the mule in front of me, clutching mutely at my knees. 'But the killers don't know that, so he's quite safe with me.'

'Why has he got his eyes closed?' Maximus enquired, and I realised that Tenuis must have had squeezed his lids tight shut ever since we put him on Arlina's back.

'Because he's not used to being on a mule. I'm taking him to Glevum to get the Funeral Guild. But first I'll have to call in on the garrison.' I explained my errand there and turned to Junio. 'You and Maximus can follow me to town and open up the shop. I'll meet you there when I've finished delivering my messages.'

'But you'll want your toga, won't you,' Junio enquired, 'if you're going to call on the commander with that kind of request? Otherwise you will be lucky if they don't make you wait for hours.'

He was quite right, of course. Wearing that badge of citizenship is not legally required, except in the forum and at public festivals, but my simple tunic marked me as the tradesman that I am. More formal dress would be a good idea. 'I'd better call in at home and pick it up – though I'll have to carry it. I'm not going to wear it all the way to town. It will get bedraggled and just be in my way.' A toga is an awkward garment at the best of times, and always likely to unwind itself into unseemly loops, so a muddy journey on a mule along a rutted, steep and treacherous forest track was hardly an ideal environment for wearing one.

'But there's a toga at the workshop!' Maximus put in, so anxious to be helpful that he interrupted us, which is not generally permitted for a slave. He realised that himself. 'Please forgive me, master, for speaking out of turn. But don't you remember, you spilt wine on it before your patron left? We took to the fullers in the town. I brought it back from cleaning yesterday. But you were in such a hurry to get back to see the vines that in the end we didn't bring it home.'

'I had forgotten, but it makes life easier,' I said. It was only my second-best toga, a little frayed around the hems, but now that it was clean it would look respectable enough. 'I'll call into the workshop so I can write the message for Tenuis to take and, while I'm there, I'll get that toga on. Tenuis will have to help me, though he's not been trained. It isn't possible to do it on my own and

108

may take some time to get it neatly draped. I'll have to hurry if I hope to get back to the garrison by noon.'

'Then you ride on,' my son replied. 'I'll call in and tell Mother that you are safe and well, and Maximus and I will put these weapons down, then follow you on foot. If we're very lucky we might even find a cart that's going our way – there's often someone at this time of day – and I don't mind paying the driver an as or two to carry us as well. Either way, we'll see you at the workshop as soon as possible.'

I nodded. 'Very well. Come on, Arlina!' And I applied my switch. There was a faint moan from Tenuis as we lurched off again, but that – apart from his involuntary squeak where the path was particularly steep and dangerous – was the only sound he uttered till we reached the city walls.

'Are we there?' he muttered, as we shambled to a stop outside the gate and I realised that he must have had his eyes tight shut again.

'Not quite,' I told him. 'But you can get down from the mule. We'll walk her through the town. It's not illegal to take an animal. The law is only for horse-drawn vehicles. Although it's probably better to . . .' But I was talking to myself. He had already ducked under my restraining arm and slithered to the ground.

'I'm on my feet again! I never enjoyed just standing up so much!' He looked up at me with such an expression of relief that I didn't have the heart to offer a rebuke. 'Can I help you to get down as well, master?' he added as an obvious afterthought.

I shook my head. I wasn't sure that he was tall or strong enough to be of any use. 'Just hold the mule,' I answered. 'I can manage well enough.'

This boast proved to be not altogether true. I used to be a skilful horseman in my youth, but I am old and stiff these days and Arlina's inclined to be contrary, anyway. So my descent was awkward and undignified – much to the amusement of the sentry at the gate. I turned my back on him and ostentatiously smoothed my tunic down, trying to look as self-composed as possible. But as I bent forward to straighten out my hems, I suddenly noticed how small my shadow fell on the wall.

I straightened up at once. 'Dear Mercury, the sun is nearly overhead. It must be almost noon!' I said to Tenuis. 'And my workshop's right at the other end of town. I don't think I've got time to get my toga first. I'll have to take a chance on calling at the garrison dressed like this. If I explain that I'm here on Marcus's behalf, they might let me talk to the commander straight away.' I gestured with my hand towards the military compound just inside the gate.

Tenuis looked where I was pointing. And boggled, visibly. 'You really think they'll let you in there, master?' he murmured, wide-eyed with disbelief.

I attempted not to preen. There is only a small garrison detachment based at Glevum now, and it does not occupy as much of Glevum as it did – most of its former land is occupied by private tenements and public buildings. But what remains is still impressive. Only the front section was visible from here, no more than the guard

110

tower and the nearest barracks block, peeping over the enclosure, but Tenuis had clearly never seen anything like it in his life. 'I've been there several times,' I told him self-importantly. 'I'm sure if I explain to the gatehouse who I am—'

'I shouldn't bother, tradesman.' I was interrupted by the sentry, who had come across to us, making no pretence that he'd not been listening. 'The garrison's been turning all visitors away, except for the town council who've been turning up in droves.' He tapped his nose. 'There's obviously something important happening. We've had imperial messengers dashing in and out since dawn.' He spoke indulgently, as though he were dealing with an innocent buffoon – no doubt the result of my ungainly exhibition while getting off the mule earlier. 'And there hasn't been a route march or shield practice for the day.'

I frowned at him, still prickling. 'That's most unusual.'

'I know it's unusual, tradesman. That's why I'm telling you.' He said it sharply. All the former friendliness had disappeared.

I instantly regretted giving way to pique. I tried my most con-spiratorial smile. 'Some preparations for the Imperial Birthday Feast, do you think? Or has the Provincial Governor decided to make a visit to the town?'

But I'd affronted him and he turned impatiently away. 'Don't ask me, tradesman, because that is all I know. I've been stuck here for hours supervising travellers in and out of town. Nobody tells the gate-guard anything. I don't suppose I'll find out any more till I am relieved.'

'Well, I'll try my luck at the garrison anyway. The commander knows me. I expect they'll let me in. If I do learn anything I'll come and let you know. Come, Tenuis,' and I took the leading-rope from the astounded boy.

The soldier shrugged and stood aside to let us through the gate, 'Don't say I didn't warn you.' He stood, hands balanced on hips and watched us through the gateway to the town.

I tried to ignore him and walked stoutly on. Once we reached the entry to the nearby *mansio* – the military inn – I turned to Tenuis. 'You stay here with the mule. I'll talk to the man on duty at that entrance over there.' I thrust the mule's leading rope at him, then went on to the gatehouse of the garrison.

It was obvious at once that the sentry at the town gate was right. There was something unusual happening. It is never easy to see inside the fort – the wall around is built to keep out spectators – but through the gateway I could see the stretch of road which led past the barrack-block, and the main administration block and guard tower just inside the gates. Through the central arch I could glimpse the inner court which sometimes functioned as a muster ground. But there were no soldiers gathered there today. Instead the town's most senior councillors seemed to be having a conclave in the open air. I craned my head to get a better look.

A bulky figure in full armour moved to block my view. 'What are you staring at, tradesman? What's your business here?' A burly soldier in the distinctive sideways crest of a centurion was confronting me. I knew several of the senior soldiery by now, but I didn't recognise this one – though I knew the type. It was written in the strutting swagger and the sneering upper lip. He was a big, ugly fellow with a broken nose and a pair of unusually narrow squinting eyes, which were looking at my tunic with undisguised contempt. But a full centurion on humble gate-duty? That was a surprise. So was the drawn sword he was grasping in his hand.

'Well, fellow?' he bellowed, raising the blade slowly until its tip was pointing at my neck.

'My name is Longinus Flavius Libertus,' I told him, though my voice came out a squeak. The three full Roman names denote a citizen, and in normal times would earn a little more respect, but it isn't easy to sound lofty when there's a sword-point at your throat. 'I am a Roman citizen,' I bleated. 'And I have an urgent message for the commander of the garrison.' It did not sound convincing, even to myself.

The eyes did not falter in their disdainful glare, but the sword-point was lowered an inch or two, so that it merely pointed at my ribs. 'Citizen, is it? You don't look much like a citizen to me. So Longinus What-ever-your-name-is, unless you have a warrant with the imperial seal—' he raised a mocking supercilious brow at me '—and I assume you don't, then you will have to wait. The commander's busy and he's not to be disturbed. Come back some other time.'

'But—'

'No buts! You heard me. Now, disappear, and make it quick.'

'The commander knows me. I'm sure he would see me if he knew it was me.' I knew that I was sounding desperate. 'Call somebody and ask him. It's about my patron, Marcus Septimus.'

The name, for once, had no effect at all. 'I will call someone in a minute, certainly.' The fleshy lips were drawn back in an unpleasant smile, revealing a row of yellow pointed teeth. 'But it won't be to ask the commander anything. It will be to march you inside and lock you in a cell. The commander is busy. I have told you that. He's not receiving anyone today. So make your mind up, citizen – if that is what you are. Are you going to go on standing there demanding an audience, or can you understand what's good for you? Go away. And that's an order.' The sword-point gave me a little warning prod. I felt it touch the handle of the knife, which I'd forgotten that I'd tucked into my belt. It was just as well that Gwellia had insisted on my putting on that cloak, so it wasn't visible – for a civilian to carry a bladed weapon was a serious offence.

I knew when I was beaten. Argument was useless. Without a toga I was nobody and if he chose to search me, he would find the blade, and I knew what that would mean. I'd spent a very unpleasant hour or two locked up in a cell in the garrison before. I turned to leave and heard the sword go back into the scabbard with a swish.

I whirled around. 'One thing, centurion. I notice that the members of the curia are here. He must have summoned them. Yet usually, I know, he'd go to them. And you say he's not receiving supplicants. Am I right in thinking something unusual has occurred?'

He flashed the yellow-pointed teeth at me again, but this time in a snarl. He reminded me of a carving I'd once seen of Cerberus, the hound who guards the entrance-way to Dis. 'Something unusual will occur to you if you ask too many questions, citizen. When decisions have been taken, you'll find out soon enough. Now . . .' His fingers were already on the sword-hilt as he spoke.

I raised both hands in surrender. 'I'm leaving, officer,' I murmured as I backed away. Then I turned and hurried ignominiously back to where Tenuis was still waiting with the mule. I felt like an idiot. No doubt the town sentry had been watching all this too. What an inglorious picture I must present, I thought.

But I need not have worried. Tenuis was too bemused by what was around him on the street to be interested in my success, or lack of it. 'Master!' he said, enthusiastically, as I came up to him. 'What an enormous place. I didn't know there were so many people in the world.'

'But surely you were sold here, at the slave-market?'

He nodded. 'That was the only time I ever came before, and I was half asleep when we arrived. It was cold and hardly light, and I was roped up between much bigger slaves. Anyway, they walked so quickly I had to watch my feet. It was all I could do to stay upright and not be dragged along. I couldn't see a thing until we got to the slave-market and not very much of that. By the time that Marcus bought us – the lot of us – it was almost dusk and they hustled us straight out of the gates into a cart. I'd never have forgotten Glevum if I'd known what it was like.'

I looked around myself. The streets were very busy, certainly, though that was only normal on a 'well-favoured' day, when all the shops and law courts and markets were operational. (On ill-omened dates – the so-called 'nefas' days – the courts and theatres were shut, and the streets were much less crowded. But even that would have astounded Tenuis, I think.)

Today had been a fairly 'ill-omened' day for me, I thought, whatever the official calendar might say. But here one could believe in pleasant auguries. There were builders whistling as they climbed their flimsy scaffolding, carrying baskets full of bricks, or cursing as their winches swung the heavy stone aloft. Traders with creaking hand-carts lumbered past, inviting inspection of their piles of wood and furs. Street vendors shouted the prices of their trays of steaming pies. There were foreign merchants in exotic clothes, women in carrying-litters, slaves with water jugs, and moving against them from the marketplace, a tide of people with their morning's purchases: eels, cheeses, bolts of coloured cloth, one man even driving a pair of mangy sheep. Nothing at all unusual, although to Tenuis, used to working on a villa farm, it no doubt seemed a jumble of colour, noise and smells.

'The town is certainly busy,' I agreed. 'And we have got to get through it quickly with this mule.

116

I think we'll go the back route, along the smaller lanes. This way, Tenuis!' And I led him down an alley to the less frequented streets.

Even then I had to urge him constantly along. He wanted to stop at every shopfront that we passed and gaze at the various carpets, vegetables, pots and leather goods displayed on tables outside the premises or spilling out onto the pavement underneath our feet. Fortunately the traders didn't bother us today. Usually they clutch your garments as you pass with urgent inducements to come and try their wares, but this morning we were spared their molestations by Arlina, who seemed embarrassingly eager to sample what they sold. Horrified traders clapped their hands and shooed us on our way. (Mercifully, with Tenuis dragging her in front and me plying the switch on her behind, we did prevent her from actually eating anything.)

All the same it took a long time to struggle through the town, and I was almost wishing I'd taken the longer route around the eastern walls, although that track is very damp and difficult – it passes close to beds of watercress and reeds, which skinny peasants bring into the marketplace to sell. But the way we'd come seemed blighted with obstacles today. So I was glad when by and by we reached the further gate, though Tenuis seemed disappointed to be outside the walls again and walking through the muddy suburb where my workshop lies.

'There it is,' I told him, pointing to my shop. 'Just between that candlemakers and the tannery. And look, there's Junio, just coming through the door. And Maximus is with him. They must have found a driver to bring them into town. They've started work already, by the look of it, and are coming to select some pieces from the stockpiles.' I gestured proudly at the heaps of different-coloured stone which were the raw materials for our tesserae. 'That's what we make the tiles for our mosaics from.'

Tenuis looked blankly at them, clearly unimpressed. I was about to explain to him how it was done when Junio looked over and caught sight of us. He left what he was doing, and hurried down to meet us, signalling to Maximus to follow him.

'You found a driver, then?' I said, as he approached.

He grinned, squeezing my shoulders in a filial embrace. 'We were very lucky there. A trapper with a wagon-load of furs. So we rode here in comfort. I half expected to pass you on the road, but of course we never did. I was beginning to wonder what had become of you, in fact. Your toga was still here, so I knew you hadn't come to the workshop and gone away again. But here you are at last, so we'll help you to get dressed, though it is getting late. You have just missed a customer, as well. A handsome contract, by the sound of it. A man who's just retired here from Londinium. He's buying the old Egidius villa and wants new floors throughout.'

I made a little face. 'I suppose he doesn't know the reputation of the place.'

The Egidius villa was a famous one – the most lavish in the district until the owner had been exiled years ago for murdering his wife – since when it had fallen into disuse and decay. It should have been seized and sold a long time ago to swell the Imperial purse, but the family fought bitter battles in the courts, claiming that it was bought with money they had lent and should revert to them. Marcus – who, as presiding magistrate had told me all of this – had prudently found in favour of the Emperor, but up to now no buyer had been found. But, finally, it seemed, a bargain had been struck.

Of course, it was derelict and had been a murder scene, and one of the ruined family committed suicide by hanging himself at the entrance in despair, so there were the usual stories of a curse. But a purifying sacrifice would see to that! And there were rumoured to be twenty rooms or more. A contract of that size was a rare event and now – because of my vain attempt to visit the commander when I did – it seemed I'd missed the opportunity. I was almost tempted to curse the Fates. But there was no point in offending supposed immortals, even Roman ones. Perhaps I had already offended them, I thought. This 'well-favoured' day, for me, could hardly have been worse. First the grisly scene at Marcus's, then my ignominious failure at the garrison, and now this!

'You showed him the pattern pieces that we keep on the rack?' I said, without real hope. I always have some samples of popular designs, stuck on linen backing for customers to see.

Junio made a regretful little face. 'He wouldn't look at them. I did the best I could but he refused to talk to me. Says he'd heard your reputation and had thought first of you, but if you weren't interested in clients he would go elsewhere. He seems a most determined individual. He'd hired a carrying-litter and come out here himself. Didn't just send a steward here or anything – though he wore a purple stripe to rival Marcus's. I found him waiting by the workshop door when I arrived, and he was not best pleased that you weren't here yourself.'

I made a rueful face. 'I can imagine that.' Patricians don't like coming to this area of town, never mind standing in the mire to wait. 'I suppose Marcus must have recommended me to him. Did you find out who he was and where he's living while he makes the villa habitable again?'

Junio shook his head. 'New to the area, that is all I know. He didn't give his name. In fact, once he found out that he couldn't talk to you, he hardly deigned to say anything at all.'

We had reached my piles of sorted stones by now and Junio paused to select some blue-veined slate, while Maximus showed Tenuis where to tie the mule. We'd found a useful ring a little way along the narrow alleyway beside the shop, and though a little further on it was a midden-heap, she seemed contented there, as long as someone provided oats and water in the broken pots that served as feeding troughs nearby, or gave her an apple, as Minimus did now.

I watched them turn the corner out of sight. 'Well,' I said. 'Well, I don't suppose it matters who the stranger was. Obviously I won't get the contract now. Perhaps it's just as well. I'm going to have my hands full with Marcus's affairs. I'll have to try to identify who did that at the house. My patron would expect me to give that priority – and, besides, I promised Minimus.'

I must have sounded sourer than I meant. 'Perhaps your mystery customer will come back after all,' Junio said, soothingly, pushing open the outer workshop door. 'I suggested that tomorrow you were likely to be here, and he won't find anybody else to match your skills. Though perhaps you'd rather that he didn't come. There was something in his matter that I didn't care for much. I don't think he'd be the easiest customer to please.' He paused. 'But the contract would be useful, Juno only knows. I kept on hoping that you would arrive. What kept you, anyway? I thought you were in a hurry to get that toga on.'

I put my hand onto his shoulder. 'I made some bad decisions,' I said bitterly. 'Let's go inside and I'll tell you everything.'

Twelve

Inside the workshop it was clear that Junio and Maximus had been busy since the customer had left. A pan of my favourite spiced mead was warming on a trivet by the fire – obviously prepared to welcome me when I arrived – and my son insisted that I drank it as we talked. 'I'm sure you need it, after the shocks you've had today!' he exclaimed. 'And you've had no chance to take refreshment since. Now tell me about this bad decision that you made.'

So while I told him the humiliating news of what had happened at the garrison I sipped the fragrant drink, though I declined to sit down on the stool beside the hearth.

'I simply haven't time. I have to try at the garrison again. I must speak to the commander as soon as possible. Though it's probably too late to have him send those messages today. The noonday trumpet must have sounded by this time.'

Junio was reaching for my freshly cleaned toga from the shelf. 'I haven't heard the signal, though admittedly from here we often don't, unless the wind is coming from the south.'

'Which it's not, today,' I pointed out, taking another gloomy sip of mead. 'And you realise that there's no guarantee that the guard will let me in, even if I do go back again. The commander

122

is obviously busy with the curia. Probably arguing with the senior magistrates about who's going to offer what at the Imperial Birthday Feast. That could go on for hours. But I can only try. Besides, it occurs to me that even if the daily messenger has gone, there may still be time to stop that ship from leaving Glevum with all Marcus's valuables aboard. Assuming that there ever was a ship, that is.'

Junio was unfolding the unwieldy piece of cloth, ready to help me drape it on. He looked at me surprised. 'Of course! We've only got the villains' word for that.'

I shook my head. 'Why did it not occur to me to ask the soldier at the city gate whether there had been a cargo delivered to the docks when the carts came in last night? A load like that would have to come by horse-drawn vehicle, which means it couldn't have come into the town in daylight hours.'

Junio looked thoughtful. 'But if there is a ship, and it was still taking cargo late on yesterday, it is quite possible it won't have sailed as yet.'

'If the wind and tide are right they will have sailed at dawn – they won't want to be travelling down river in the dark.'

'Of course they would be anxious to be gone, especially if they've got stolen goods aboard. Though the captain may not know that, I suppose, so there's just a chance he won't be hurrying.' He brightened suddenly. 'I think you're right and it is worth a try. If Marcus's possessions are still here, even if they're already loaded in a hold, one word from the commander would be enough to have them seized. And, of course, you need to see him anyway.'

I nodded. 'Really, I ought to go down to the docks myself, in any case. There might be something I could learn, even if the ship's already sailed. But I need to get Tenuis to the Funeral Guild as well, and that can't wait all day.'

Junio grinned. 'Don't worry about him. That's something I can do, thanks to you teaching me to read and write when I was young.' I knew he meant this as a genuine compliment – not many masters do that for their slaves – but these expressions of gratitude discomfort me sometimes.

'We've still got that old wax-tablet block upstairs and there's a stylus somewhere too,' I said, speaking briskly to disguise my slight embarrassment. 'You can write the letter, then seal it with my seal. You know where to find the seal-block and the pot of seal-wax. Though when you've written it, you'd better get Maximus to show Tenuis where the slave-guild is. The land-slave's only little and doesn't know the town. If you just give him directions he's likely to get lost.'

Another cheerful grin. 'Better than that, I'll take him there myself, and speak to the leader of the guild. That way we'll even get the writing tablet back. Now leave all that to me. You worry about getting to the garrison. Let me help you into this. Someone there will have to talk to you, at least, once you are wearing it.' He held up my toga and shook it out to its full length. It smelt of fulling liquid – urine-bleach and lime – but, I had to own, it looked presentable.

'And take this knife, for Mars' sake, and put it somewhere safe,' I said, as I took off my cloak and revealed it at my belt. 'I nearly got myself arrested for wearing it when I was at the garrison.'

Junio took it from me and turned it in his hand. 'You were lucky no one caught you wearing it. No one could mistake this for a dining knife, which is all you are allowed to carry in the street. Though it's a very splendid one. Look at the handle – made of horn and beautifully etched. Where did it come from?'

'Marcus's kitchen,' I replied. 'I picked it up when Tenuis shook the gate and I thought the thieves were coming back. I'd better take it back where it belongs.'

'Let's hope that you're not spotted doing it,' he said, placing it carefully out of sight on the shelf above the fire. 'Now, what about this toga?'

I held out my arms and allowed my son to drape the awkward garment round my portly body and over my left shoulder in the accepted way, then adjusted the folds to make it hang becomingly. It's no easy matter, but he'd been my slave for years and was adept at it, so by the time the boys came back from dealing with the mule, I was resplendent in my whitened finery. Tenuis, who had never seen me in this guise, looked gratifyingly startled and impressed.

'Master!' he said, awestruck. 'I didn't . . .' He lapsed into silence and looked anxiously around. I suspect he was wondering if he ought to kneel to me, as he would have done to Marcus, but he took his cue from Maximus and simply bowed his head.

'Now listen, boys,' said Junio, taking charge at once. 'Here's what we're going to do. Maximus will go with Father to the garrison.' He saw that I was likely to protest at that, and held up a warning hand. 'Take him, Father. You'll need an attendant slave if you want that guard to treat you like a proper citizen.'

'But what about the shop?'

He shook his head. 'I know it means there won't be anyone here while I am gone, but that won't be for long. I'll be back as soon as I've delivered Tenuis to the guild. I'm sure your mystery client won't come back today – and it would make no difference if he did. It doesn't matter if I'm here or not. In any case he'll only deal with you.'

I nodded. My son, as usual had reason on his side, and – all things being equal – I wasn't sorry to have my little slave with me. 'Then we should leave at once,' I said.

Maximus was already pulling on his cloak with a delighted grin. A stroll to the garrison with me was clearly a more pleasant prospect than one spent sorting stones and fetching water, stoking up the fire and sweeping the chippings from the workshop floor – which is what he would have been doing otherwise. 'Ready when you are, Master,' he said eagerly, darting to the door to open it for me.

'But the citizen told me I was to stay with him . . .' Tenuis' childlike tenor followed us, and as we walked out into the street I could hear Junio beginning to explain.

'Don't worry, Tenuis. I'll take care of you and take you to the guild . . .'

But there was no time to linger. 'Come then, Maximus!'

We did not take Arlina, but hurried off on foot. This time our passage through the town was quick – it is amazing what difference the Roman dress can make. Traders who had blundered into us or blocked my way before, now stood politely to one side to let us pass. Only a group of citizens in dark mourning robes delayed us as they crowded down the street, deep in solemn conversation and taking up the whole width of the pavement and the road: rich people by the numbers of slaves attending them, and oblivious to anybody but themselves. They turned into the forum, on their way to the basilica to listen to the formal reading of a will, I guessed, and after that we met no hindrance. In no time at all we had reached the garrison.

The same centurion was still on duty at the gate. I'd rather hoped he would have been relieved by now. But there he was, as large and ugly as before. As soon as he saw us, he came lumbering across, but this time there was no drawn sword in evidence. Indeed, to start with, he was unctuously polite.

'I'm very sorry, citizen,' he murmured, with a courteous inclination of the head. 'But the commander . . .' He tailed off and finished, in a different tone of voice. 'Great Mars, it's you again!'

'Indeed.' I gave him a smile of huge beneficence. 'Citizen Longinus Flavius Libertus, as I believe I told you earlier.'

'You don't give up, do you?' he said sourly.

'I might do, on my own account,' I said. 'But I'm here on business for His Excellence, Marcus Septimus Aurelius. I think I mentioned that before as well.' I thought I saw a glimmer of recognition in his eyes, so I stressed the point a little. 'Perhaps you haven't heard of him. But if so, I'm surprised. His Excellence is the senior magistrate in this part of Britannia and a friend and personal advisor to the Emperor Pertinax. In fact he's gone to Rome to visit at this very time – and something terrible has happened.'

Cerberus (as I had named him to myself) looked at me with interest suddenly.

'Marcus is my patron,' I added helpfully. 'And my business is urgent, as I said before. I've something very important to report. I need to send a message through the imperial post to Rome – and to Corinium as well. Today if possible. And I'm anxious that the commander should impound the cargo of a ship for me – if it's not already sailed. So this time,' I emphasised the words, 'I would be obliged if you would let us in.'

This strategy was more successful than I could have dreamed. Centurion Cerberus turned positively pale. 'A messenger to Rome? This concerns the Emperor?' He sounded horrified.

'I didn't quite say that,' I backtracked hastily. 'Though I'm sure that Pertinax would support me if he knew. My message is to Marcus Septimus.' I could not resist a little boast. 'Though that's no slight matter either. He is likely to become the most influential man in all the Roman world. After the Emperor, I mean.'

There was no response to that, though I could

see that my words were having an effect. The centurion was biting his upper lip with his yellow lower fangs.

I judged that he was weakening and I plunged in again. 'So you appreciate that the matter is significant. May I see the commandant?'

My plea was interrupted by the sudden thud of hooves and an Imperial courier came riding down the road from the direction of the praetorium – the commander's private quarters behind the barracks block. He did not pause as he approached – just galloped at us so we had to leap aside. Cerberus had barely time to move the gate away before the rider was through it, scattering us with dust. I almost felt the movement of his cloak as he rode by, but he did not even glance in our direction as he passed.

'What . . .?' I looked at Cerberus, but the guard made no reply, just stared after the rider, shaking his head from side to side like a demented bull.

'Now, look here, centurion,' I said impatiently. 'If you had only let me in at once, I could have sent my message with that courier. What do you think your commander's going to say if he learns that you've insisted on turning me away? And what will Marcus do when he finds out, do you suppose? When he discovers that you've been impeding me – when this is a matter of murder, robbery and fraud. I wouldn't be surprised if you got an Imperial reprimand . . .'

But Cerberus was already stirring into speech. 'Dear Jove, what should I do?' He looked round wildly as if seeking inspiration from the walls.

I followed the direction of his glance and

realised that the crowd of councillors had gone, or at least they were no longer in the inner court. Either they were somewhere else within the fort, or they had all dispersed. In fact, the whole compound was unnaturally devoid of life – none of the usual training cohorts forming up, or groups of conscripts busy on fatigues. Only a solitary foot soldier could be seen, sitting at the doorway to the nearest barracks block – a stoutish auxiliary with large, hairy knees, industriously buffing up his helmet with a mix of lard and sand. That gave me an idea.

'Summon that fellow to ask the commandant,' I said. 'He gives the orders. If you doubt me, he'll tell you what to do.'

Cerberus looked at me for a moment with the return of something like the old contempt, but then he put two fingers to his lips and blew, letting out a whistle that made the arches ring – rather as I've heard a shepherd whistle for his dog. The effect, in fact, was similar: the soldier dropped his polishing and leapt up at once. He hastened over, pulling his helmet on as he approached.

'You signalled, sir?'

Cerberus looked at him, disdainfully. 'Take a message to the commandant. Apologise for my disturbing him. Tell him I have a citizen out here who claims his patron has new influence in Rome and wants the garrison to send a message there. Say that I've asked him twice to go away, but he is insistent the matter cannot wait. Oh, and he's brought a slave with him, as well.'

The soldier saluted and made to move away.

'Tell him it's Libertus,' I shouted after him, but I wasn't sure he heard. He didn't glance in my direction, just marched through into the inner court.

We waited. Cerberus said nothing and I said nothing back. Maximus edged closer, clearly ill at ease. After what seemed a lifetime, the soldier hurried back.

'I'm to take him to the guardroom,' he said breathlessly. 'The commandant will send someone to have a word with him.'

'I want to see the commandant in person,' I complained.

The fellow looked at me. 'You're very fortunate to see anyone at all. The commander has refused to admit anyone today except the senior members of the curia and the priests – and that's because he sent for them himself. Everybody else who's come here has been turned away. I think it was the mention of your name which did the trick.'

I glanced triumphantly at Cerberus but he was studiously looking past me at the wall.

He contented himself with snapping at the messenger. 'Well, man, what are you waiting for? You have your orders, I believe – however odd they seem. If the commander says so, take the citizen inside.' He bared those horrid yellow teeth at me again. 'Though the slave will stay out here. I don't recall that any mention has been made of him.' He gestured to Maximus, who had been waiting anxiously a pace or two behind.

'Go back to the workshop,' I murmured to my slave, who looked relieved at this. 'Tell my son that I've gained audience, and I'll be back as soon as I've finished here. Though, on second thoughts, perhaps I'll look in at the dockside on the way.'

Maximus sketched a bow – mostly at Cerberus and the soldier, I surmised – and hurried off as fast as his legs would carry him. It seemed that fetching water and sorting stones had become a more attractive prospect suddenly.

Cerberus found his voice again. 'Pass, then, citizen. It seems you've got your wish.' He stood aside and let me through the gate.

I was inside the garrison at last.

Thirteen

I was expecting to be escorted through the arch and into the lower offices of the guard tower, where I had been taken several times before. There is a familiar bench beside the window-space in the dim-lit room downstairs where visitors are often asked to wait, and I was preparing myself for a another lengthy period of twiddling my thumbs – no doubt under the incurious gaze of several junior officers. There was generally an *octio* or two, sitting at one of the tables in the room, writing up reports or calculating requisitions and supplies, or simply warming their chilled hands beside the fire.

But to my surprise my escort led me past the guard tower and out towards the range of buildings in the very centre of the garrison compound. This was the heart of the whole establishment, where the central administrative building, the *principia*, lay, and – directly opposite – the commander's private quarters, with its own kitchen, courtyard and latrine. So that was where my guide was taking me? I had been invited to the residence before, but I hadn't been expecting to visit it today. Perhaps the chief officer was in there talking to the town councillors?

I was about to murmur something of the kind when a shouted order and the stamp of half a hundred feet in unison drew my attention to the exercise ground nearby. This was where the soldiers' daily training sessions took place, mock skirmishes with wooden swords, javelin contests, and endless rehearsals of field manoeuvres like the *testudo* – the creation of a 'tortoise' by close formations interlinking shields.

Obviously, something of the kind was happening now – over the palisades I could see the helmet tops of serried ranks of soldiers as we passed. Almost the whole contingent, by the look of it. That explained the absence of troops elsewhere, but instead of engaging in any military drill, they seemed to be listening to a fat centurion, who was standing on a makeshift dais at the end – obviously reading something from a scroll – under the metal standards of the signifers.

I was not allowed to linger. 'This way, citizen,' my guide said, in a tone that brooked no argument. But instead of going to the praetorium where the commander lived, I found myself following him towards the administration block.

I had never been in the principia before. It is not a place civilians would expect to be. Its contents are a mystery to mere citizens like me, but I've heard that it contains the regimental shrine, as well as its treasury, and record scrolls. So it was a complete surprise when the soldier led me straight inside the portico and tapped at the door of a little ante-room that gave onto the entrance lobby.

A muffled voice replied, 'Who's there? Identify yourself.' It did not sound like anyone I knew.

'Auxiliary Lucus Villosus, returning with the

citizen as commanded, sir,' the soldier shouted back. He contrived to holler deferentially, though still addressing the stout wood of the door.

'Very well. Enter.'

Villosus – the name means 'shaggy' and it suited him – pushed the door open and stood back to let me in. 'This is the individual, with your permission, sir.' He gave a smart salute. There was no attempt at the customary rigmarole of invoking the Emperor by all his titles first. Perhaps my escort wasn't used to carrying messages to senior officers. I blinked in the cool gloom of the ante-room, trying to make out how senior this one was.

I did not have long to wonder. The man who rose to meet me from the desk was none other than the commandant himself. 'Libertus! You may leave us, soldier.' He waved a dismissive hand at Villosus, who gave another hesitant salute and sidled out again.

'So citizen, we meet again,' the commander said, without enthusiasm. He was as elegant as ever, his armour gleaming in the light of the candles burning on the desk, but his lean and weather-beaten face was drawn and lined and his air of easy authority had abandoned him. 'You insisted you must see me. Something about a messenger to your patron, I believe.' The accent was patrician, as it always was, but the voice was flat and near-expressionless – not a bit like his usual light, educated tone. No wonder I had not recognised it earlier. 'I trust this is a matter of some consequence. I'm not in general seeing anyone, though I have made a special exception in your case. I am occupied with urgent business, as no doubt you can see.'

He gestured to the table-top, which was littered with half-opened vellum scrolls and rolls of bark-paper. The pots, which had obviously contained them, lay strewn around the floor, though it was clear where they had come from: there were shelves of similar containers ranged around the walls, some of them with empty spaces here and there. Evidently this was a storage room for records of some kind and he had been taking them out and sifting through them with some haste.

I made a deepish bow – more than the token inclination of the head which etiquette required. I was still reeling with surprise. I had been expecting an interview with a centurion, at best, and here I was with the most senior-ranking officer in half Britannia. I recognised that this was a compliment to Marcus, rather than myself, but I did appreciate that it was done at all. Besides, I have learned a personal respect for this tall, athletic man. 'I'm sorry if I disturb you at an inconvenient time, commander,' I began, apologetically. 'But thank you for agreeing to see me anyway.'

He cut me off impatiently. 'Spare me the formalities, just tell me what you want.' This brusque response, like the disorder in the room, was most untypical. I knew him to be aesthetic, calm and disciplined, but now tension was etched in every feature of his face and his thinning, but normally neatly barbered hair was all awry – he kept running his fingers through it as I watched.

I began to feel distinctly uneasy about this interview.

'It concerns my patron, Worthiness,' I began. 'You know he's gone to Rome?' I was almost sure he did. He often dined with Marcus, both at the villa and my patron's apartment here in town – and travel arrangements were certain to have been discussed.

A curt nod answered me.

'Well, there has been a terrible incident at his country house. Somebody who clearly knew he was away.' I outlined the grisly details of today's discoveries.

The commander stood with his hands behind his back, and heard me out, his face expressionless. I had hardly expected exclamations of dismay but this complete impassiveness was not what I'd anticipated, either.

'So most of my patron's valuables are gone and all his household slaves are dead,' I finished, to re-emphasise the facts. 'It's fortunate his land-slaves have escaped. This loss will be a dreadful blow to him – not just financially. You can see that this is a meticulously plotted fraud, by someone who knows him fairly well.'

'Lot's of people knew that he was going away.' The voice continued to be emotionless.

'But not the details of what he had in every room,' I pointed out. 'It had to be someone familiar with the house. And Marcus should be told as soon as possible. That's why I've come to you, in the hope that you could send a message with the imperial couriers – and one to his wife Julia in Corinium as well.' He remained impassive, and I said urgently, 'I understand it's probably too late for that today. But there's just a chance that we could intercept that ship . . .' I paused, expectantly

For a long moment the commander made no reply at all. Then he made a helpless gesture with his hands. '"We", Libertus? What do you expect that I can do to help?'

I stared at him in honest disbelief. 'But, surely, commander, even if you can't spare the men yourself, a single word from you and the dock authorities would search the hold for us. Even a sealed letter that I could take down there myself would be enough – your seal alone would ensure that it was done. Marcus is likely to lose a fortune otherwise.'

He sat down heavily on the small three-legged stool. It was much too low for him, and it occurred to me to wonder – belatedly – why he had chosen to come here and read the scrolls instead of having them sent to him in his usual upstairs office in the guard tower. Not that the room there was luxurious at all. It was so masculine and soldierly it bordered on the austere (this one, if anything, had more amenities), but it suited his nature. He'd chosen that unconventional location for himself, and its contents were designed for him, including a handsome desk-table, efficient oil lamps and a stool of better height. So why was he sitting in discomfort here?

And why was he looking through the scrolls himself? Usually there'd be a dozen octios to search out what he required. Surely there could be no lack of personnel – the whole of the garrison was at his command.

138

I would have liked to ask him, but I did not dare. In any case, before I could say anything at all, he got to his feet and began to pace restlessly around the shelves. When he spoke it was still in that strangely neutral tone.

'I'm afraid he is in danger of losing more than you suppose. And as for sending messages, I have no communication to relay to Rome today. It's probably too late to reach him anyway. When is he scheduled to reach the capital?'

It was such an unexpected question that I shook my head. Surely the commander knew that sort of thing. 'I couldn't tell you, Worthiness. I only know he set off before the Nones of Mars – and we are well into Aprilis now. How long it takes him will depend on roads and weather, I suppose – and whether the rivers are in spate or not. If the mountain tracks or bridges are impassable it could take the best part of another moon, but with favourable conditions he could be there by now.'

The commander had paused by the table and was staring into the candle flame like someone in a trance. I heard him mutter, almost to himself, 'That would make things very difficult.'

'Forgive me, Worthiness. I don't mean to contradict, but you'll remember that he still has property in Rome. I believe a distant cousin is occupying it, but there is always accommodation there awaiting him, so whenever he arrives that's where he plans to stay,' I explained, although I was fairly sure that the commander was well aware of this. 'So it shouldn't be hard to locate him once he's there.'

139

I glanced at the officer for some acknowledgement, but he made no reply, just went on frowning
at the candle flame.

Something was clearly troubling him, but what?
Perhaps Marcus had really not discussed his plans
and I was foolish to have come at all. I have
never travelled outside of Britannia myself – the
slavers who captured me had put me in ship, but
only to bring me to Glevum from my homeland
in the south – but I understand that Gaul is very
big indeed. There must be a score of roads that
lead to Rome, so if he really didn't know which
one Marcus planned to use, how could a courier
hope to intercept him on the way?

'I understood he had your letter of authority to
use the military inns for accommodation and fresh
horses when he needed them,' I supplied, to fill
the silence.

The commander still said nothing.

Perhaps an open letter was all that was required
and Marcus had not identified the towns where
he hoped to stay. 'It's the same route that he took
when he went to Rome before.'

I knew that I was burbling, but my companion
made no remark at all.

'He's travelling fairly lightly. He's arranged with
an old friend in Gaul to hire a travelling gig, and
a couple of slaves to ride aboard the luggage cart,
plus he's taken a four-man mounted escort of his
own in case of any bandits or brigands on the
way,' I blundered on. 'He'll travel by river where
that's possible, I suppose, but otherwise he'll have
to stick to major military roads, and even a little
retinue like that will attract a certain amount of

attention as it passes by. Any mansio he used would know where he was heading next, so a messenger could easily track him through the inns. It should not be hard to trace him, if he's still travelling.'

'I wonder if we can catch up with him in time?' the commander murmured, as if talking to himself.

I stared at him. I did not dare point out the obvious – that even a light gig and single baggage cart would obviously take much longer than one man on a horse – let alone a skilled imperial courier with a change of horses every hour or two and automatic priority over everyone on the roads, including the Roman army, where it was on the march. The commander knew that better than I did myself.

'I think it's likely that he's still somewhere on the road,' I said. 'If he'd got to Rome already, he would have sent a message back.' That sounded foolish, as I saw at once, and I added hastily, 'Though of course it would take a little time for that letter to arrive.' Then I fell silent. Really, there was nothing more that I could add.

There was a pause so long it seemed to fill the room. The commandant had moved to the far side of the table now, and was standing with his back to me, examining the painted frieze of wild beasts on the wall. At last I heard a murmur. 'I wish I could be sure exactly where he was.' One thin hand clasped the other by the wrist. 'I have had no letter from him since he left.'

'Last time we had word from him, he was just leaving Gaul,' I proffered, helpfully, but was obliged to add, 'though admittedly that was written days and days ago. Before the Kalends of Aprilis, I believe.'

The commander turned round sharply and fixed his gaze on me. 'But he did send at least one message back from the Gallic provinces? So, there might have been some substance to that letter to the steward, after all?' He had obviously been listening carefully, despite appearances. 'It did come under his personal seal, I think you said. And you mentioned that he had acquaintances in Gaul. So he may indeed be planning to set up a villa there.' He sounded almost hopeful.

I shook my head. 'I don't believe so, Worthiness. In fact it has just occurred to me, that the message saying so was suspect from the start. Marcus has been writing mostly to his wife, sending messages with anyone he can – and she sends them on to the villa where appropriate. I was shown one by the steward a day or two ago. It was the most recent, but there was no mention of any change of plan.' It was mostly about vines, although I didn't mention that. 'I did not see the fake – I've only heard of it – but I am doubly certain now that it was a forgery. If it had come through Corinium, as it should have done, Julia would have sent some communication with it, I am sure – the contents were so unexpected and so star-tling. But the steward didn't question it, because it bore my patron's seal.'

'And that does not convince you?'

I shook my head. 'Someone contrived to steal his ring, or make a counterfeit.'

Another uncomfortable silence fell.

142

I felt I had to fill it. 'If the thieves had been content to simply steal the goods, or even sell the servants in the slave-market, I might have been persuaded that my patron ordered it – though I would have expected to have heard something of his plans myself, from Julia, at least. But murdering the household? And contriving to have the land-slaves quartered somewhere else meanwhile, then keeping them busy collecting useless wood? Why go to all that trouble, if not to ensure there were no witnesses?'

He nodded. 'You are quite right, of course. Marcus would never have countenanced the slaughter of his slaves. He was very proud of how well they'd all been trained and how valuable they had become as a result.' There was not a vestige of irony in his words. 'He wouldn't have ordered their destruction, he'd have had them sold. So I fear that your suspicions are correct. But I'm afraid I cannot help you very much.' He went back to his desk and sat down on the stool, making a little pyramid of his finger-tips. 'Citizen Libertus, I will not mince words with you. I was prepared to see you because I thought that you might know where Marcus was by now, and whether he was staying somewhere with a trusted friend – in which case I would have sent a courier with your message willingly. I wanted to send him a warning letter of my own.'

'A warning, commandant? You mean you knew some trouble was afoot? Perhaps you know who did this – or could make a guess? All the more reason, surely, to send a messenger – even if it only reaches him in Rome.'

He shook his head all the more emphatically. 'What happened at the villa is no part of it. I can see that it has disturbed you very much, and another day, perhaps, I would have felt the same. But frankly, citizen, I have no time to deal with such minor incidents today.'

'Minor?' The protest escaped me before I could resist.

'Forgive me, Citizen Libertus.' He ran his hand through his thinning hair again. 'Minor in comparison – that is all I meant.' He raised one eyebrow at me. 'I know that you are greatly in your patron's confidence. I imagine that he told you why he went to Rome?'

I shrugged. 'He thought the Emperor needed his advice. Said Pertinax was far too honest to succeed. That he would cut out the excesses of the previous Emperor and he wouldn't try to bribe the Praetorian Guard.'

'That is exactly what he said to me. And it turns out he was right. So if you have any care for him at all, you will not repeat what you've just told me, outside of this room. Marcus will have enemies enough under the new regime. It must not be thought that he was party to the plot.'

'Plot!' I cried out in astonishment. 'The new regime?' The Roman must have seen the dawning horror on my face. 'Something has happened to the Emperor Pertinax?'

'Pertinax is no longer Emperor. We received a messenger from Rome first thing today – there have been horsemen riding day and night across the Empire with the news.' Suddenly the neutral tone had disappeared. There was a bitter anger in his voice and I almost thought it trembled as he spoke.

'He's been deposed? Imprisoned? Exiled?'

'He's been assassinated – by that same Praetorian Guard, and for the very reasons that your patron had foreseen. They were his personal protection and they turned on him. It's the story of Galba all over again – only worse, if anything.'

I had only the vaguest notion of Roman history from a century before, but I knew what they said of Galba – 'one of the finest Emperors of Rome, if he had never ruled'. And I knew about his fate. 'You mean that both Galba and Pertinax were assassinated for the same thing: refusing to pay the guard the excessive bonus that their predecessors had done?'

A nod. 'Apparently Pertinax attempted to reason with the men. Insisted on going to face them and trying to explain that he really could not pay because there was not enough money in the treasury. Commodus had spent it all on luxury, he said. Typical of him to take a brave and rational approach. But reason did not help him, in the end. It almost did. He was beginning to persuade them, so our informant said. But not all the guards were swayed by argument. One man lost patience and threw a spear at him. Then all Dis broke loose. Pertinax fell wounded to the ground and, at that, all the other guards surged up and stabbed at him as well. And these are the chosen men who take an oath that they'll defend the Emperor until their dying breath! What has become of the old Roman values, citizen? Duty, bravery, honour and rational debate?'

I shook my head. 'I can't believe it.' I couldn't. It was scarcely three moons since Pertinax was hailed as Emperor by all the populace around the Roman world. More than hailed – joyfully acclaimed. Celebrations everywhere had lasted half a moon, and there were grateful sacrifices to the gods because we had an honest Emperor at last, and the corrupt and cruel Commodus had been overturned. 'The entire Empire had such hopes of him!' I said. 'And now . . .?'

'So swiftly passes the glory of the world – as the old adage says.' The commander spread his hands in a gesture of despair. 'I could not believe it, either. In fact when the first intelligence arrived, I refused to send on the messenger to the Iscan settlements till the news was confirmed by someone I could personally trust. But now it has been – several times – and more disturbing details are emerging all the time. The last courier reports that when he left the Imperial capital, the soldiers had cut off Pertinax's head and were carrying it in triumph around the city on a pole.'

I could hardly take it in. 'So, who has been acclaimed as Emperor in his place? His son will not be old enough to take the purple yet. And I suppose they wouldn't want his family anyway.'

'That, citizen, is almost the worst news of all. It almost happened that his influence went on. Pertinax's father-in-law looked likely to succeed – he was prepared to offer the praetorians what they were asking for – and that would at least have kept a semblance of propriety. He was the Chief Prefect, promoted to the post by Pertinax himself, and would have been the obvious successor. But while he was in the palace making his offer to the guard, another candidate announced himself outside the gates – shouting that he would pay a higher sum. The two of them began to make promises of gold – bigger and bigger promises – to the praetorians.'

'All this in public – so that anyone could hear!' I don't know Rome, but Marcus has described the Imperial court to me and I could visualise the scene – even though I could scarcely credit it.

'All this in public, citizen, as you rightly say. It seems that our rulers have no shame or dignity at all. In the end Didius Julianus made a bid that his rival could not match, and his succession has been ratified.' He looked at me and for the first time I could see that he was close to tears. 'They auctioned the Empire, citizen – and we who supported Pertinax have lost.'

Fourteen

The enormity of this was almost too dreadful to take in. The praetorians – the select Imperial Guard – openly selling the Empire to whoever agreed to pay them most! I found myself staring, speechless, at the commandant, as if Jove had struck me with one of his famous thunderbolts and I'd been turned to stone. I was so shocked that I could hardly think at all, but one clear realisation surfaced in my brain: I could abandon hope of getting help in dealing with Marcus's affairs. Nothing else would matter to the commandant now.

That recognition must have been written on my face. 'I see that the implications are not lost on you,' he said. 'You'll understand now, citizen, if I don't seem as sympathetic as you might have hoped to the local troubles you report, however dreadful you may feel they are.' That dead and neutral tone was back again, but I now realised that this lack of outward emotion – as with the mask-like expression on his face – was the product of iron self-control. Inwardly the man was seething with outrage, grief and shock.

I found my voice sufficiently to say, 'You think this will affect us a great deal, then, even in Britannia?' This was the most far-flung province of them all, and the most removed from the customs and fashions of the Imperial Court – as Marcus had often scathingly pointed out to me.

The old soldier looked me. 'What's just gone on in Rome affects everyone in the Empire – even us in Glevum, citizen. For you and your little workshop perhaps not very much. People will still want pavements, I expect, and if there are wars they probably won't reach as far as this – though there may be extra taxes, by and by, which everyone will feel. But for me . . .?' He tailed off. 'It all depends on who's advising Didius.'

I stared at him. 'But surely . . . you have had an impeccable career. And you have kept away from politics. Marcus told me that you'd chosen to be posted here, instead of seeking a comfortable senatorial seat in Rome like most people of your rank and seniority.'

He made a wry face. 'A praetor cannot altogether escape from politics, citizen. I have long been outspoken in my praise for Pertinax and I have no friends in the Praetorian Guard. I shall be lucky not to be recalled to Rome and – at best – relieved of my command. If I am less fortunate . . .' He left the sentence hanging in the air, but it was quite clear what he meant: even his life might be in question – and his fortune, certainly.

I swallowed hard. Here was this senior Roman officer speaking frankly of his fears to a humble Celtic ex-slave in a toga, whose future was likely to be more secure than his own. An hour ago I would have said that was impossible. Suddenly the whole ordered world was turning upside down. 'That's why you're searching through the records?' I was hesitant, but anxious to make clear I'd understood. 'Looking for proof that you've done nothing wrong?'

149

The officer gestured to the littered documents on the desk. 'I'm looking at accounts of my career, trying to predict what imaginary failure of duty the new Emperor is going to charge me with! And trying to find anything that I can use in my defence! Ah!' He untied the strings that held together yet another scroll and let it unroll gently between his hands. 'This might be of help – a commendation from someone that I served with once, but unlike me went into politics. He's kept his own counsel over many years, so he is likely to retain his senatorial seat and still have a voice in government. I saved his life once and he's not the sort of man who would forget. I'll send to him. If necessary he might speak in my support.' He began to roll the letter up again with care.

There was no possible answer I could make to this. It was clear that the commander was in earnest about this. Yet this weather-beaten soldier had always seemed to me the picture of a successful, well-born, well-respected military man. I had always thought him a model of a good commander, too, ready to listen and not too quick to judge. Without his presence Glevum wouldn't be the same. I shook my head. 'You really think . . .?'

'Citizen, you're not familiar with the Imperial Court.' He was carefully retying the letter as he spoke. 'If a new man seizes power the first thing he must do is weaken the influence of his prede-cessor's friends. Anyone in politics will tell you that. Sometimes this is done by semi-legal means – imposing exile or a seizure of lands and property

– or sometimes by arranging a convenient demise. Failure to do so is always a mistake, as Pertinax has discovered to his cost. He was too lenient when he assumed the purple, not only with exiled criminals (he offered several pardons where he felt his predecessor's decrees had been unjust), but also with the powerful men of Rome: both those who served Commodus while he was in power, and those who planned his overthrow. When Pertinax was first installed, he should have made an example of them all, but in fact he executed very few of them, and that was his downfall in the end. Men who bring down one Emperor with impunity tend to imagine they can do the same again.'

This was another shocking new idea to me. I had always regarded the Roman Emperors – even the half-crazed Commodus himself – as creatures set apart by destiny, close to being the deities they sometimes claimed to be. (Not that Pertinax had ever called himself a god!) This view of them as calculating and ambitious predators – human spiders spinning a web of treason and deceit and clinging to power by devouring enemies – was disquieting. 'So what do you think the new Emperor will do?' I managed.

'Knowing Didius, he'll do what he's advised,' the commander said. 'Left to himself, he'd rather bribe and flatter than make enemies. So let's hope that he surrounds himself with people of like mind and they tell him to try and buy support rather than wreak vengeance on Pertinax's men and run the risk of popular revolt.' He set the chosen letter to one side as he spoke, and began to gather up the other documents. 'I wish I knew which people were advising him. It would make your patron rather safer too.'

I stared at him in horror. That aspect of events had not occurred to me. But, of course, it should have done. Marcus was no mere supporter of the murdered Pertinax – he was an intimate. He counted the late Emperor as his patron and his friend. And he was at this moment on his way to Rome, if he was not there already – an obvious target for this Didius.

'That is why you agreed to see me!' I exclaimed. 'And why you said that Marcus stood to lose more than just a houseful of possessions and some slaves. You think he is in danger of his life?'

'Of his rank and fortune, anyway. I wanted to discover where he was so that I could warn him,' the commander said. He was absently re-rolling another of the scrolls. 'Of course he may have heard the news already and decided to turn back of his own accord. The whole of the Empire will be buzzing by this time, and Marcus is days nearer to events in Rome than we are here. Let's hope he doesn't carry on to the Imperial Court and try to be heroic by making public speeches against the overthrow. He'd find himself in prison, or in exile – or worse. If he comes straight back to Glevum he should be safe enough, provided he doesn't thrust himself into the public consciousness. The new Emperor is not a man to worry about what is not underneath his nose.'

'You sound as if you know this Didius.'

The commander shrugged his shoulders. 'I've

met him once or twice. He commanded the twenty-second Primigenia for a time.'

I nodded slowly, trying to weigh what this might mean for us, his subjects now. Probably nothing in particular. Almost all Emperors have been military men, ever since Caius Julius, and the support of the army is obviously what keeps men in power. 'So he will have the loyalty of the Germanic legions, as well as the praetorians, if there is revolt?'

The vestige of a smile played round the handsome mouth. 'I'm not so sure of that. He was no soldier really – more interested in politics and power, even then, though his subsidiary officers were excellent and built a reputation for him, which he did not personally deserve. But he has powerful allies. He was raised in the court of the Aurelians and Marcus's aged mother was his patroness. So it did not surprise anyone when he rose like cream and was promoted to be governor of a string of provinces, each one a little bigger and more important than the last.'

'Always ambitious, then?'

He put down the rewound scroll, glanced briefly at another document, then began to roll that up as well, as if his life depended on activity. 'I think he always dreamed of being Emperor one day. He was accused of conspiring against Commodus, once – and I expect he did.'

'And yet he lived?' I was astonished. Scores of others down the years had suffered nasty, lingering deaths, simply for being half suspected of that crime.

The commander nodded. 'He was acquitted and

had his accusers executed instead. As I told you, he has powerful friends.'

'So we can expect him to be ruthless?' I murmured doubtfully, thinking of Marcus and what his fate might be in Rome.

'He has a reputation for it, certainly.' The old soldier laid the second rewound document neatly by the first. 'But I am not so sure. When he was governor of Beliga he once put down a rebellion with some force – that's why he was promoted to the consulate. Yet he really did no more than sit in his provincial capital and sign the papers that the army brought to him. It was the officers in the field who quashed the rebel force. But Didius knew how to word the dispatch back to Rome so that he made himself look like a hero and a patriot.'

I was still trying to get a mental picture of the man. 'Obviously he's clever and has a way with words.' That was a serious asset, I could see. Romans greatly value argument and rhetoric and a powerful orator can often sway the crowd.

'Clever enough, at least, to pay someone to pay somebody who does. I'm almost sure, from what I knew of him, that he didn't compose those dispatches himself. Any more than I think he prepared his own defence in that treason case.' He found the storage jars he wanted and laid the rolls inside. 'He used to keep a secretary in his retinue, a man who was born to noble rank, in fact, but had been obliged to sell himself to slavery and who had the education and skill to frame the words for maximum effect. Didius made no secret of the fact. He boasted of having paid a handsome sum for him. No doubt he still keeps someone of the kind. He's has never been afraid to use his wealth for his own advancement.' He stuffed a bung into a storage jar with unnecessary violence. 'And now he's bought himself an Empire.'

I heard the crackle of emotion in the voice and felt I must say something comforting. 'So let us hope he goes on using bribery and he'll simply try to buy allegiance from people who used to follow Pertinax.'

'Gold would not tempt Marcus very much, I think,' the commander said, as if he were considering the matter carefully. 'But perhaps he could be bought – a position in the new Emperor's retinue, perhaps.'

I tried to imagine Marcus as a magistrate in Rome. Perhaps that was the fate that I should wish for him. It would mean at least that he was well and safe – for a little while at least. And no doubt he would fulfil the role with skill and dignity. But I realised suddenly how much I'd miss the man. He was thoughtless and high-handed now and then – 'arrogant and impulsive' was what Gwellia would have said – but I was oddly fond of him. And how would I manage without his patronage? Any pavement-maker needs some wealthy man to be his advocate and introduce him to affluent prospective clients.

The thought reminded me of the customer I'd missed and – despite the seriousness of events in Rome (or perhaps because of them) – I found myself wondering selfishly how lucrative that Egidius contract would have been. With Marcus gone, I'd probably never get a big commission of that kind again. And now I'd almost certainly lost the opportunity. I sighed. The client was clearly not the type to tolerate delay, and – whatever Junio had said – was unlikely to call on me a second time.

I was brought back to the present by the commander's voice. 'It wouldn't surprise me if Didius did begin by trying bribery. After all, it has already got him where he is.' He got abruptly to his feet. 'But he won't be able to sustain it, if he does. There are too many people who supported Pertinax, and not enough in the coffers to pay even what he has already promised to the Guard. And he won't keep their support if they don't get the gold. It's a dilemma, citizen. If he isn't harsh and ruthless, he will not last very long. It takes a stronger man than Didius to run an Empire.'

I swallowed. 'So what do you foresee?'

'I'll tell you, citizen.' He walked over and put the storage jars back on the shelf. 'There will be wars and uprisings all round the Empire – till someone has succeeded in seizing power from him. One of the provincial governors, I expect. Maybe even the governor of Britannia – he has as good a claim to the purple as Didius Julianus has. I'm half expecting to receive a message saying so and urging me to move in his support. Perhaps I ought to think of writing to him first, suggesting it. Though Jove alone knows what the local populace would think.' He looked wearily at me. 'Or what they'll think about any of these events, in fact.'

'This news from Rome has not been publicly announced here?' I said, though I knew the answer even as I spoke. There'd been no evidence of public disturbance on my way, as there surely would have been if the death of the Emperor were known.

The commander shook his head.

'But there's been an announcement to the garrison,' I said, suddenly realising why Cerberus had abruptly changed his mind when I talked of dreadful happenings and needing to send an urgent messenger to Rome.

'I told the senior officers at once,' he said. 'We made a placatory sacrifice to Jove, and decided that the news should be passed on to the other ranks.'

'That was what was happening when I came in, I think.'

'Exactly. But we haven't released the information to the town. The soldiers will all be sworn to secrecy meanwhile, as they always are in anything which touches on the safety of the Emperor, and I'm refusing to see anyone from the *colonia* today, though of course there'll have to be a public proclamation later on. Exactly when, I couldn't say. I have left that decision to the curia.'

'Really? Isn't it really a matter for yourself?'

He ran a distracted hand through his thinning hair again. 'It affects the civic powers as much as anyone – and besides, citizen, I am in need of their support.' He said it simply, but I could see the force of it. 'I called them here as soon as the message was confirmed,' he went on, 'and they went away to discuss exactly what to say, and when – though they want me to put troops out on the street when the announcement's made. And I agreed. It would be a wise precaution. There were civic riots when Commodus was deposed.'

I nodded. 'I have vivid memories of that night. I was almost trampled by excited crowds.' Almost lynched, was nearer to the truth. They had been dragging down a statue of the hated Emperor and setting fire to anything that had his name on it: sign-boards, carvings – even coins – while anyone who didn't join them in these activities found themselves in danger of being set upon. The frenzy of that violent mob had been terrible to watch – like some sort of new-hatched monster which uncoiled itself and devoured anything which crossed its path.

'That night was frightening,' I said. 'But Commodus was loathed – Pertinax is . . . was . . . well-respected, if not exactly loved.'

'Which makes it very likely to be worse this time, unless we fill the streets with soldiers first – and even then it might be difficult to maintain control. Pertinax was governor of this province once, and gained a name for justice and fair play, so Mars alone knows what disturbances this news is going to cause. And if I don't handle this with care – if a citizen gets injured or a soldier killed – I'll give the new authorities the opportunity they need to have me relieved of duty and recalled to Rome.'

I could see his dilemma. 'So you are in no hurry to have the news proclaimed.'

He had taken up station by the wall again. 'Frankly, I would prefer to do it as soon as possible – I don't want to be rebuked for reluctance to acknowledge Didius. But I suspect that the announcement may be made at dusk, when the gates are due to close to travellers and most people are abed. Let's just pray to all the gods that rumour doesn't get there first. There must be traders on their way to us by now who have already heard the news elsewhere.'

'Then wouldn't it be wiser to insist?' I said, defying convention by proffering advice. 'Rumour seems to spread faster than messengers can ride. And the tales will just get more exaggerated all the time.'

He did not turn around. 'And no doubt Didius will claim it's my fault, if they do. I shouldn't have delayed when the first courier arrived. But I think that I can prove it was the magistrates who didn't want the announcement to be made at once. There's a long will to be read out in the forum, today.'

I could not see the relevance of this, but I nodded anyway. 'I believe I saw the mourners gathering,' I said, remembering the dark-clothed citizens and their slaves who'd crowded me off the pavements while I was coming here. 'Oh,' I added, remembering suddenly, 'that will be Gaius Publius, I suppose.'

Gaius had been a councillor himself but when he died last moon he left a fortune and not much family, and there were conflicting rumours over his estate. It was said that many wealthy men had been promised a bequest in return for favours

159

previously received, while other gossips said he'd left his money to the town for public works in the hope of having his name inscribed on some of them. Still others said he'd spread these differing stories purposely to ensure a good attendance at his funeral and at the reading of his testament.

The commander nodded. 'Gaius Publius – exactly, citizen. And some of the richest men in Glevum will be there. The curia felt it would be better to let that group disperse before the dreadful information is released – out of respect for the dead man, if nothing else. They didn't want to interrupt the reading of a will with something that was likely to create a riot. I did not press the point. I dare not offend the curia over this. I shall have sufficient charges at my door.'

Of course! Several councillors would have an interest in that will themselves, I thought – and not only in relation to the public purse. They would not want the legacy delayed or set aside, as it might be if the augurers declared the reading was ill-starred because it was interrupted by the dreadful news from Rome. I was about to say so to the commandant when we were interrupted by a tapping at the door.

The commander turned abruptly and went over to the desk. He picked up the letter which he'd said might be of use, and put it inside his breast-plate, out of sight. Only then did he reply, as he had done before, 'Identify yourself.'

A muffled voice responded. 'Auxiliary Lucus Villosus returning with a message, sir.'

'Enter, Villosus!' And the soldier sidled in.

160

'In the name of . . .' he began, and trailed off hopelessly. I understood now why the formal exchanges had been missing, earlier.

'The Emperor Didius Julianus – till you hear otherwise,' the commander said, so coolly it was difficult to recall how unwelcome that official formula must be.

'In the name of His Imperial Excellence, the Emperor Didius Julianus,' the soldier repeated in an obedient tone, 'I am sent to tell you that there is another messenger – this time from the Governor's palace in Londinium.'

The commander raised an eyebrow at me, saying 'I told you so' as plainly as if he'd said the words. What he did say was rather a surprise. 'Show him to my usual office. I will see him there. And find the duty octio while you are gone. Get him to send a couple of his men to tidy up in here. I have finished with the records.'

Villosus looked ready to salute and hurry off, but the commander checked him. 'And when you've done that, report to the guardroom and accompany this citizen to the docks. I've already posted a soldier down there – just in case of rumours coming in by boat. Tell him to make an announcement that no ships must sail today. All captains are to report to the forum before dusk and await a proclamation from the curia.'

'You'll send a written message, sir? Otherwise they might not credit what I say.'

The commander shook his head. 'There is no time for that. I'll send a *tubicen* along with you to blow a trumpet blast – that will give you all the status that you need. The signal will make

161

the sailors and the dockers gather round, so the soldier can tell them what they are to do. He's not to say what's happened, even if he knows – just that something of international importance has occurred.' He gave me a curt nod. 'It's not much, citizen – but it's the best that I can do.'

The soldier looked startled. 'The guard will want a watchword, sir, to take commands from me. I wasn't on duty when it was announced – I have been on infirmary fatigues.'

'The watchword for the day is "let us be soldiers".' The commander raised a sardonic brow at me. 'Ironically it is the one that our late Emperor preferred.' He turned back to Villosus. '"Let us be soldiers",' he repeated, pensively. 'Remember those words, soldier, whatever happens to the Empire from now on.' He turned to me. 'I shall be sending a courier to Londinium later on, and he'll be changing horses at Corinium. I'll get that message to the lady Julia, for you. So now, with your permission, citizen, I'll ask you to retire to the usual waiting room. Your escort will be with you as soon as possible.'

And I was ushered out of the principia, accompanied to the guardroom block again and left on that all-too-familiar bench to wait.

Fifteen

My presence in the guardroom caused little interest today, though usually there was at least one octio to stare. Now all eyes were on the flamboyant messenger from the provincial governor in Londinium, who was already waiting on the bench when I arrived. Even when he had been shown up the steep stone staircase at the back, which led up to the commander's offices, none of the junior officers gathered in the room so much as glanced at me. Instead, with one accord they stopped their calculations and their scribblings and seemed to be trying to will themselves to hear the interview – although, of course, that was impossible.

Nobody spoke, but there was an air of suppressed tension in the silence which ensued and I knew that every soldier there was wondering about what was happening upstairs and whether the messenger was bringing a request for military support for the provincial governor against the upstart emperor in Rome, thus forcing decisions about their loyalties.

If so, there could be battles here in Britannia soon.

However, I did not have very long to worry about this. After a few moments Villosus hurried back, now swathed in a handsome military cloak. He was accompanied by a sulky-looking youth in uniform, carrying a *tuba* – the long straight trumpet which the Roman army uses for signalling.

'Citizen, if you would accompany us now?' The auxiliary sketched a bow and opened the door for me to pass. His earlier diffidence had wholly disappeared. His voice was suddenly stentorian and he held his chin unnaturally high – almost pink with self-importance at having been selected for the current escort task. He swaggered proudly beside me to the gate, while the trumpeter trailed morosely after us. 'Let us pass, please, sentry,' Villosus almost barked, then seemed to notice that the man on duty was a full centurion, and therefore greatly his superior, of course. 'We have an urgent mission to perform, special orders from the commandant himself,' he added, in a more conciliatory tone.

Cerberus looked dispassionately at him, and then at the unwilling tubicen and finally at me. 'Ah, you, citizen!' he said, in a tone which made it clear whom he held responsible for this breach of discipline. 'I should have guessed as much!' He turned to Villosus. 'Watchword?' he demanded.

Villosus gave it – smugly – and the sentry moved aside, though I heard him muttering underneath his breath. 'A tradesman, an auxiliary and a horn player – who else would be entrusted with an "important mission" by the commandant? The Empire has gone crazy!' But he let us past.

It was strange to move out of the tension of the camp and into the normal hubbub of the town. The streets were still bustling with the business of the day, the inhabitants oblivious of the dreadful news from Rome. Our little party attracted some curious stares, of course – the young trumpeter in particular was an unusual sight – but people were too busy with their errands and their trades to do much more than gawp and nudge their neighbours as we hurried past.

We did hurry. Villosus saw to that. He was taking his role as courier very seriously and, being a trained soldier and used to route-marching, kept up a pace which I soon found impossible to match.

'You'll have to slow down, soldier,' I managed, between heaving gulps of breath. 'I'm just an old tradesman. I'm not used to this.' I clung to a pillar in a portico and tried to get some air into my gasping lungs. I knew my face was scarlet with effort, and my toga was threatening to dislodge itself and fall in embarrassing festoons around my knees. I hitched it up. I felt ridiculous – even the horn-blower was looking half-amused. Despite his awkward instrument, he'd kept up easily, without so much as seeming to bestir himself. 'Let me rest a moment here,' I pleaded, breathlessly.

Villosus looked doubtful. 'We can't be too long, citizen. Any message from the commander must be delivered with all possible dispatch – every messenger will tell you that. Besides, we don't want any shipping slipping out of port because we contrived to miss it while we were loitering here.'

It was a point I hadn't thought of and I acknowledged that – though only by a nod. I was still

165

too out of breath for unnecessary words. After a little, when I'd stopped gasping like a landed fish, I let go of my pillar and we started off again, though mercifully a fraction more slowly than before. Fortunately the docks are no great distance from the garrison and we were soon walking down the only broad main street that meets the riverside.

The wharf is always a busy area and today was no exception. There were people everywhere – sailors, merchants, moneylenders, overseers, slaves – while outside the busy warehouses and wine shops, the usual street vendors wove nimbly through the crowd, offering hot pies and oatcakes from their greasy trays. A bored soldier stood in the centre of the quay, obviously on watch and leaning on his spear – though he was too busy looking at a plump prostitute (draped against the doorway of a drinking house and dressed in the tell-toga) to notice we were there.

'There's the guard,' said Villosus and went to walk that way, but I held back a moment, peering at the quay. Was there a likely ship there, or had we come too late?

Despite the crowd it was possible to see several vessels tied up at the dock. Two were being unloaded as I watched, and their crews – assisted by gangs of slaves from the nearby warehouse – were already scuttling to and from the quay, carrying sacks and boxes into store, loading dried fish onto waiting handcarts for the market stalls, or teetering down unsteady planks balancing precious amphorae in their arms while their masters shouted instructions from the decks.

Another ship stood idle, its single sail dangling loosely from the mast and its rows of wooden oars shipped inboard – awaiting cargo by the look of it, since it rode a little higher in the water than the rest. Only a single watchman seemed to be aboard. I shook my head. None of these seemed likely candidates as hiding places for Marcus's effects, yet they were the only sea-going vessels in the dock. All the rest were smaller, purely local craft: eel-boats and the little one-man coracles that ply between Glevum and the islands in the river, bringing back mud crabs and mussels for the marketplace or for use as bait for local fishermen.

I shook my head. I was almost certain that, after all, I would find nothing here. We had arrived too late. In fact, when I considered it more carefully, perhaps I should have anticipated that. It was only that false message to the land-slaves yesterday which suggested that the ship was still in port. Or even, come to think of it, that there had ever been a ship at all. What had ever made me think that the goods were bound for Gaul? Only that forged letter to the household slaves!

'Citizen!' Villosus was tugging at my arm. 'We must go and see the guard and tell him about the announcement for the sea-captains.'

I gave an inward groan. If trade were inter-rupted unnecessarily and these ships were all delayed to no useful purpose, it would be my doing, I thought despondently – though only the commander and myself would be aware of that. But there was nothing for it now. I nodded at

Villosus. 'Very well, lead on,' and followed him across the quay to where the soldier was.

The man had sensed us coming and had dragged his eyes away from the dumpy prostitute. I was surprised that he was interested in her – she was no longer very young and her hair was so dyed with henna that it was getting thin. But he must have been, as she was obviously licensed and there was nothing illegal in her looking out for customers provided she did not actually approach them and operated only in the registered premises. Perhaps he was hoping to purchase her favours later on, when he was off duty and had an as or two to spend. He was a legionary soldier, by his uniform, and not looking pleased at our interruption of his reverie.

Villosus did not even wait for him to speak. He offered the watchword with self-conscious pride, and explained what the commander had ordered him to do. The soldier sighed. 'So we can expect the docks to be full of idle men all night!' he muttered. 'Very well, then – sound the trumpet, tubicen.'

The sulky youth stepped forward and raised the *tuba* to his lips. It was not much shorter than the trumpeter himself, and he held the body of it upwards so it towered overhead. People were already turning round to stare, but as the clear notes sounded, everybody stopped and expectant silence fell.

The legionary gestured to a passing slave to bring across a wooden box that he was carrying. 'Put it on the paving over there. I want to stand on it.'

168

The slave looked startled, but did as he was told and the legionary climbed onto his temporary dais. 'Citizens, friends, strangers – gather round. There's an important proclamation I've been asked to make.'

There was a general scurry as the crowd complied, and the murmur of conversation began to rise again. The trumpeter, who had come suddenly to life, glanced at the soldier for permission to proceed, and – having gained it – gave another piercing tuba blast. This time the silence was immediate.

The legionary, who was clearly enjoying his unexpected role, struck a pose – one hand on his chest and the other in the air, as one sees lawyers sometimes do – and declaimed the message in a ringing voice. 'No departures from the port are authorised today. Captains of all vessels are to report to the forum shortly before dusk. There will be an announcement of great importance then.' Realising that there were mutterings of discontent, he added, more feebly, 'This is by order of the garrison. Disperse.'

Far from dispersing, though, the crowd was thickening. People were appearing from dwellings, warehouses and the maze of narrow lanes around the quay, and even the clients in the drinking shop put down their cups of watered wine and hurried out to see what the disturbance was. Among the throng I saw a man I recognised, an ancient steward named Vesperion, who worked at one of the larger warehouses nearby. In fact, I remembered hearing he was now effectively in charge, as the business had changed hands (as a result of an unfortunate incident I'd been able to resolve) and the new purchaser knew little about the import–export trade.

It occurred to me that Vesperion would know – if anybody did – what ships had come and gone from Glevum in the last day or two and what they were carrying. And I'd done the new owner of the premises a favour once (in fact, it was probably my doing that he owned the place at all) so I felt justified in going there first to ask for help.

I turned to Villosus. 'Thank you for your escort, officer.' He was not an officer, but flattery of that sort never comes amiss. 'I see the very man I hoped to meet.' And before he could protest, I had left his side and begun to work my way across the quay to where Vesperion stood talking to a resplendent citizen in an embroidered cloak, who – alone on the dockside – had his back to us, clearly intent on whatever was in hand.

I grinned. It looked as if the new arrangement was working perfectly. The citizen, who was obviously very affluent, was waving both hands emphatically while the wily steward stood simply shaking his grey head – driving a hard bargain, by the look of it. I even wondered if I ought to interrupt, but I continued to work my way across the crowd.

But then – perhaps I was moving against the general flow – Vesperion noticed me. He was an aged man, very stooped and thin, and rather slow and careful in his activities. But to my surprise, he reacted instantly. He murmured something to the citizen, then began to come to meet me, shuffling his way surprisingly nimbly through the throng, using his bony elbows to ward off pie-sellers and lifting his skinny sandalled feet to step carefully over the treacherous rope-coils that lay underfoot.

He was panting by the time he reached my side. 'Citizen Libertus!' The crowd was surging round us, jostling, and he had to raise his cracked voice and fairly shout at me – though even then it barely reached me over the general clamour of the crowds. 'This is a surprise and privilege. Were you in search of me?'

'I want some information, that's all,' I shouted back, though my voice too was almost lost amid the din. 'But don't let me interrupt. I see you already have a customer.' I gestured vaguely towards the warehouse, though the press was so great I could not turn to look.

Vesperion glanced over there, then shook his thinning locks at me. Whispering was quite impossible, but he mouthed the words at me. 'I think he's gone.' He made a cancelling gesture with his hands. 'No prospect, anyway.' A group of drinkers from the tavern barged past as he spoke and pushed him roughly into me, so that his face was forced unnaturally close to mine. He seized the opportunity to murmur in my ear, 'Let's go into the warehouse, citizen, where we can talk – and breathe – more easily than here.'

I nodded and he began to lead the way, hobbling through the ever-increasing throng and elbowing a path. I was glad to leave the situation on the dock. The crowd was getting more vociferous all the time – murmurs and complaints about missing

171

wind and tide, and indignation at being required to wait to find out why. There was beginning to be a nasty mood abroad and I feared for the three soldiers if no move was made to reassert authority quite soon.

Obviously, they'd seen the danger for themselves. As we reached the warehouse the trumpet sounded again, and continued sounding until uneasy silence fell. The legionary had climbed on his makeshift dais angrily, and was shouting at the crowd. 'You have been given the order to disperse. Or do you wish us to arrest the lot of you?'

There was a lot of scuffling and – very slowly – people started drifting reluctantly away. Vesperion's old hand tugged at my toga-folds. 'Come in here, citizen. I have an office at the back where we won't be disturbed. Let's go in there and you can tell me what it is you want to know.'

He shuffled into the warehouse, and I followed him.

Sixteen

I had been in this building several times before, but even so I was unprepared for the cool, aromatic quietness of the interior. After the noise and clamour of the dock, it seemed extremely still and peaceful here, and the mingled odours of fur-skins and exotic spice, together with the dimness of the light, gave it almost the atmosphere of a shrine.

However, by the smoky light of the torches, which even at this time of day were burning in stanchions on the wall, I could see the evidence of distinctly mortal enterprise: the sacks, boxes, crates and racks of amphorae, which were the stuff of trade. Each commodity was neatly stacked in one of the partitioned areas into which the whole huge space was sectioned off, and divided from other types of goods by wooden barriers a foot or two in height which had the names of the articles stored in that zone roughly chalked on them. I noted potted dormice, a stack of rough-sawn timber, and huge jars of olive oil and wine, and that was just in the four compartments I could make out from the door. Business was doing very nicely, it appeared.

'You know where I have my office area, citizen, I think?' Vesperion was leading the way along the central aisle, walking as quickly as his old legs would allow. 'I'll sound the gong and have the house-slave bring . . .' He broke off as a spotty slave, whom I had seen here before, came out of the living quarters at the back and hurried down to us.

'Your pardon, steward, but you have a visitor.' He must have recognised me, but he gave no sign of it – or even that he'd noticed I was there. 'I showed him to your office. I hope that was correct.'

Vesperion nodded.

'Obviously a wealthy citizen,' the pimply one went on. 'I offered him refreshment but he motioned me away.'

'Well, you can bring some watered wine for this citizen instead,' my companion said. I suppressed an inward groan. The steward was intending to be courteous, but this hospitality was going to cost me time.

However, it would be discourteous to refuse and if I wanted information from him, I could not offend. 'I'll be very happy to taste a sample of your wares, of course,' I replied. 'Thank you, steward. But I cannot tarry long. I have an important engagement later on.'

'Well, boy – you heard the citizen.' The old man clapped his thin, veined hands together sharply, as men sometimes do when shooing geese. 'Don't stand there lingering. Go and fetch refreshments as quickly as you can!'

The boy looked disconcerted but departed with a bow.

Vesperion looked at me. 'He can't get used to thinking of me as a man to be obeyed,' he murmured, deprecatingly – though I detected a certain pride. 'But my new owner has put me in charge of everything. He's even given me the use of the accommodation block, and that slave to go with it. It makes a change from all those years of sleeping on the floor, keeping watch at night the way I used to do. There is a special guard who comes and does that now – and if things go well I get my freedom in a year or two.'

'Then I mustn't keep you from your visitor,' I said. 'It may be the customer that you were talking to before, and he looked like too wealthy a client to offend.'

The steward shook his grizzled head at me. 'It won't be him, I'm sure. He didn't really seem to want to do business anyway. Pretended to be interested in some wine we have in store, but would not make up his mind – kept asking questions I don't know the answer to, and when I refused to quote a lower price, snapping that, he wanted the proprietor, and couldn't do business with an underling.'

'I'm surprised that he troubled to come down here himself,' I said. It was not unknown for wealthy men to choose their wine in person, but generally a really rich man likes samples brought to him. However, there seemed to be a fashion for rich customers condescending to visit humble premises today – no doubt the augurers (if they knew) would claim this was an omen of the general collapse of order in the Empire. Perhaps it was.

'It would have been much easier to deal with a member of his staff,' Vesperion was saying, in his faded voice. 'He kept demanding the proprietor, though I told him that my master may not even be back here again today – he was called to an urgent meeting of the curia somewhere – and he doesn't come down to the warehouse every day, in any case.'

I nodded. Of course, Alfredus Allius, the new owner of the export business was a curial councillor, and quite a senior one – no doubt he'd been summoned to the garrison. I hadn't noticed him when I looked through the arch, but Alfredus was not a man to stand out in a crowd.

Vesperion misinterpreted the nod. 'In the end I told the patrician that, since I obviously couldn't help, he would simply have to call again another day to see my master – which displeased him very much. And then I saw you and excused myself. Frankly, I was glad to get away. I was clearly about to get a diatribe against impertinence – I don't think he's the kind of man who likes delays, or inconvenient truths. But I'm fairly sure he wouldn't come in here to find me after that.'

'This caller must be someone different,' I agreed. No patrician that I ever met would deliberately seek to be humiliated twice.

'One of our usual customers looking for some olive oil, I expect, if the news is round Glevum that there's a shipment in. Well, we shall soon find out.' He was about to lead the way towards the office area when he realised that I was hanging back. I hadn't wanted to ask my questions with strangers listening in and run the risk of starting rumours in the town.

Vesperion seemed to guess my feelings. He glanced at me uncertainly, and paused. 'You are looking doubtful, citizen. Perhaps the information that you want is something that you wouldn't wish to share with anyone?'

'I think I'd rather ask you privately,' I owned. 'Is there a quiet corner where we could talk out here?' Not only was it likely to be more discreet, I thought, but perhaps I could be excused the time-consuming formalities and wine which politeness would otherwise require.

Vesperion looked flattered by the prospect of intrigue. 'Follow me.'

He led the way into the right-hand corner of the store, where there was an empty storage compartment, screened from the rest of the warehouse by a pile of fleeces higher than my head. He patted an empty box invitingly. 'Sit down here a moment, citizen, and tell me what it is you want to know. We won't be overheard – even if that wretched slave comes out again.' He gave me a sly grin and squatted on the stone floor at my feet. 'If it's about the market price of anything, I'm sure my master wouldn't mind me telling you.'

He thought that I was hoping to make a profit on some deal! 'Nothing of that kind.' I returned his smile. 'All I want are the names and destinations of any sea-going craft that left the harbour in the last few days. I assume that you would know. And – if possible – whether any of them had unusual private loads aboard – tables, statues, gold and silver ornaments, fine furniture, and personal effects?'

He gave me a sharp suspicious look. 'What makes you ask? Are you in the market to buy or sell these things?'

I leaned back on my makeshift stool and found my back in contact with the soft wool of a fleece. 'The truth is, steward, this is delicate. I'm trying to trace something which has disappeared since His Excellence, Marcus Septimus, has been away.'

This was a massive understatement, of course. I was trying to trace a whole houseful of goods, though I was not going to tell Vesperion that – the fewer people who knew what I was looking for, the more chance I had of finding it, and – with any luck – discovering the thieves. But as a slave himself, I knew the steward would sympathise and understand why even a single missing item would be troubling. A man who's left in any way in charge – as I had been – is generally accused of theft or negligence if something disappears in his patron's absence.

That was an uncomfortable thought, in fact, now it occurred to me. Not that Marcus was likely to blame me for the crime itself: fraud and theft on this scale was obviously planned by somebody outside – and by someone with sufficient wealth and influence to afford that number of horses, carts, and men to do his work. But would he think that I should somehow have prevented it? I shook my head. No one could possibly have guessed at such a scheme. My patron – surely – would realise that at once.

For the moment, though, my obvious concern and thoughtfulness convinced Vesperion that I was serious. He frowned a moment. 'Private goods? Not that I can think of, citizen. The only ship that left here yesterday was carrying wheat

178

and wool, most of it from our warehouse – from where you're sitting at this moment, actually – in exchange for a few bottled dormice, and some olive oil and wine.' He gestured to the stores that I had noticed earlier.

'There's no chance that there was any other hidden cargo, too?'

He shook his head. 'I oversaw the loading of the hold myself, so I can assure you there was nothing else aboard. I'm sorry I can't be more helpful, citizen.'

'And what about the ships that are in harbour now?' I asked, fidgeting with the curls of wool beside my neck and finding my fingers damp with lanolin.

'They both came in this morning while the wind was light – and they are only just discharging their cargo as you saw. There's been no opportunity for smuggling goods aboard. And I'm certain that there's nothing of that kind in store in any of the other warehouses round here. I walk around each morning to see what goods our rivals have and what their prices are – and of course they do the same to us. No good asking a denarius for oil if someone else is selling it for half the price.'

'But you'll keep an eye out for me when the ships begin to load – in case something is brought in from the town?'

'Gladly, citizen, but I doubt that they'll be doing that until tomorrow, now. This proclamation will have seen to that. No point in having perishable goods stored in a stuffy hold any longer than you need.'

I made a sympathetic face. I'd spent tormented days and nights chained up in a stuffy hold myself when I was first captured into slavery. It was a memory that still recurred to haunt my dreams.

Vesperion mistook my grimace for disbelief. 'The wind has not been favourable for going downstream today, though I know that at least one of the captains was hoping it would veer round later on so he could catch the breeze and get away again. But there is a favourable tide. That's why there's so much discontent at being made to wait. I presume it's something urgent? People were muttering it might be some new tax, on ships perhaps, and that no one was to leave until it had been paid.' He darted an uncertain glance at me. 'It's said that Emperor Pertinax, hail to his mighty name, is attempting to restore the public finances.'

He was obviously hoping that I'd enlighten him, but I said nothing. I simply did not dare.

'You came here with the trumpeter, I think. I thought perhaps you'd know.' He paused. 'And possibly that you'd exchange your news for mine?'

It was an awkward moment. I had not – like the soldiers – been sworn to secrecy, but I knew that the commander expected it of me. If word of the assassination of Pertinax got out, the news could be all over Glevum in an hour – and if there were riots I would be responsible.

I shook my head. 'I know there is some urgent news from Rome,' I hedged. 'Something significant, which is to be proclaimed throughout Britannia. There'll be an announcement in the forum later on.' It sounded uncommunicative – as indeed it was – but I did not want the steward concealing facts from me in turn. So I smiled, apologetically, and got up as I spoke. 'I think the captains have been ordered to remain because it's felt they ought to know before they leave.'

'Something political? Or warnings of a bad storm threatening?' His cracked voice rose an octave with anxiety as he, too, got stiffly to his feet.

Both, I thought, bitterly, but I merely shrugged. 'I can't tell you any more than that. I'm sure those two soldiers know exactly what's afoot, but they didn't talk to me. They've been sworn to silence till the proclamation's made. It does not concern new taxes, I'm certain about that.'

What I had said was literally accurate, of course, but it disguised the truth, and was intended to. I offered a mental apology to the ancestral gods – I usually set great store by honesty.

Vesperion, however, appeared quite satisfied. 'And I'm sorry I can't help you more with your enquiry. But those are the only two ships that are in port – as you can see.' He began to lead the way back to the centre of the room.

'What about the smaller one?' I murmured, padding after him. 'That was empty, by the look of it.'

He laughed his cracked old laugh. 'You are observant, citizen. I'd forgotten about him. He's often at the quay. He brings in shellfish from the coast and he waits for a consignment of something to take downstream again. He's been here two days already, but he's empty, as you say.'

I frowned. 'I thought all shipments were contracted in advance.'

He chuckled at my obvious innocence. 'Oh, he doesn't deal with exports, citizen. The captain is not a trader of the usual sort, he's just a river craft, and holds himself for hire, plying between Glevum and the sea. He takes people too. Anywhere on the Sabrina where you want to go – he's available to take you, if he's going that way. But he was cursing just this morning that he'd been disappointed of a fare, and now he could not find anyone or anything to take – showed me the hold, so empty there was not a straw in it. I'm afraid what's missing from your patron is not aboard. I am quite sure of that.'

So was I. Many of the missing items were made of gold or bronze – and with the items of furniture as well – would have filled that little vessel to capacity. 'Well, thank you for your help, Vesperion,' I said, reaching into my draw-purse to find a quadrans as a tip for him. 'At least I can ignore the possibility that what I'm looking for has left town on a ship. So I'll start to look elsewhere.' We had reached the central passageway by now, and I held out my hand to him. 'And now I'll—'

I was about to say I'd leave him to his customer, but we were interrupted by a strident shout. 'There you are, steward. What are you thinking of? Are you deliberately intent on compelling me to wait? And don't say you didn't know that I was here. I sent your slave to find you quite a time ago and instructed him to tell me when he'd passed the message on. I shall tell your owner when I meet him and see that you are flogged!'

We had turned as one man in the direction of the voice. The speaker was standing in the doorway of the office space. This was obviously the visitor the slave had spoken of.

The warehouse was in shadow at the inner end, but even in this light it was clear that Vesperion had been wrong. This was indeed the wealthy citizen that I'd seen earlier. Though he was in the shadow by the door I recognised the gold and silver decor-ation on his cloak, which was glittering in the light of the flickering torches over-head. He'd obviously got tired of being made to wait and had come out to investigate the reasons for the delay. Perhaps he had heard our voices as we approached, I thought – mentally thanking Jove that we had gone elsewhere to talk.

I looked at the man more closely. He was large and stout and paunchy, and clearly of patrician birth – the width of the purple toga-stripe indicated that, and would have made him conspicuous enough even without his embroidered finery. He was angry too. As he stepped further forward into the full glow of the torch, it was clear that he was dangerously annoyed. His mouth was set in an irritable line and the dark eyes were furious and glittering.

I caught my breath. I recognised that slack and florid face. I had seen it wear exactly that expression once before – when its owner had nearly run me down in his carriage yesterday.

Seventeen

Vesperion, with a look of horror on his face, was already shuffling forward as quickly as he could, murmuring deprecatingly, 'Citizen Patrician, I do apologise. Please come through into the *locus tabularum* again.'

He led the way into the little office room where all the records and accounts were kept. It was gloomy and airless and devoid of ornament, and I could understand why the visitor had not cared for waiting there. However, there was a handsome ebony stool beside the writing table – evidently provided for the patrician citizen – and Vesperion produced a plain three-legged one for me.

'Please, citizen, be seated.'

I was ready to comply but the visitor pointedly declined to sit, which naturally meant that I could not – it would have been improper for my head to have been higher than his own. The steward (who, as a servant, did not count, of course) began fussing about with a bunch of tapers from a hook on the wall, as though more illumination might somehow dispel the tenseness of the atmosphere.

'I heard there was a caller awaiting me, patrician,' he said, lighting one of the candles from the oil lamp on the desk and positioning it in a holder for maximum effect, 'but since you'd said you hoped to speak to the proprietor direct – of course, I did not guess that it was you.'

'So you preferred to deal with this other customer?' Fancy-Cloak looked derisively at me – clearly he hadn't recognised me from the day before. 'You thought, perhaps, that he had precedence?'

'He has had dealings with the establishment before.' Vesperion's old voice was cracking with anxiety.

It was clearly intended as an explanation and defence, but Fancy-Cloak chose to see it as a piece of impudence. 'Then I shall tell your owner of your priorities.' He was still staring loftily at me, as one might look at a tray of damaged goods. 'Who is this . . . person . . . anyway? Apart from claiming to be a citizen, of sorts.'

The arrogance and rudeness stung me into speech. 'I am Longinus Flavius Libertus,' I said, using my full titles for the second time today. 'And we have met before. I believe you know my patron, Marcus Septimus – I think I saw you outside his villa yesterday. I was on a mule and you almost knocked me down.'

I had hardly expected an apology, but his response was start-ling. The haughty gaze completely disappeared, to be replaced by a look of bad-tempered bafflement. 'Mighty Jupiter! The man who impeded my carriage – that was you!'

'You did not recognise me in a toga, Citizen Patrician?' I enquired smoothly, moving forward into the candlelight. 'It was me, indeed, but fortu-nately no actual damage was sustained. I'm sorry that you felt I was impeding you. I was merely attempting to tell you that my patron wasn't home, though I imagine you had probably

185

discovered that by then. I take it you received no answer at the gate?'

'None at all!' There was a pause while he glanced at me sharply, his small eyes glittering and his thin lips pursed tight. Then, 'Perhaps – as his client – you can offer an explanation for that breach of common courtesy?'

I looked thoughtfully at him, wondering anew if his presence in the lane last night had been merely a coincidence. Was it possible that he was responsible for what had happened at the villa after all? He looked the sort of man who might slaughter slaves without a second thought, if that sort of thing had still been legal nowadays. What he didn't look like was a man who needed gold or the sort who'd stoop to stealing if he did. He was more likely to bully some hapless inferior into offering a 'gift'. Nor, surely, would anyone have coolly challenged me to explain the lack of a gatekeeper if he'd just hanged the man in his own cubicle. It was just possible that it was a bluff, but if so, it was a convincing one.

And he was genuinely waiting for my response, it seemed. I was not about to tell him what had happened at the house. No one else should know that until Marcus did. So I simply muttered, 'I can't explain it, citizen.' I was aware that I sounded like a fool.

My meekness seemed to dissipate his disapproval, though, and a moment later he was offering a half-apology by lowering himself onto the stool and saying with a grimace that might have been a smile, 'Well, perhaps it is no matter. Probably the gatekeeper was using the latrine, but I own that I was angry – I'd been travelling all day, and visiting the villa was a detour as it was. But I had some business with Marcus Septimus.' He looked at me bleakly. 'News I think he would have been surprised to hear – as surprised as the Provincial Governor in Londinium was – or the senior Decurion at Corinium, yesterday, when I lunched with him.'

I squatted uncomfortably on the smaller stool, and tried to look impressed. In fact, I was feeling simultaneously disappointed and relieved – disappointed that I had not found the perpetrator of the crime, and relieved that I was not obliged to confront this rich and powerful citizen. Because he'd unknowingly disposed of my suspicions straight away.

If what he said about being in Corinium was true, Fancy-Cloak could not possibly have arrived at Marcus's country house more than a few moments before I saw him there – long after the thieves and murderers had left.

'Lunched?' I tried to sound admiring. 'You were favoured then.' Lunch is usually a fairly frugal meal, and only usually shared with intimates. Important guests are entertained at dinner, as a rule.

'Oh, I arranged the food,' he said, dismissively. 'Just cheese, bread and fruit, and a flask of decent wine, by way of thanks. He'd agreed to be a witness for some land that I had sold. I wanted it done properly, the old-fashioned way, with five witnesses and a pair of copper scales. Quite a little ceremony, but well worth the expense.'

So it was almost certain to be true. There was

no point in lying about a thing like that – too many people would have witnessed it. No guilty person would offer such an alibi. It was too easy to prove that it was false. (I would check, of course – a query to Julia would probably suffice. That kind of gossip would be all over the town. But I was sure I'd find that Fancy-Cloak was where he said he was at noontide yesterday.) Of course he could not be aware of how significant his little boast had been. He was simply attempting to make clear that he moved in the highest social circles possible. I shook my head.

He'd seen the gesture. 'It's true, I turned up at the villa unannounced, but one does expect a gatekeeper at least, even if the owner is not in residence.'

My mind was racing along a different route by now. If he had called on Marcus bearing news which he'd already shared with dignitaries elsewhere, dare I ask him what the news concerned? For a moment I wondered, like an idiot, if he'd somehow learned that Pertinax was dead. But I dismissed that as the foolishness it was. That news was far too recent to have reached him yesterday. He would have left Londinium days and days ago, so he could not have heard it there, and the message would not have reached Corinium until he'd left. Anyway, that bulletin was carried by imperial couriers alone – under imperial seal, and for named recipients. They would never have dared disclose it to anybody else, even an important purple-striper such as this. His 'news' must be regarding something different, and presumably something quite significant – though he was clearly not disposed to tell me what it was. Not for the ears of humble tradespeople, it seemed.

I tried a different approach. 'You were in Corinium? You did not think of calling at my patron's town house there?' I forced myself to smile. 'You would have saved yourself a detour, and you would have found a gatekeeper to let you in. His wife is due to have a child and has moved her household there.'

For the first time, the man looked less than confident. 'Indeed? Nobody told me that. But surely Marcus isn't in Corinium? Hasn't he gone to seek preferment overseas?'

I had no time to answer before Vesperion spoke. 'Not for ever, citizen. He's gone to Rome to see the Emperor himself, so my master tells me, but he is coming back again – though he may be away for many moons.' He was clearly proud of having information to impart and anxious to ingratiate himself, after having been rebuked before.

He might have saved himself the effort. Fancy-Cloak did not even deign to glance at him. 'I was talking to this citizen,' he snapped. 'If I want information from you, steward, I shall ask for it.'

'However, Vesperion is right,' I confirmed. 'Marcus is merely making a short trip to Rome. But he may be back sooner than originally planned.' I was placatory, hoping to soften the implied rebuke to poor Vesperion – but then wished I hadn't said anything at all.

'A sudden change of plan?' The patrician was looking at me searchingly.

I cursed my wayward tongue. Until the news

189

from Rome was publically announced, I was not in a position to explain. 'Something unexpected has arisen which is likely to bring him home before he planned,' I proffered, lamely. 'When he comes, Citizen Patrician, I'll tell him that you called. Whom shall I have the honour of saying that you are?'

The patrician did not answer that at once. Instead he whirled his body round to stare at me, while I held his gaze and tried to look as nonchalant as possible. After a moment he turned to Vesperion again. 'Leave us, slave.' He flapped a dismissive hand. 'I wish to speak privately to this citizen.'

'But – citizen, you wanted to enquire about some wine?'

'You heard me, steward. Kindly leave the room.'

The steward gave me a beseeching glance – obviously a good sale would be another step towards earning the promised freedom by and by, and the profit might even add a little to his *peculium*. But I could do little except nod my head.

'If this concerns my patron, steward, I must hear him out. Any wine purchase can be dealt with later on,' I said. I was not anxious for private conversation with a man who did not even have the courtesy to vouchsafe me his name, but it occurred to me that this message which he claimed to have may have been an attempted warning which arrived too late. Though surely the enemies of Pertinax could not have tentacles that reached as far as this?

The steward gave a defeated little bow and backed out of the door. As he did so the spotty slave appeared – finally arriving with the promised tray. Vesperion was about to shoo him testily away, but the lad forestalled him. 'I'm sorry, steward, to have been so long with this. But I was delayed by a disturbance on my way – somebody shouting and hammering on the door. I'm surprised you didn't hear it for yourself. I had to put the tray down and find out who it was.' He glanced triumphantly around. 'Turned out to be another visitor. Says he is the servant of the citizen who's here, and he must see his master urgently. Won't say what it's about. I've left him at the door, but you'd better let him in – he's got a most impressive-looking scroll with him, sealed with the biggest seal-box that I've ever seen.'

Vesperion looked enquiringly at me, but I shook a doubtful head – Minimus would not be carrying a scroll. The patrician, however, was on his feet again. 'That will be my attendant, I expect. Bring in that tray, slave, and put it there.' He gestured to the desk. 'Then go and summon him to me at once.'

The pimply slave-boy hastened to comply, and – after a brief hesitation – Vesperion followed him.

'So our private conversation will have to wait,' I said, rising respectfully to my feet again, as courtesy required.

The patrician gave me a disdainful look. 'On the contrary. Cacus has been with me since he was a boy. He is entirely in my confidence and I'd be glad of his advice.'

My face must have revealed the astonishment I felt. I could think of no one more unlikely to discuss things with an underling.

'Cacus is no ordinary servant, as you'll see. I bought him from his parents when he was just a boy fishing in poverty in one of the smaller islands in our sea. I saw potential in him even then and he has proved me right a hundred times. He's very gifted – for a slave. Much like yourself, I suppose.' I was about to protest that I had ceased to be a slave ten years or more ago, but he waved a jewelled hand to silence me. 'I take him every-where. He often assists me in conducting my affairs. In fact, he has been dealing with some urgent family business on my behalf today. I'll have him in, and I want you to tell him what you have been telling me. Ah, here he is!'

I turned to look, and saw what he had meant. This was indeed no ordinary slave.

The man who filled the doorway was an impres-sive sight. He was half the age that I am, but almost twice as tall – and broad to match, though there was not an *uncia* of fat on any part of him. His skin was the colour of burnished bronze and the muscles and sinews in his legs stood out like knotted rope. He wore a striking ochre-coloured slave-tunic and cloak, and a pair of high-laced sandals dyed to match. It was a uniform designed to emphasise his master's wealth and rank, but actually the short garments merely served to accentuate his size and draw attention to the colour of his skin.

'Come!' his master ordered, and the apparition came into the room, though he was so tall he had to duck his head to get in through the door. He strode across to us, his arms and shoulders rippling as he moved. There was none of the usual clumsiness that accompanies great size: if this was a giant, it was a most athletic one. As he came forward into the light of the candle I got a clear look at his face.

It was like one of the beaten masks the cavalry sometimes wear – handsome, hardened and expressionless, and the same gold-brown as all the rest of him. I could see why his master took him everywhere. This was no mere slave, this was a bodyguard. And his presence answered a question I had not thought to ask myself, why a patrician of such noble rank was travelling without an armed and mounted escort at his side. This man would have seen off any hungry wolf or bear, and the sight of the cudgel stuffed carelessly into his belt as if it were a trifling thing and not a heavy club, would have dissuaded bandits very fast indeed. But today he was acting as messenger as well. In one gigantic hand he held the promised scroll.

Pimply-Face was right – that was an imperial seal-box, by the look of it.

The giant did not even glance at me. He threw himself upon his knees before his owner, bowed his head and held the scroll out, saying urgently, 'Your pardon, citizen—'

'Thank you, Cacus,' his master interrupted impatiently. 'You can give that to me. I'll put it where it's safe.' He lifted his toga folds and put it carefully into a long, deep leather pouch that was dangling from a belt around his waist

– obviously designed for carrying the document. He carefully concealed it beneath his drapes before he spoke again. 'Rise, man, rise. I have a task for you!'

Cacus – it occurred to me that he'd been appropriately named after the monstrous son of Vulcan – scrambled to his feet. He towered over us. 'Master, I fear that I could not finish what you asked. Your brother—'

'Never mind that now. This is the citizen, Libertus,' his master interrupted with that chilly smile of his, gesturing to me with one pudgy hand. His fingers were covered in ostentatious jewellery, one ring at least on each – I noted two fine seal-rings and a mourning ring in jet – and underneath the cloak I saw that he wore a stack of thick gold bracelets on each upper arm. I mentally applauded his sagacity – it's a safer way of carrying your wealth than as gold pieces in a luggage cart, since any market will exchange a given weight of precious metal for its worth in coins. And there was clearly lots of weight. He must have been carrying a small fortune on his arms.

Cacus inclined his head a moment in a bow, then looked at me with that impassive, mask-like face. More than looked, in fact. He examined me so fixedly – studying my features as though he were trying to learn a task by heart – that he could almost have gone away and painted a likeness of me from memory alone. 'This is the citizen that you were speaking of?' he said. The Latin had a faintly foreign ring to it.

The purple-striper nodded. 'There'll be need

for you to call in at his workshop now. By great good fortune, I encountered him myself. But I'd like you to listen to what he has to say.'

'You planned to call on me?' I was so astonished that I interrupted him. 'It wasn't you who came into my workshop earlier today wanting mosaics for a country house?' It seemed so likely when I thought of it, that I wondered why this had not occurred to me before. 'If so . . .'

But the patrician shook his head. 'I have no need of pavements, citizen. I have no home in Glevum nowadays. Revisiting the place, I'm rather glad I don't. The town is nothing but a trading post and a retirement *colonia* for the soldiery, and a remote and backward one at that. I have spent a fruitless morning in the town attempting to find a senior member of the curia. But it seems that none of them is willing to be found.' He gave me that peculiar bleak and twisted smile again. 'I take it that not all of them have followed your patron's example and gone away to Rome?'

It was intended as a challenge, but I answered peaceably. 'As it happens, citizen, I can help you there. There's been an extraordinary meeting of the curia today,' I said. 'They were summoned to the garrison. The commander wanted their advice on making that proclamation that was just announced outside.'

The sudden change in his demeanour startled me. Within an instant he was furious again. The florid face grew redder than before and the small eyes glittered angrily. 'How do you come to know that, pavement-maker? You visited the garrison?

195

You must have done. Of course, you were with those soldiers when the trumpet call was made! They accompanied you here. I saw you with them when Vesperion so rudely left me and hurried off to talk to you instead – though of course I did not realise at that point who you were! What were you doing at the garrison?' He was so incensed that he was in danger of turning more purple than his stripes. I saw him look at Cacus, who shook a warning head.

'Master, he must have met the soldiers on the way. At the garrison everyone was being turned away – I told you that.'

So he'd been refused entry to the garrison himself! No wonder Fancy-Cloak had been so furious, I thought. I had been afforded more preference than his representative. I shook my head. I had no wish to offend a powerful man like this. 'I was turned away as well,' I said, with truth, if not with total honesty. 'But I would have supposed that the imperial seal . . . Ah, I see!'

The exclamation escaped me before I could control my tongue. A piece of the mosaic had just tumbled into place.

Eighteen

I had not managed to keep the triumph from my voice, or the smile of satisfaction from my lips. That was not wise of me.

'Something is causing you amusement, citizen?' The patrician's voice was dangerous.

'Only that I think I've come to understand.' I was only too eager to explain. 'Apart from the property that you were mentioning, you have some other legal interest to register, I suppose. I presume your scroll relates to something of the kind?'

He looked astonished, then bewildered, but to my delight he nodded.

So I had been right. Why had I not thought of it before? Obviously the treasured scroll was an official document emanating from the now-dead Emperor. That was not required for mere sale of property, even of the formal variety, so the document which bore the seal must relate to something else. Probably a travel permit or an imperial judgement on some disputed will.

Perhaps I could even guess which will it was, given what was happening in the forum at that very moment! And it was obvious why the citizen was so urgently seeking to register his scroll with a senior magistrate, or some other member of the local curia. 'That's why you were looking for my patron, yesterday?' I said.

'You are as perceptive as they say you are, citizen!' he said. Was I imagining it, or was there a tone of genuine astonishment? 'It was indeed in connection with the scroll that I was attempting to call at the villa yesterday.'

And was probably why he had called in here today, I realised – in the hope of finding the town councillor who had bought the warehouse recently. In which case, his lofty remark to Vesperion had not merely been a snub, he genuinely could not deal with an underling. Only a member of the curia would suffice. But the old steward had been right in one respect at least: there was never any interest at all in buying wine. The poor old fellow was going to be disappointed of his sale.

Fancy-Cloak was clearly a person with violent shifts of mood. He exchanged a look with Cacus then turned and met my eyes. His own had lost their angry glitter and now seemed half-amused. 'Your powers of reasoning are impressive, citizen – though I should not be surprised. I'd already heard of you. You have a lively reputation in the town, both as your patron's trusted confidant and as a puzzle-solver of considerable skill. In fact, the relative with whom I lodged last night told me that you were the cleverest man for miles. I see that you deserve that accolade.'

Perhaps it was the unexpected flattery that prompted me to venture my second wild surmise. 'If your imperial letter of authority concerns the will of Gaius Publius, by any chance, they are reading it on the steps of the basilica as we speak.'

'Are they indeed?' The news had taken him aback. 'I was not aware of that. Thank you, citizen. So if I wish to make a challenge, I should present myself at once?' He turned to Cacus. 'You see what this implies? I think we can forget our other errands in the town – for the moment anyway – and get over there as soon as possible.' He gave me another of his chilly smiles. 'You cannot guess how much your words have simplified our business in Glevum, citizen.' He even extended a ringed hand for me to kiss.

This sudden civility emboldened me again. 'There will be many claimants, as I understand – all of them expecting something out of the estate. I believe it is a lengthy will with lots of small bequests, but Gaius seems to have made conflicting promises about the bulk of his estate. People were predicting legal battles in the courts – though your imperial decree will give you undisputed claim, of course. But there are likely to be wrangles, even with your scroll.'

'So?' He withdrew the hand, impatiently.

'Since you are too late to register your claim before the reading starts, you won't be able to do so till the end. So before you go, with your permission, there's something I might ask . . .?'

'About what, citizen?' The voice was sharp again.

'Only that I wondered why you'd meant to call on me.'

'Ah!' He looked at Cacus and raised a questioning eyebrow at his slave. I thought for a moment he meant that his bodyguard should answer me – but, to my surprise, it was simply a signal to bring the refreshments from the desk. There was, of course, only a single goblet on the tray – intended for my use – but the patrician picked it up, as if of right, and held it out for his manservant to fill, then sat down on the stool again and motioned me to take the other one.

I sat, reluctantly, cursing my tendency to talk too much. I had not intended to create a long delay. Evidently the patrician was in no hurry any more – presumably the prospect of a legal brawl in the forum did not appeal to him – but I still had unfinished business in the town. However, this leisurely interlude was entirely of my own creation and I did not dare offend a man of rank.

He raised the metal drinking cup and smiled at me – an almost friendly smile. It seemed the news I'd given him about the will had softened him. When he spoke his tone was more relaxed. 'It's true I planned to call in at your workshop later on. Having not found Marcus I was hoping to find you. And here you are in person – before I even look – and already you have given me invaluable advice.' He took a sip of wine. 'It seems the Fates are smiling on us both.'

That was ironic, given the terrible happenings today, but I did not tell him that. I simply said, politely, 'But I still don't understand, patrician, why you should come to me at all. I'm not a magistrate – in fact I have no legal authority of any kind – so I could not help with registering your claim.'

He made a face as though the wine was poor – which probably it was. The sample was not intended for a person of his rank. 'Surely, citizen, with your skill at solving problems you can work out what I was going to ask of you?'

Challenged like that, of course I saw at once. A mere ruling on a will – even one that carried the imperial seal – was not likely to surprise either the provincial governor or the chief decurion of Corinium. 'You had some news for Marcus – apart from seeking to register your scroll – and you hoped to entrust me with conveying it?' I said, and earned a swift approving nod. 'I should be honoured to do so, naturally. But if my patron is already on his way back here, as now seems possible, it may be more convenient to wait and deliver it yourself.' He gave me a peculiar look, and I added quickly, 'Assuming that you are still in the vicinity by then. Are you intending to be in Glevum long?'

'I have already been here longer than I meant. I hoped that my business would be finished yesterday.' He gave me another of his chilly smiles. 'I originally intended to be away from here by dawn with a view to reaching Isca by tonight. Clearly that is no longer possible. But once I've settled what is owed to me I shall leave at once. And, I fear, I shall not be this way again. So tell your master when you see him that I spoke to you – and that I'm sorry I failed to call in at his town house in Corinium yesterday.'

I frowned. 'That is all the message? I thought that there was news.'

'Since you have told me about the reading of the will, the other information is no longer relevant. If the estate is settled and I get what I am owed – and I have every confidence – I shall be content to regard my business here as done.' He drained the cup and held it out for Cacus to take, and when the slave had replaced it on the tray, got sharply to his feet. 'Your patron knows me well. He had a lot of dealings with me once and my fortunes in these last few years I owe to him alone. I could not come to Glevum without attempting to repay a little of the debt.' He held out his ringed hand for me to kiss again, which I did by simply scrambling to my feet and bending over it. 'Tell him Commemoratus tried to call on him. You won't forget the name?' He smiled at the jest: the name means 'well-remembered' or 'recalled to mind' and he was teasing me.

'I won't forget,' I said, with dignity, though it would have been more polite of him to offer his full title, as I had myself.

'Good. I'm sure he'll understand. You can tell him that I came to call on him, but you met me at the gate and I hadn't been able to gain admittance to the house. I wouldn't like your patron to suppose I hadn't tried.' He did not wait for an acknowledgement, but pulled his embroidered cloak more closely round himself and raised a parting hand. 'So, farewell citizen and thank you for your help. Come, Cacus. I think our business is concluded here.'

'At your command, as always, master. Do you wish me to obtain a carrying-litter for you, or are you content to walk?'

'It isn't far to the basilica,' I said. 'Just go to the corner and follow the main street.'

'Even so we should make haste before it is too late,' the golden-skinned slave said in his lilting Latin. He was so tall that he'd been looking idly through the window space – though it was built

202

deliberately high up on the wall to keep out intruders and casual prying eyes – but now he came across the room and opened the door for his master to go through, and bowed his handsome head towards me in farewell.

There was no sign of Vesperion or the spotty slave outside, though I'd expected them to be hovering right beside the door – if not actually trying to overhear the talk within.

The same thought had obviously occurred to Commemoratus, who paused to call imperiously to me. 'Please make our apologies to the steward, citizen,' he said, loudly enough for half the dock to hear. 'I don't know where he is. He can't be far away – it would be discourteous not to escort me from the premises – but I'm not disposed to wait till he arrives. Thank him for the sample of his wine on my behalf, but tell him I decided that I didn't want to purchase any more.' I'm sure I heard him chuckle as Cacus closed the door and they moved down the warehouse towards the outer door.

That put me in a slight dilemma, naturally. Now I was more or less obliged to wait and pass the message on, but Vesperion was nowhere to be seen and I was in a hurry on my own account. Then it occurred to me that I could write it down – the steward was as literate as I was myself and there was chalk-stone on the desk. I was in the act of sitting down to scratch a note when the door flew open and the spotty slave came in.

He did not trouble with the usual courtesies, but burst out breathlessly, 'There's someone asking round the docks for you. A youngish tradesman, by the look of it. He says it's urgent that he talks with you, but Vesperion said I had to ask you first. Thought that he'd be interrupting a private interview, but I see the fellow in the fancy cloak has gone.'

'He said to tell you that he didn't want the wine.' I gestured to the tray. 'Perhaps he did not enjoy the sample that you sent.'

The boy picked up the glass and sniffed at it. 'He should have done – it is the best we have.'

I should have been flattered, since it was meant for me, but my mind was too busy with other things to pursue the thought. Who was this 'youngish' tradesman who'd come to look for me? It wasn't Junio, surely – he had taken Tenuis to the guild and had promised to look after the workshop afterwards. But I could not think of anybody else who knew that I was here.

'Well, I'd better see this visitor,' I said.

'You want to stay here in the office?' The slave picked up the tray. 'I don't know if that is convenient. Vesperion will be wanting to get in here later on. There's lots of new goods to be entered up.' He paused as the old steward appeared in person at the door. 'But I suppose that it'll be all right, if you're not very long.'

I turned to Vesperion. 'I gather there is a visitor for me – though I don't know who it is. It seems that he has urgent news. May I use this record room a little longer, so that we can talk?'

Vesperion looked startled. 'But of course you can, citizen. I don't know what my owner would say otherwise. He always says he owes you every-thing. Sit down on that better stool and the

204

house-slave will bring you another jug of wine. And another drinking cup for master Junio.' He turned to the spotty slave who was staring at us like a landed fish. 'Don't goggle at me, boy. He's only in a workman's tunic, but he's a citizen – just like his adopted father here.'

The slave-boy gave him an astonished look, and trotted off at once.

I was quite as astounded as the spotty slave had been. Junio! So it was him, after all! What by all the immortals was he doing here? I was about to ask the steward what he knew, but before I could utter a single word there was an urgent rapping at the door and Junio himself was standing there.

'I apologise for coming in here unannounced,' he said, in a peculiar voice. 'But I had to see my father.' He was obviously agitated, and as he came over to where I was sitting at the desk, and so into the better light the little candle threw, I could see that his face was white and tense and his eyes were filled with tears. 'Father,' he said, 'you'd better come at once. It's little Maximus. There's been some sort of accident. I am afraid he's badly hurt.'

Nineteen

'Maximus? Accident?' I repeated stupidly, scrambling to my feet. The day, which had been terrible so far, was fast becoming worse. 'What's happened? Where is he? Is he going to be all right?'

They were idiotic questions, as I realised instantly. Of course, if this had been a trivial affair, Junio would never have come rushing halfway across the town to find me here and he would never normally burst in before he was announced. Obviously this was something serious. And if he knew what caused the accident he'd have told me straight away. I braced myself, ready for a harrowing account.

But Junio said nothing, simply shook his head. That was more alarming than graphic description would have been.

'Great Jupiter!' I cried. I found that I had seized my son by both his upper arms, hard enough to make him wince. 'Don't tell me that he's dead.'

Junio gently disengaged himself, but if I hoped for reassurance he could not offer it. 'Not quite, when I left him – but he may be close to it. I found him on the workshop floor when I got back. It looks as if he'd tumbled down the attic stairs – though what he was doing up there I cannot begin to guess. It looks as if the ladder had moved away from him and he was lying in a crumpled heap. He's clearly hurt his head. I tried to rouse him, but he did not stir, and I could find no sign of life. I had to hold a polished mirror to his lips to see that there was any breath at all.'

'And you left him lying there?' Another stupid question. What else could he have done?

But Junio shook his head. 'Not unattended, Father – at least not for any longer than I could avoid. I made him as comfortable as I could, then rushed next door and fetched the tanner's wife. She wasn't very gracious but she agreed to come, and when she saw what had happened to the boy she changed her attitude. Sent me round to fetch a couple of their slaves to help. When I left she had them warming water on the fire and fetching soft cloth and healing herbs to wash the wound, and strong wine to dribble in his mouth.' He made a despairing gesture with his hands. 'I even offered an oblation of it on the household shrine in the hope of invoking the mercy of the gods, so everything that could be done is being done for him. But I'm not sure how successful it will be. I think you should come as quickly as you can.'

I was almost too shaken to think of anything, but the habits of courtesy enabled me to say, 'Excuse me, steward, but you will realise that this requires my presence at my workshop instantly. So pardon me, and thank you for the offer of the wine but – like Commemoratus – I really cannot stay.'

Vesperion waved my apologies aside. He was already leading the way out onto the quay. 'Never mind Commemoratus. He means nothing to me, despite the flattering name. But I'm sorry to hear about your troubles, citizen. If it's in my power to help at all, send word to me and I'll do anything I can. I'm sure my owner would agree at once – I'll tell him what's happened as soon as he arrives. He thinks most highly of you, as I think you know, and if we have any useful herbs or unguents in store, I know he'd be glad to make a gift of some.'

This unexpected kindness took me by surprise. Perhaps it was the sudden brightness of the day after the gloom of the interior – I am not in general a sentimental man – but I found my eyes were watering and I had to blink them hard. I swallowed the lump that was rising in my throat, managed to murmur, 'Thank you, Vesperion – and farewell, for now,' and followed Junio out onto the dock.

The quayside was still very crowded, much to my surprise, despite the previous orders from the soldiers to disperse. Those who remained had homes or business here, perhaps, or simply worked the ships – though most of the unloading activity had ceased. Groups of people stood in sullen huddles here and there, murmuring discontentedly about the forced delay. My mind was so concerned with Maximus that I might not have noticed what surrounded me, except that several muttering clusters were standing in our path, and we were attracting vicious whispers and suspicious looks as we attempted to weave our way towards the major road.

'Where do you think you're going, citizen?' one of the captains called. 'Planning to escape the town before they slap this new tax on us all?' The shouts and cheers that greeted this emboldened him, and he came and stood directly in our way. 'I shouldn't bother to try and run away. The tax collector will find you in the end.'

There were hoots and jeers from several in the crowd then someone shouted, 'He's one of them. He was with those soldiers earlier. I saw him come into the dock – he was accompanied by that trumpeter. I swear to Jupiter, he'll know the truth about this tax.'

The cry was taken up from all around. The mood was getting restless – which was dangerous. It was still hours before the proclamation would be made. I looked around to see what had happened to the guard, and saw him at the corner of the main road into town, with his baton drawn, trying to placate a group of angry traders who were jostling him. Villosus and the trumpeter were no longer to be seen – presumably they had gone back to the garrison by now. I devoutly wished that they had not. The presence of three soldiers would have been enough to ensure that this disturbance didn't escalate.

Someone grabbed my toga and I tore it free, and turned to try to reason with the crowd – though I could not help remembering events in Rome, and what had happened to the recent Emperor when he attempted something similar.

'I know nothing of any tax,' I said. 'But I can tell you this. This proclamation is because there's been a courier from Rome and the same announcement is being made throughout the Empire.' My denial had no effect at all. People were still crowding round me, insisting I must know. I had an inspiration. 'I think there may be a public holiday declared,' I said.

In fact, that was very likely to be true. The accession of an Emperor is always marked by some special festival – an occasion much welcomed by the general populace, as – apart from the sacrifice at the imperial shrine – it gives them an excuse to feast, often on food provided by the state. Didius would doubtless see the value of the bribe and declare a day of celebration very soon.

I must have spoken with enough conviction to impress my audience. The captain who had been taunting me stepped back a pace or two so that his face was no longer inches from my own, and there were one or two ragged cheers from elsewhere in the crowd. 'But this is only hearsay,' I added hastily. 'You'll have to wait for confirmation in the forum later on.'

But people now surged round me more closely than before and there was no move to let us through. I began to regret what I had said. Any moment somebody would ask what the public holiday was for – and my refusal to tell them might result in violence.

It was Junio who saved me. He held up his hand. 'What my father has just told you is joyful news, of course. But he has no cause to celebrate himself. Some of you know that I came here seeking him, and that it was an urgent message that I brought. One of his valuable slaves is lying hurt. Let him past, so he can go and tend to him.'

I would not have bet a quadrans on the success

of this appeal, but to my surprise the crowd began to part, allowing sufficient room for us to pass. The mutterings and jeers had ceased as well, and it was in awkward silence that we reached the corner of the major thoroughfare where the soldier was still waiting with his baton drawn.

'Citizen! A word!' He stood and barred my way.

I felt my heart sink to my sandal straps. It was obvious that he'd been turning people back and not allowing them to leave the quay that way. And now it looked as if he was going to do the same to me, and I would have to force my way across the dock again to one of the stinking smaller alleyways that served the area, some of them ankle-deep in putrid mud and sediment.

I turned to the soldier. 'I thought we had received an order to disperse? You know that I was given an escort to come here by none other than the commandant himself. It's clear he personally approved my visit to the dock, as no doubt your colleagues can confirm. Do you intend to thwart him and prevent me leaving here?'

The man looked startled and appalled, as well he might. He took my arm and led me closer to the wall, saying in a murmur that could not be overheard, 'Citizen, I intended nothing of the kind. There was indeed an order to disperse, and anyone who had no business in the dock has gone. But that still left the sea-captains and the owners of the warehouses – and their slaves of course – and they are beginning to show open discontent. I was advised to keep them here an hour or so, instead of letting them rampage directly into town – apparently there's some important will-reading going on. But though there are lots of other alleys into town, preventing people leaving this way almost caused a riot. One patrician almost burst with rage – and I thought his bodyguard was going to flatten me.' He gestured vaguely in the direction of the crowd.

I looked where he was pointing, and realised who he meant. Over the heads of some of the assembled men, I could see the towering figure of Cacus backed up against the wall – with a no-doubt furious Commemoratus at his side, though he was hidden by the press of onlookers. 'I've met that bodyguard,' I said. 'More than a match for several ordinary men.'

The soldier nodded. 'I've sent the auxiliary and the trumpet player back to the garrison, asking for reinforcements to be sent – but nothing's happened yet. I was hoping you might go there and speak on my behalf – you obviously have influence with the commandant – and ask him to send somebody as soon as possible.'

I shook my head. 'I'm sorry, that is quite impossible. I'm sure he'll send as quickly as he can. But I can't go to the garrison myself. Did you not hear what my son was saying to the crowd? There's a member of my household staff who's lying, badly hurt, back at my workshop – and I need to go to him. But there is one favour that I can do for you.' I nodded to where Cacus could still easily be seen, moving in the opposite direction now, but towering over every other person in the crowd, and looking over his shoulder towards us with a frown. 'If that's the servant of the man you mean, then I can vouch for them. His owner's not a trader, he's an important visitor, here to attend the reading of that very will. He has an imperial warrant of claim on the estate – I'm astonished that he didn't wave it in your face. If you value your skin, soldier, I should call him back and let them through at once.'

At the mention of the warrant the soldier had turned pale. 'Thank you, citizen,' he murmured fervently. 'I'll do as you suggest. You!' he beckoned to an urchin who was hovering nearby. 'Go tell that giant with the golden skin to come back here at once. And you, citizen, of course may continue on your way. And may you have good fortune with your slave.' He stood aside to let me pass and sketched me a salute.

I turned immediately and was about to set off up the street, when I heard the clatter of marching hobnails on the paving stones ahead. The promised reinforcements had obviously arrived. I stepped into an entrance-way to let them pass – twelve of them – armed with shields and with their daggers drawn. They did not glance at me, but marched resolutely on. The soldier on the quay would have no trouble now.

Once they were safely past me, I set off again, hurrying towards the town centre and the north gate beyond as quickly as I could. Junio had been trapped on the quayside by the arrival of the troops, but I expected that he would follow very soon. Yet I'd walked almost half a block before he caught me up. I did not pause to talk but raised a questioning brow at him.

'Sorry, Father,' he apologised, as he came up

beside me and matched his pace to mine. 'I got caught up by the guard. If the soldier hadn't spoken up for me, they would have kept me there. They're going to let people out in twos and threes, it seems, and there's to be no assembly till the trumpet sounds again at dusk – people can gather in the forum then. Jove knows what that's about. Maybe it is a tax or some new law that's introduced. But I'll tell you one odd thing that caught my eye. That enormous slave you pointed out – he must have taken fright. When he saw that the pie-keeper was on his way to him, he began to edge away, and when the troops arrived he didn't turn to watch like everybody else. He started forcing a passage through the crowd the other way – really pushing people roughly as he went – and taking his owner with him, by the look of it.'

I glanced at him, struck by a sudden doubt. 'You got a sight of the patrician, then? It wasn't the man who called in at the workshop earlier?' Commemoratus had denied it when I asked, but I wasn't sure I trusted him to tell the truth.

Junio shook his head. 'Definitely not. That was an altogether older person, though not wholly dissimilar in build. And just as belligerent, by the look of it. I wonder why they didn't come back when they were called.'

I shrugged. I had no interest in Commemoratus now. All my thoughts were with little Maximus. 'Expecting trouble from the guard, I suppose,' I said, dismissively. 'Perhaps they shouldn't have been so threatening before. The soldier said he thought the slave was going to knock him down.

Just as well he didn't, it would have sparked a riot – just what the commander didn't want.'

Junio gave me a peculiar sideways look. 'So it was true what they were saying on the dock? You did get into the garrison, after all. Several people have told me it wasn't possible – that no one but the curia was admitted there today. And I suppose you really were escorted down here by a trumpeter? And what you said about a public festival was true? I thought that was just a clever ploy to get away.'

Of course, I had forgotten – in my anxiety – that Junio had no idea about the news from Rome. 'I'll tell you when we get back to the workshop,' I promised, walking briskly on. 'I can't go into details until we are alone. The town will be full of rumour soon enough. But I did see the commander, and got his promise that a message would be sent to Julia today, though getting one to Marcus will be more difficult. It's even possible that he's already on his way back home. But enough of that for now. I can't walk quickly and talk at the same time. Anyway, it's your news that I'm most concerned about. Tell me about Maximus – everything you can.'

Junio shook his head. 'I wish there was something more that I could say, but I've already told you everything I know. I came back from taking Tenuis to the Funeral Guild – they're taking him back to the villa with them, you'll be glad to know – and went into the workshop to wait for you. I didn't realise anyone was there – obviously I thought that Maximus was with you at the garrison – so I decided I'd try to finish off that

215

piece we're working on. So I went into the inner room and poked up the fire and used it to light the tapers so that I could see – and there was Maximus lying on the floor. I went and knelt beside him – I thought that he was dead. And the rest I've told you. That's really all I know. I came to find you.'

I nodded. It was all that I could do. We had almost reached the centre of the town by now, but the effort had left me too breathless for coherent speech. 'You didn't. . . try . . . garrison?' I managed, finally.

Junio, being young, had no such problem. When he answered, it was in a normal tone, as though we were not hurrying as quickly as I could. 'There was no point in my trying at the garrison dressed in workman's clothes – after what happened to you a little earlier. But you'd said that when you finished you might come down to the docks, so this is where I came. I was prepared to have a lengthy search for you, but you'd obviously been noticed, because several people told me where you were. Though, once I remembered that you know Vesperion, that's probably the first place that I would have tried, in any case. Great Jupiter, what's this?'

He paused as a crowd of people all in mourning clothes came streaming from the forum by every lane there was.

Twenty

There were several members of the curia I recognised among the little crowd, including Alfredus Allius, the owner of the warehouse I'd just visited. He was walking with a youngish, pleasant-looking man I hadn't seen before, both of them wearing dark-coloured mourning togas in honour of the dead, and accompanied (at a respectful distance) by their personal escort slaves. Alfredus raised a hand in greeting as we passed, and almost looked as if he meant to summon me, but – much as I would have liked to stop and catch my breath – I did not slacken pace to talk to anyone.

It was just as well, perhaps. We were near the forum, where the toga is obligatory dress for anyone entitled to be wearing it, and mine was threatening to unwind itself and festoon around my knees in a most unRoman fashion. It was also hampering my steps. If I had been somewhere private I would have stripped it off and carried it. It is not a garment suitable for anyone in haste.

'They've come from . . . the reading of the will . . . of Gaius Publius,' I told my son between panting gasps of air, clutching at my disintegrating folds.

He raised an eyebrow at me. 'The one you were talking to the guard about? Then it doesn't look as if your friend Commemoratus and his slave

217

have managed to arrive in time to challenge it. From what you were saying to the guard back there, I fear they won't be pleased. How did you come to know about that Imperial warrant, by the way?'

I shook my head at him. 'Later!' I wasn't refusing to tell him anything, but that more was beyond my current powers of speech

Junio understood. 'Of course. In the meantime, let's cut down the side street of the silversmiths – and avoid these crowds. We'll get back quicker that way,' he said and led the way without waiting for a response.

The little street was narrow, but without the throng we made quick progress and very soon we were through the northern gate and out into the muddy streets of the busy suburb where the workshop was. As we approached it I tried to quicken my pace, but my poor old heart was pounding painfully – though whether mostly from exertion or anxiety it would be hard to say. Strangely, when we reached the door, I almost felt I didn't want to go inside – but suddenly it opened and a skinny slave I'd never seen before came rushing out to us.

'Oh, masters, come quickly – or you will be too late. My mistress has done her very best for him, but I think he's near to death.'

Little Maximus! I could not believe that this was happening. My hesitation vanished and – despite my breathlessness – I rushed into the shop, skirted the counter and ran through into the inner partitioned space which was my working area. By the dim light of several tapers burning in a jar, and the flickering of the fire, I could discern the stout form of the tanner's wife kneeling by the hearth. She was bending over a little crumpled form, which was lying motionless, with a piece of bloodstained linen wrapped about its head.

She raised her eyes and looked at me, but did not seek to rise. 'Ah, Citizen Libertus, there you are at last. I've done everything I can to cleanse his wound and given him what comfort I could find, but – as you can see – only the gods can help him now.'

I nodded, too full of grief for speech. She had found the blanket-cloak and thrown it over him, but even in the dim light I could see that the boy's face was ashen pale. His eyes were closed and when I bent to take his hand, it was as cold as death. I shuddered and put my fingers to his lips.

'He's breathing, just.' The tanner's wife got slowly to her feet. She was a sour-faced woman, whose tunic, hair and face had long since been dyed brown by tanning smoke. Our neighbourly relations had not been happy ones – she still held me responsible for the loss of an old slave – and she was famous for her irritable ways, but there was no trace of anything but gruff concern in her demeanour now. 'Poor little fellow. Who did this, do you think?'

'Did this?' I found that I was staring at her in dismay. 'I understood . . . it was an accident . . . he'd fallen from the attic . . . when the ladder slipped away from under him.' Still gasping I turned to Junio who was standing at my back. 'Is that not what you told me?'

He nodded. He was looking as startled as I felt. 'It's what I thought myself. What else could it have been? Maximus was in here on his own – though I did wonder why he'd gone up to the attic, suddenly. It is not a place we very often go.'

It wasn't. Once upon a time that upper room had been my home, but a fire in the building had put a stop to that, and – though the roof was patched enough to keep the weather out – the area was only used for storage now, and only for things that weren't in common use.

The woman's face had taken on its more familiar scowl. 'You say the ladder "slipped away from under him". Who moved it, then? Did you?'

Junio shook his head. 'Why should I move it? It wasn't in the way. Obviously I saw that it had fallen, but I didn't pick it up. I was too worried about Maximus. I left it where it was.'

She looked at me with a sort of gloomy triumph. 'Well, citizen pavement-maker. You're the clever one. You look at that ladder, and tell me what you think.' She gestured to where it was lying, just on the other side of the piles of sorted tesserae, which were waiting to be placed into the piece of pavement pattern we were working on.

A little more recovered from my exertions now, I took up the taper, picked my way around the workpiece and stones and went across to what had previously served us as the attic stairs. It is a simple ladder of the usual basic kind – a central strut with pieces fixed across at intervals to give a step at either side – and at first sight I could find no fault with it, though the footholds at one end were badly scuffed as if they had made violent contact with something as they fell. I looked up at the aperture into the attic room, and down again, and saw what she had meant.

'Dear gods,' I murmured. 'It can't have fallen there.' I turned to Junio. 'Where was he lying when you found him first?'

'About where you are standing. You can see the blood – near the mark on the floor where the ladder used to stand,' he said. 'Dear Juno, should I not have moved him? Have I made it worse? I thought to put him closer to the fire.'

'Nothing could have made this worse,' I said, 'But the tanner's wife is right. It was no accident. Look where the ladder's lying, then look at the little groove it made when it was properly in place. If the bottom had simply slipped away from him and landed over there, it would have run into that heap of tiles and you would see the track it made as it pushed them aside. But there's no sign of anything like that. They've not been disturbed at all.' My voice was trembling. I have seldom felt so helpless and angry in my life.

'I'm sorry, Father. I should have seen that for myself.' Junio was genuinely contrite and upset. I've long encouraged him to use his eyes and head and try to make logical deductions from the evidence and he prides himself on his abilities. 'I was too concerned about his injuries to think of it, I suppose.'

I gave him a sympathetic look. 'I am not surprised. I would have been myself. But you can see it now? And look at those scuff marks on the upper rungs – they've banged against the opening several times. You can see the marks around the aperture. It seems that someone either picked the ladder up and deliberately shook it till he fell, or – more likely I suspect – clubbed the boy so violently that he collapsed half dead, and then yanked the ladder loose and arranged the scene to make it look as if there'd been an accident. The intruder probably supposed he'd murdered him.'

Junio was staring at me in dismay. 'But who would want to murder Maximus? He was just a slave. He hardly knew anyone outside the family. Except that he once worked for Marcus, I suppose.' He looked at me sharply. 'Dear gods! The orchard! You don't suppose . . .?'

I knew what he was thinking, and I interrupted him. The tanner's wife had a careless tongue and an appetite for gossip which was famous in the street. 'There must be a connection,' I said bitterly. 'But for the moment I can't see what it is. Maximus was not at the villa yesterday.' I meant, of course, that he was not a witness to what happened there, and so a potential danger to the conspirators, as my patron's household servants would have been – though I avoided saying this. Even at a dreadful time like this, it was important that my patron's business was not bruited round the town.

I watched my son's face as he worked out for himself the implications of my words. 'You don't think that they mistook him for Tenuis, somehow?'

'I suppose that's possible,' I said. 'It had not occurred to me. Though they obviously didn't

222

know that Tenuis had seen them yesterday, or they certainly would not have let him go. Anyway, what on earth would make them look for Tenuis here? No one knew that he was coming . . .' I broke off, suddenly. 'Except for Georgicus!'

'Is that the fellow who came calling here today?' I had half forgotten that the tanners' slaves were there, but the one who'd met me at the door was clutching at my sleeve. 'We could describe him, if you need a witness, citizen. Couldn't we, Festus?'

His companion, who was standing with his mistress by the hearth, shook his small head energetically. 'I didn't see anything. I had work to do.'

I recognised the terror in his voice. It reminded me of Tenuis when we first questioned him. This Festus was unwilling to say anything at all.

The other slave, however, seemed oblivious. 'Of course you did. You must have done. We saw him from the yard – some sort of patrician, with a stripe as wide as this.' He indicated the imaginary width by holding up a finger and thumb and spreading them apart.

'If you mean the patrician who came here asking about mosaics before noon, I spoke to him myself,' Junio said, soothingly. 'Came this morning in a carrying-litter, didn't he?'

The slave-boy shrugged. 'I didn't mean this morning, citizen. I think it was past noon. We'd been working inside the tannery since dawn, scraping an ox hide that had finished in the soak – it's a lengthy business and it must have taken hours, but we did it in the end. When it was done

223

the master sent us out to hang it on the outside rack and that's when I glimpsed your visitor.'

'You can't be sure what time it was!' The other slave was looking mutinous. 'We didn't hear the midday trumpet sound today. It could easily have been this man who wanted pavements done.'

'But I didn't see a carrying-chair. He seemed to be on foot – that's why I thought it was peculiar. And there's another thing. He had a slave-guard with him – an enormous man. He was taller than a tree and his face was the colour of the mixture that we brew to tan the skins.'

I stared at Junio. 'Cacus!' we said together, like the chorus in a play.

'Now look what you've done. They've worked out who it is! Why don't you keep your mouth shut?' Festus said angrily, abandoning pretence. 'If they call us as witnesses we'll end up being questioned by the torturers. And if that big slave gets to hear of this, he'll come back in the dark and finish what they started – so you'll never speak again.'

'You think the slave-guard did this to Maximus?' I demanded.

My would-be informant was looking doubtful now. 'I just saw him standing in the street. I don't know if he came into the workshop, though I suppose his master did.' He realised I was giving him a sad, reproachful look, and he hastened to excuse himself. 'I thought nothing of it – it's not unusual for a slave to wait outside, and I didn't realise that you weren't here yourselves. Anyhow, I couldn't stand and watch, I had my tasks to do. Just as I have now. I'm sorry, citizen, I've told you everything I can.' He hurried over to join his mistress and Festus at the fire and turned his back on us. It was obvious that we'd get nothing more from him.

'So it looks as if it was the patrician himself who came in here and made this unprovoked attack on Maximus,' Junio said soberly to me. 'Though I can't imagine why. It can't be anything that Maximus had done. He's always courteous. What makes a wealthy man like that attack a humble slave? Most people of that rank would hardly stoop to notice he was there. But it looks as though that is what happened all the same.' He turned to me. 'Was it Commemoratus, do you think – given the fact that Cacus was outside?'

I shook my head. 'It isn't possible. Commemoratus was already at the dock when I first got there, and – according to Vesperion – had been there for some while, asking for Alfredus Allius and wasting everybody's time by pretending to be interested in purchasing some wine. He could not possibly have come here, done this and got away, between your leaving here and my arrival at the docks. I was quite a short time at the garrison.'

'So perhaps it wasn't Cacus after all?'

'There can't be two of them!' I was bewildered now. 'But Cacus was running an urgent errand with that scroll – they wanted it registered before the will was read, though his master doesn't usually move without him, it appears. He would not have had the time to come down here as well – in fact, he said as much. They were going to come and see me later on with a message for

Marcus, if I hadn't met them there. Yet I can't believe it's just coincidence. I wonder if the tanner's slave has got his timing wrong. You're sure Commemoratus is not the man who came here earlier?'

'Absolutely certain.' Junio was emphatic. 'If he's the man you pointed out to me with Cacus on the dock, that's not the person who wanted pavements made. The two are not dissimilar in a lot of ways, I suppose, and certainly both wore a wide patrician dress, but your Commemoratus looks nothing like the man who came out here. He was much younger and had a different colouring.'

I glanced towards the fireside. The tanner's wife was on her knees, still totally absorbed in tending Maximus – I doubt that she had heard a word of this exchange. Her slaves, however, were simply standing watching her. I beckoned them across.

'One more question – answer it, and I won't ask any more. If it helps me find the culprit, I'll give you a reward. A half-sestertius.'

The boys exchanged a glance. It was the skinny one who answered. 'What is it, citizen?'

'Did you notice the colour of the patrician's hair?'

This time the look that they exchanged was a bewildered one. Then Festus shrugged his shoulders. Obviously the promise of the bribe had done it's work. 'Just ordinary hair. The one thing that I noticed about the purple-striper that we saw was that his face was very pale, as if he never went outside into the sun and wind at all . . .'

226

I had just time to reluctantly conclude that this could not be florid Commemoratus after all, when we were interrupted by the tanner's wife calling from the hearth. 'Citizen Libertus, I think you'd better come.'

Great gods! I had been chattering all this time while Maximus was hurt! I scampered across the workshop as quickly as I could, scattering tesserae in all directions as I came. I think I was in time. I took my poor slave's hand and held it in my own, and I still believe there was the faintest pressure from his fingertips and that a suspicion of a smile curved the bloodless little lips before the hand went slack and the face expressionless. I picked up the copper mirror which was on the floor nearby, where Junio had dropped it earlier. I held it despairingly before my slave-boy's mouth, but – though I kept it there for minutes – no blessed mist appeared.

My beloved little red-haired Maximus was dead.

Twenty-One

I staggered to the stone pile and sat down heavily. To any outsider my distress would no doubt seem ridiculous. My patron had been robbed of goods worth millions of denarii, his household slaves had all been killed, Pertinax was murdered and the Empire was in shock, but the loss of Maximus – a mere slave of the kind that you could pick up from any slave-market for not much more than the price of an amphora of good wine – hit me harder than any of the other horrors of the day. I closed my eyes and buried my head between my hands. I have no idea how long I stayed like that, but after what seemed an eternity I was conscious of a hand on my shoulder and a soft voice calling me.

'Father?' I looked up, wearily. Junio was beside me, carrying the remnants of the mead, re-warmed and steaming in a metal drinking cup. 'Drink this.'

I shook my head. 'I don't want anything.' I tried to say the words, but my voice had failed.

'Maximus mixed the spices in for you – almost the last task he performed on your account. So, don't make his efforts appear to be in vain. Drink it – as he meant you to!' My son spoke so severely that I did as I was told.

There was not a lot of mead but it was strangely comforting, though the act of drinking what my dead slave had so lovingly prepared almost made me weep. But my grief was mingled with an anger too – a bitter fury so intense it gave me strength. I would find the culprit and I would make him pay, even if I had to go beyond the law.

The law, I knew, was of little use to me. The killing of another person's slave was an offence, of course, and if I could find the culprit and convince a court, I could demand the maximum legal penalty for such a crime: a compensation of three times his market price. No doubt there were excellent slave-boys available for less, but no amount could buy me another Maximus. I did not want a substitute – I wanted something much more like revenge.

But first, I had to find the murderer, and there seemed to be only one place to begin: Cacus, the giant with the muscles of a human Hercules, who could break me in two across his knee as easily as I could snap a twig. I looked around the inner workshop, ready to ask Festus and his friend to tell their tale again – no new questions, since I'd promised that, just a recapitulation of their first account, with the inducement of another half-sestertius if they did. But the room was empty except for Junio and me and that shrouded form which had once been Maximus, his injured head now tenderly covered by my cloak. Four lighted tapers burned around the corpse.

Junio had followed the direction of my glance. 'The tanner's wife and her two slaves have gone. There was nothing further she could do for Maximus – we'd closed his eyes and called his name three times and set the candles up, but she had a business to attend to, and naturally she wanted to get back to it. She was very good – even offered to leave Festus with us to start up a lament, but I said that we'd prefer to take the body home and do these things ourselves.' He looked sadly at me. 'I presume I guessed that right. She promised we could have her slave again if we changed our minds.'

I shook my head. I had always supposed that Maximus would be one of the bearers at my funeral. It had never occurred to me that I might find myself arranging his. (Of course, many slaves are simply buried without ceremony at all, as very young children are, but I held Maximus in too high a regard for that.) But it left me a problem. Unlike Marcus, I had not paid contributions for my servants to the Slave Funeral Guild: I had not even considered whether they would prefer a Roman pyre or to be interred in a proper grave as I hoped to be myself. I would like to think of little Maximus entire, dressed in a gold and silver gown and with a jewelled circlet on his head, happily living in the Celtic Otherworld, but he was born into a Roman household, and – if he had a preference – it would probably be for a version of the cremation rite. As paterfamilias, that meant I could officiate at the pyre myself – an idea which was heartbreaking in one respect, of course, but also comforting. There would be no funeral oration or lamentation pipes, but I could make sure that he enjoyed some dignity in death.

'We'd better get some purifying herbs,' I said,

making an effort to turn my mind to practicalities. 'We'll do it properly. Cleanse the body and purify the room, and put him in his newest tunic, cloak and shoes. We'll break his bowl and spoon and put them on the pyre, and Minimus can . . .' I broke off. I could not bear to think of what Minimus would feel. The two boys were not related, but they had seldom been apart since Marcus bought them several years ago – and had grown so close they could often finish each other's sentences.

Junio understood what I could not find words to say. 'Speaking of herbs,' he murmured. 'We had a visitor. Vesperion came here bringing a gift of healing herbs and unguents that they had in store, which Alfredus Allius sent to you, but I had to tell him that he'd come too late.' His voice wavered for a moment, and I realised how hard Junio, too, was finding this. But he recovered and went on in a calmer tone, 'He's gone to tell his owner what has happened here – and he promises some funeral herbs instead. He'll be back with them as soon as he can collect them, he declares. That is why I roused you when I did.'

'Vesperion?' I murmured stupidly.

He took the now-empty drinking cup from me. 'He will be back quite quickly, Father, if I am any judge. Are you now sufficiently recovered to receive him when he comes?'

I nodded. 'Help me to my feet. I'll go to meet him in the outer room. It isn't seemly to ask him to come into a room of death like this.' I was a little ashamed of my unmanly show of grief and tried to emulate my son's example, and be

231

controlled and businesslike. 'I suppose we'll have to think of how to purify the shop – and ourselves as well – otherwise people will avoid this place as being cursed and the workshop will be ruined. And news will get about. The tanner's wife was very kind indeed, but I'm sure she was partly driven by curiosity and the prospect of a thrilling tale to tell.'

Junio extended a strong arm to lean on, and I struggled to my feet. 'Vesperion promises that his herbs will deal with all the cleansing rituals – they have imported purifying mixtures in their stock, presumably destined for the undertakers and arrangers of public funerals. If Alfredus Allius genuinely makes a gift of those, Minimus will have as fine a send-off as any slave could have.'

'That would be some comfort to me,' I allowed. 'And I'll find out who did this if it's the last thing that I do.' I managed to summon up a rueful smile. 'As I suppose it might be. The presence of Cacus is the only clue I have – if he did not come into the shop himself, he must know who did. I don't relish the idea of confronting such a giant, but I'll have to find him and try to talk to him – though I don't quite know how. He and his master are no doubt on their way to Isca by this time.'

Junio frowned. 'Though if they missed the reading of the will, perhaps they'll linger long enough to lodge a legal challenge with the magistrates.'

That was sensible and I pounced on the idea. 'It's possible Alfredus Allius will know – perhaps I'll go and ask him before I leave the town, but

I can hardly do so with my toga in this state.' I was attempting to straighten the garment as I spoke, but my efforts had the opposite effect. The folds, which had been tending to unwind earlier, were hanging down around me in untidy loops, and there was little for it, but to start again.

Junio put the cup down on the shelf above the fire and came across to help. 'You think that Cacus was responsible?' he asked.

I shook a doubtful head. 'I've been thinking about that. It would obviously be no problem for a man of his size and strength – he could have felled little Maximus with a single blow, and wrested the ladder from its restraining cords and tossed it over there with no more effort than it would take for me to squash a fly. But there is quite a lot of blood, as you pointed out to me. I've managed to get it on my feet from simply standing there.' I pointed to my sandal-prints which were clearly visible. 'You would have thought that Cacus would get it on himself as well, but when I saw him shortly afterwards, his gold-coloured tunic was impeccable.'

'Which is more than you can say about your toga,' Junio said, coming across to help me with rearranging it. 'There are several bloodstains on the hem.'

'I'll use it as a winding-sheet for Maximus,' I said. Legally that was probably a terrible offence – slaves are prohibited from wearing Roman dress. But I no longer cared. It simply seemed appropriate to wrap the boy in something that was mine – and there was nothing else of sufficient size available.

Even Junio was looking slightly shocked.

'Not for the funeral itself,' I added, 'but for when we take him to the roundhouse later on. It won't look like a toga if we fold it properly – just a piece of woollen cloth. That way we can lay him on the mule with decency, and it will not matter if it gets stained again. I'll have to send Maxi . . .' I trailed off, hopelessly. 'I'll have to take it to the fullers for a second time,' I corrected. 'But for the moment, help me take it off. I can't wear it as it is.' I meant it. I could not bear to think of bearing splashes of my servant's blood, though that put paid to my calling on the councillor tonight. It would not be proper to call on a curia member in my working clothes. 'I'll have to delay calling on Alfredus Allius,' I said.

'You can send a message with Vesperion, perhaps, when he comes back again,' my son replied, helping me to shuffle off my awkward garment as he spoke. 'Or better still, I'll go to the west gate and enquire. If they've really gone to Isca they'll have their travelling coach, and Cacus would attract attention anywhere he went. If not, presumably they are still in town.'

I nodded doubtfully. 'I need to talk to Cacus. He's the only lead I have – assuming that he was the one the tanner's servant saw.'

'Either way, there's nothing more that you can do today,' my son went on. 'It would take too long to trace them and it wouldn't be proper to abandon Maximus. You'll have to catch Cacus tomorrow if you can. But when we've finished here, we'll put the body on the mule. It means you have to walk, but there are advantages to that. If I'm quick with my enquiries, I can catch you up.'

I was loath to give up the idea of finding Cacus, but this suggestion was clearly sensible and Junio was right: the first task was to see that Maximus was safely taken home. So with Junio's help I spread my toga on the floor, and with the greatest care we swaddled the poor dead slave in it.

'I've washed his hands and feet with water from the jug,' my son said, soberly. 'The rest of the cleansing will have to wait till we get to the roundhouse later on. All we need now is for Vesperion to come back with . . . Ah! There's a knocking now.'

So I went out in my tunic to the outer room and Junio opened the front door of the shop. To my astonishment I saw that there were two men on the step. The old steward was accompanied by Alfredus Allius himself, still wearing the dark toga that I'd seen him in before.

I had recovered something of my wits by now, and was in a slight dilemma about the proper courtesies. The little outer area is a narrow space, where – when the shutters are removed – the open counter looks out on the street: hardly a place in which to receive a curial councillor. The slats had been absent when I first arrived, but had obviously been replaced when Junio left the shop, and not been taken down again since then, so only my son's taper offered any light – though he busied himself at once with rectifying this and opening the counter to the light of day. That helped a little, as the afternoon streamed in, but there was nowhere I could ask the magistrate to sit except the little three-legged wooden stool which the slave-boys sometimes use when Junio and I are busy on a piece, so they can watch for prospective customers.

What on earth had brought him to a place like this? With some embarrassment I gave a little bow. 'Citizen, you do too much honour to my humble shop. I fear we're not equipped to entertain you properly.'

I need not have concerned myself. My visitor waved my apologies aside in a way that Marcus never would have done. 'Citizen, I'm very sorry to learn that your young slave is dead. And, since you were at my warehouse when the first tidings came, convention and courtesy demands that I should call.' The councillor had a distinctive flat and nasal voice, and always came close to peer at one with weak, short-sighted eyes. I was glad that we had thought to take the shutters down. 'One can't be too careful with the spirits,' he went on.

I nodded. There is a superstition that the spirits of the newly dead can walk abroad, seeking those who should have attended them at death but did not come. By calling at my workshop in this way, perhaps Alfredus Allius was hoping to ensure that his warehouse was not troubled by the ghost of Maximus.

I murmured that his visit here was very kind, but that Maximus had not died until after I returned.

'So I understand,' he said, to my surprise. 'But this is a house of death and I had promised herbs.' The curial councillor had turned slightly pink. 'I

236

had a corpse in my own warehouse, as I think you know, and business was blighted until I obtained some special herbs from Rome to cleanse the place. Fortunately I still had some in store.' He gestured towards the aged steward as he spoke. 'Vesperion, you have something for the citizen, I think.'

The old man shuffled forward to present me with a casket of dried herbs, his aged knees and hip-joints creaking audibly. 'There may be enough to prepare your poor servant for the funeral pyre, as well. With my master's compliments, citizen.'

I hardly had to glance to know this was a handsome gift. The little chest itself was beautiful, and the herbs and spices it contained were ones which I could never have afforded for myself. I could detect basil, rosemary, myrrh and frankincense – as well as the usual hyssop, lavender and myrtle. I gazed at Alfredus in astonishment.

But my surprises had not ended. My caller spoke again. 'I have sent to the priest who cleansed my property for me – and for the wise woman who advised me what to do.'

I looked at him, alarmed. 'But citizen – the fee. I am a humble tradesman—'

'I will be honoured,' he interrupted me, 'to pay them for their services, citizen. The woman, especially. She was the one who told me to wear this.' He fingered a silver chain around his neck, hung with phalluses and other lucky charms. 'It has served me very well.' He gave his timid smile.

I looked at him suspiciously. Why should he do that? He was not especially noted for his generosity – or indeed for anything at all. Alfredus

Allius was not a man to stand out in a crowd, being of average height, of medium build, and of middle-age – thirty-five or forty, perhaps. His hair was mousy brown and his features, though regular, were unremarkable at best, and the dark-coloured mourning toga that he wore today did not flatter him, making him look more than usually plain. He was resolutely unexceptional in every way, but I'd never thought of him as devious. Yet this offer was far beyond the call of courtesy. What was he up to?

I shook myself. I should be thanking him, not thinking doubtful thoughts. Junio, however, was ahead of me.

'Thank you for your generosity, citizen.' You can see my father feels it very much.'

Alfredus made a dismissive gesture with his hand. 'He is a client of Marcus Septimus. His Excellence would be displeased if he returned and found I had not helped. Wasn't the dead slave a gift from his own household, after all? Unfortunate that this should happen while he isn't here. Some sort of fatal accident, I understand.'

'What affects my father most is that this was no accident,' Junio said softly.

I shot a warning glance at him, but he was right, of course. There was no point in our attempting to disguise the facts. The tanner's wife had worked out for herself that the ladder had been deliberately moved, as she would no doubt be telling everyone with pride.

Junio's words had caused a little stir. Vesperion gasped aloud. 'You can't mean that your servant killed himself?' He glanced at his own master.

238

'That might make a difference to the herbs . . .'

I shook my head. 'I mean that someone murdered him.'

This time even Alfredus Allius looked shocked. 'Then I hope you find whoever is responsible,' he said. 'That boy would have grown up to be a valuable slave. It will cost you quite a lot to replace him even now. Which reminds me that I have another purpose here.' He looked embarrassed and turned a little pink. 'I have been asked to recommend a pavement-maker who could be relied upon to do a large job quickly and efficiently, and I thought of you. But there is an element of haste involved, and obviously you have recently sustained a nasty shock, so perhaps you feel that you could not undertake the task . . .?'

I could only boggle at him stupidly. Not because he'd thought of recommending me – such a thing is not unusual: a stranger moving into a town will often ask (or even pay) some local worthy for advice about which tradesmen to employ – it gives the man concerned a chance for patronage, and limits the chance of the newcomer paying a high price for shoddy workmanship. What had surprised me was that he'd bothered to come here himself, just as this morning's customer had done.

Alfredus Allius was still urging me. 'A deliberate killing is upsetting, naturally, even when it just concerns a slave, and perhaps you would prefer that I didn't bother you with ordinary business matters at this time. Though possibly – with your financial loss – a profitable contract would be good news for you?'

I looked at Junio who had darted me a glance. Obviously his thought had been the same as mine. I just had sufficient presence of mind to exclaim, 'So it was you who proposed me? That was very kind of you.' I saw that the councillor was puzzled so I added, hastily, 'This does concern the Egidius villa, I presume?'

Twenty-Two

'By all the deities, citizen, are you a sorcerer?' Alfredus Allius was so surprised he sat down on the stool, though it was far too small for him and much cruder than appropriate for a person of his rank. 'How did you know? That is indeed the property in question.' He shook his head. 'Marcus always boasts of how astute you are, but how could you possibly have guessed?'

'It is no guess,' I told him, as Junio hastily brought other seats for us to ensure that our heads were decently below the councillor's. 'The new owner called here earlier today in search of me.' I squatted on the little stool which Maximus had used, while Junio perched on a block of wood we used for cutting tiles. 'But unfortunately I was not here when he came. There was a problem at my patron's villa which delayed me very much.'

Something in my manner had alerted him. 'I wish I'd sent my wise-woman to visit you before. You clearly need one of her talismans to ward off ill luck today. It was a serious problem at the villa, from the way you talk of it,' he said.

I was having a fairly serious problem of my own right now, in fact. My balance on the stool was quite precarious and I was in danger of dropping the precious casket of dried herbs. It would have been the worst of omens to have broken it. I managed to lean over and put it down on the counter of the shop, which was available now that the central shutters had been taken down. Only then was I able to consider a response. 'More serious than you can imagine, councillor,' I said, shuffling myself more securely on the seat.

Alfredus Allius frowned. 'I suppose it was a fire? Most unlucky, since Marcus is away.'

That was a sensible surmise, in fact. Buildings (and people) were destroyed by fires almost every day – as indeed this very workshop had once been. But, since we were now within earshot of the street, I hesitated for a moment before I answered him.

Alfredus was not expecting a reply. He had only paused to touch his precious amulets and before I could say anything he went on at once, 'In fact, it's turning out to be a very ill-starred day . . .' He glanced around and seemed to check himself '. . . as you will doubtless find out for yourselves. An announcement will be made in the forum very soon – now that Gaius Publius's will has been read out and the crowds attending the forum have dispersed. There's been sad news from Rome.'

'If you are referring to the Emperor, I already know,' I said, and saw Junio share his look of startlement. 'The commander of the garrison told me when I went to call on him – but I have not had the opportunity to tell my son as yet.'

'Then I had better do so,' the councillor replied. 'But close the shutters up. Vesperion will help. We don't want the street to hear.'

I nodded. The tanner's wife had found a reason for hovering nearby, coming out in person with a jug to buy milk from a stout girl selling it from a wooden pail. The arrival of the magistrate had clearly been observed, and there had already been some curious glances aimed at us.

Junio fetched the slats of wood and, with the assistance of the steward, slid them into place, while I moved the box of herbs to safety once again. It plunged the little area into gloom once more though fortunately the candle had not quite gone out.

Alfredus seemed to feel the need for dignity. He rose slowly to his feet, blinking his weak eyes against the shadowy dark. 'If the commander has already told you what has happened, citizen, I feel there is no harm in my repeating it and telling you the latest information that I have,' he said. 'It may affect what you decide to do – it might be wise to leave the town as soon as possible. I fear the guards may lock the gates tonight before it's dark – there is a general feeling that there may be riots.'

'Why, what's happened, Excellence?' Junio asked, squatting uncomfortably on his makeshift seat again and remembering to add the honorific title just in time.

Alfredus told the story, or rather, declaimed it as though he were a public orator, with dramatic gestures to give graphic emphasis. It was much the same account that I'd already heard, but in greater detail – including the omens which had been observed in Rome the day before the murder of the Emperor.

'It's said that when Pertinax (may I not disturb his memory by my words!) was sacrificing to the household gods, the fire on the Larian altar flickered out and died,' he made a fluttering gesture to imitate the flame, 'instead of flaring up as usual when oil was poured on it.' He paused dramatically. 'And the sacrifice he offered was found to have no heart! Imagine that! And as if those signs were not enough, when he turned to speak to those attending him, there were no pupils visible in his eyes at all.'

Vesperion had been listening to this account aghast – evidently it was new to him as well. He stared at his master as though he were a messenger from Dis, then spat on his finger and rubbed behind his ear, in the age-old gesture for keeping off a curse. 'Dreadful omens! May we be preserved.' He glanced round nervously, obviously expecting to be rebuked. 'If you'll pardon the interruption, master. I forgot myself.'

Alfredus did not reprimand the man – as Marcus would have done – for joining in the conversation of his superiors unasked. Indeed, he nodded in agreement and fingered his good-luck amulets again. 'Vesperion is right. It's almost as if the deities were warning Pertinax, but he did not heed the signs. Though he was thrice reminded that the auguries were bad, he insisted on doing all his usual duties for the day. With terrible results. And so we lost an admirable Emperor.' He sighed and sat down on the stool again – this was clearly the end of the formal oratory. 'Who knows what kind of man this Didius will be. Another Nero, or a Commodus, perhaps – though all honour be to his Imperial name, of course.'

This last remark, I realised, was not some ritual incantation to ward off bad luck – though given the councillor's superstitious instincts it might well have been – it was to protect himself against potential mortal listening ears. Everyone had learned to do that when Commodus ruled. It used to be rumoured that there were Imperial spies in every house, and the citizen who spoke ill of the Emperor, or was even reported to have done so, was liable to suffer a very painful death, often as an after-dinner spectacle for Commodus and his current favourites, it was said, as a reminder that it could be their turn next. Under Pertinax, this constant spying had been much less prevalent, but with this newest Caesar now in power in Rome who knew if such times were likely to return?

'Don't worry, councillor,' I said. 'No one can now hear us from the street, and there are no informers here.' I decided that candid frankness was the best approach. 'The commander does not think that Didius will last – that he will either try to bribe his way to power, and not be able to fulfil his promises, or simply be deposed by someone else more ruthless than himself. But either way there are unsettled times ahead.' I looked directly at the councillor. 'For all of us, I fear. My best hope is that Marcus will come directly home and not get as far as the capital at all. Though, the gods know that there is grief enough awaiting him back here.'

'So the fire was a substantial one?' Alfredus

Allius asked. 'I thought with a water source nearby, it might have been contained.' He saw me hesitate. 'I owe you and your patron a great deal, citizen. If there's anything that I can do, I would be honoured to assist. It happens that I know a fine property for sale not far from his town house in Corinium, if the villa is too damaged to rebuild at once.'

I looked thoughtfully at him. I was still nonplussed by Alfredus Allius. He must have some motive for coming here today with these expensive herbs and cleansing rituals for a low-value slave. I did not quite believe that it was simply generous. Perhaps it was a kind of test of loyalty – wondering where my sympathies would lie if Marcus fell from grace. Is that why he had been so frank with me, even conde-scending to reveal the story of the Emperor before the formal announcement had been made? Well, I was tired of dissimulation on my own account today – several times I'd given only a version of the truth. This was surely a moment for outright honesty.

'The villa building is undamaged, councillor. The problem is with what my master kept inside.' I gave him a full account of what I'd found (and failed to find), including what I'd learned from Tenuis, some of which Junio had not heard before.

I had almost forgotten, in my grief for Maximus, how terrible and shocking these events would sound but the reaction of my listeners soon reminded me. Even Junio, who already knew the worst of it, looked pale, and the other two stared at me with shock and incredulity. When I'd finished there was a little pause.

Vesperion was rubbing spit behind his other ear. 'More deaths!' he muttered in that cracked voice of his. 'The gods are angry. Such dreadful auguries!'

The curial magistrate caressed his amulet again. 'Vesperion's right, again. So many killings all at once cannot be a coincidence. It must be a message from the gods. What are they trying to warn us all against?'

I shook my head. 'I agree it's not coincidence. But I don't blame the gods. I suspect a human hand. In fact, begging your forgiveness, councillor, I believe that it all hinges somehow on that man to whom you recommended me as a mosaicist. How well do you know him?'

Alfredus Allius made a doubtful face. 'Not very well at all. I've met him once or twice. He used to have a villa near Corinium – in fact he also has a town-house there and served for some years on the local curia. He was a distant relative of Gaius Publius – or at least of his dead wife – and it was at her funeral that I first encountered him, though he's had some dealings with the warehouse since. But I can't believe that he's connected with these deaths. He's a pleasant fellow, and extremely rich. If he wanted precious ornaments, he wouldn't stoop to stealing, he would buy them for himself.'

'That's true,' I agreed glumly. 'But the same could be said of anyone of high degree – as I presume he is.'

'Oh, indeed. Risen from the most successful *equites* in Britannia – and he's even wealthier now. He's one of the few people to really benefit from the reading of the will today. I think he knew he would be, despite the various claims. That's partly why he's bought the house near Glevum – there will be estates to manage – though of course he's kept a town house in Corinium as well. Rather like Marcus Septimus, in fact.'

So the challenge to the will had been presented after all, I thought. I was about to say so, but Junio spoke first.

'But I understood that he had come here from Londinium,' he murmured with a frown.

'Londinium?' Alfredus Allius gave him a puzzled look. 'Not that I know of, citizen. What gave you that idea?'

'That's what he told me – almost the only information that he was willing to divulge. Once he had discovered that my father was not here, he would not even consent to give his name,' my son exclaimed.

Alfredus raised his mousy brows at me. 'How extremely odd. I've always found Scipio Drusus rather talkative. When did you speak to him?'

Junio shrugged. 'He called here this morning. He was waiting when we . . . when I first arrived.' He had suddenly remembered Maximus, and it affected him. He gulped, but went on steadily enough. 'That must have been a little before noon. My father got here shortly afterwards.'

But the councillor was hardly listening any more. 'That's not possible. I met Scipio Drusus by arrangement near the northern gate about the second hour. I actually saw his travelling coach draw up – it's a distinctive one – and he'd clearly just arrived. He was to come to my town apartment to refresh himself (and incidentally to bargain for some wine) but as it happened I could not stay with him. I'd just been summoned to a meeting of the curia.'

'That was the meeting at the garrison?' I said. 'So by your own admission you weren't with him all the time. He could have called here, while you were being addressed by the commander, couldn't he?'

'In theory, citizen. But I had my slave attend him to my flat, and that's where he was when I came back later on. According to my servants, he had been there throughout. They had given him refreshment and assisted him to wash his feet and change his clothes. He'd brought his mourning toga with him for the reading of the will – he didn't want to wear it in a dusty coach.' He shook his head. 'When I came back I took him to the forum straight away. So all his movements are accounted for. He could hardly have been here at the time that you suggest.'

'And you are quite sure that he's the man who purchased the Egidius house?' I said.

Alfredus nodded. 'Absolutely sure. He didn't want the villa that Gaius Publius owned – it's on the unfashionable northern side of town and doesn't have a bath house, or a hypocaust. And there's a problem anyway. Gaius Publius let it just a little while ago when he became too frail to leave his house in town, and the tenant claims there was a contract saying he could buy. Scipio will look into that of course. He may have to fight for possession in the courts. But even if he wins it, he intends to sell.'

'The Egidius house is more convenient,' I agreed. 'It used to be quite splendid, I believe.'

Alfredus Allius gave one of his rare smiles. 'And will be again, so Scipio declares. He's moving his whole household into it today, including many of his effects, I understand – though some items from the house have been in storage for years and they were included in the purchase price.'

I made a little face. I wasn't sure how much I trusted this account. 'Then he's rather careless with his money, isn't he?' I observed. 'Buying goods and property that he has never seen.'

'He may be wealthy, citizen, but he is not a fool. Of course he came to see the place before he parted with a single quadrans. Though I would not like to live there, I agree.' Alfredus fingered his amulets again. 'I warned him of its bad reputation, but he did not seem to care. Laughed and said it was a bargain at the price – he would buy some cleansing herbs from me to set the ghosts to rest, and even pay a priest to come and purify the place. In fact, I have promised that I'll send my priest and wisewoman to him later on today when they have finished here.'

I made a little bow 'You are generous, again.'

'Ah, with him it is a business arrangement, citizen,' he said, meaning that Scipio had

250

promised a fee for finding a suitable priest to undertake the task. No doubt there'd been another one for recommending me.

But it raised another question. If it wasn't Scipio Drusus who called here earlier – and according to Alfredus it could not have been – who was it? Someone else anxious to earn a fee for recommending me, perhaps? That would make a kind of sense, and might be a reason for the man not offering his name, since he was only hoping to act as agent for this Scipio. Had our visitor this morning actually claimed that he had bought the Egidius house himself, or only that it had found a purchaser, and that new pavements were required? Probably the latter, from what Junio had said.

So who else could have known that the villa had finally been sold? Any patrician who knew Scipio, it seemed – since he'd been to look at it and had made no secret of his interest in the place. Anyone but Commemoratus, who had not been here at all, and had witnesses to prove it, including Junio.

I frowned. These thoughts were leading nowhere. Even if I found this morning's visitor, that might have no connection with the murder of my slave. My only link was Cacus, the slave of a man that I'd been talking to when Maximus was killed. Was it possible that Commemoratus had a twin, perhaps, and therefore seemed to be in two places at once?

But of course that was no answer. Quite the opposite. The person I was looking for – according to two different witnesses – did not resemble Commemoratus much, apart from the colour of his toga-stripe. Perhaps Cacus had simply followed him around to try to register the objection to the will? He'd said that he was looking for a magistrate. But what was the purple-striper doing in this neighbourhood? Supposing that it was really Cacus that the tanner's slave had seen!

I shook my head impatiently. None of this was making any sense.

Alfredus saw my impatience, and misinterpreted it. 'Of course you will be anxious to begin the rites if you wish to leave the workshop before the gates are shut. I wonder what's delayed the wise-woman and priest? They should be here by now. I sent my personal page to fetch them urgently.'

I almost smiled at his patrician certainty. It did not appear to have occurred to him, even for an instant, that they'd refuse to come, or that they might have other duties to perform before they did. He simply assumed that they'd obey his summons instantly. Such, I suppose, is the privilege of rank.

'Perhaps, councillor, they would not hurry – for a slave?' I ventured.

Alfredus looked at me disdainfully. 'They would hurry at my orders, or so I should expect!' He gestured to his steward. 'Vesperion, go out onto the street and see if you can see them anywhere.'

The old steward hurried out to do as he was told, but he'd not been gone an instant before he shuffled back, closed the door carefully and made an awkward bow. 'There's no sign of those two, but someone else has just arrived. He was going to come straight in, but I made him wait outside. A slave-boy, by the look of it. Not your attendant, Master Alfredus.' He turned to me. 'Little red-headed lad. I think it's one of yours.'

Twenty-Three

'Minimus!' I murmured. It could be no one else. I began to scramble painfully from my precarious seat, but Junio had shot me an agonised glance and was already on his feet. By the time that I'd regained my own, he was re-opening the door.

'Minimus! It's you!' I heard him cry. 'I thought you were assisting in the house today. What brings you here instead?'

'The mistress sent me. There's been important news!' My little servant sounded out of breath. 'I'm glad to find you here – I've run most of the way, but when I got here I saw the shutters up and thought you must be gone. And then that old slave I didn't know came out, and wouldn't let me in. What's happened? Are the master and Maximus inside?'

Poor creature. He had no idea what dreadful news awaited him.

Junio was obviously thinking the same thing. I heard him say softly, 'Your master is. He'll tell you everything. You'd better come inside.' He opened the door wider and gently propelled Minimus towards me as he spoke.

My young slave blinked a moment against the sudden gloom, then peered around. 'Your pardon, citizen,' he murmured, seeing Alfredus, and bending one knee in an awkward bow, continued, 'I did not realise that my master was receiving visitors. And in mourning robes, I see.' He turned to me. 'Has someone of importance died today? There's obviously something happening in town. Lots of people wearing dark togas like this citizen, and groups of armed soldiers on guard in every street. I had quite a problem getting through the gates. Had to tell them who my owner was, where I was going and what my errand was, and even then he was not keen to let me pass.' He turned to me. 'It was only the mention of His Excellence that changed his mind, I think.'

'Your message concerns Marcus? There hasn't been more trouble at the villa since I left?' The words were almost startled out of me.

Minimus shook his tousled auburn curls, a familiar gesture that made me swallow hard. Maximus had done the selfsame thing a thousand times. 'Well, it's good and bad news, master. Mostly good – I think. A letter came by courier from Corinium. We think it said the lady Julia has safely had her child, and both of them are well.'

'You came all this way to tell me that?'

A breathless nod. 'I've brought you the tablet it was written on so you can check if we are right. The courier took it to the villa first, of course, but there was no one there except Georgicus and he cannot read, so they brought it to the roundhouse and my mistress and the courier did the best they could. The rider claims that the baby is a girl, but I'm not sure if the message mentions that.' He handed me the tablet from inside his tunic-top. 'My mistress isn't quite sure that she deciphered it aright, but she thinks the last line is something you should see.'

I undid the ties that secured the writing block and read the message scratched into the wax. It was written in Julia's eccentric female hand – no wonder my poor wife had found it hard to read. Much of the spelling was erratic and individual as well, but it did confirm that the newborn was a healthy female child, born on the Kalends of Aprilis, several days ago, and that the mother had survived the birth. But Gwellia was right. The last line was the most important one. There was a spotted fever in Corinium, and Julia was fearful for the baby's health, so as soon as she and the child were strong enough, she planned to journey back. The message was to alert the household to the plan and ask them to be ready for her imminent return.

'Dear gods!' I murmured. Obviously Julia had sent this courier long before my message had arrived. I knew that spotted fever was a dreadful thing – those that it did not kill, it often scarred and blinded dreadfully – and could spread as quickly as a fire. Julia would want to get her children safe as soon as possible, not only her new baby but her little son as well. Yet the villa here could not receive them as it was, bereft of slaves and proper furniture. I could only hope that my message had arrived in time and she was not already on her way. Fortunately my patron had a town apartment too, so she would not find herself without a place to stay – though the slaves there wouldn't be expecting anyone. I would have to send them word.

However there was a much more pressing problem to be dealt with here. I passed the writing

256

block to Junio, and turned to Minimus. 'Come here,' I urged him gently. 'There's something I must tell you. You must be very brave. You know what we discovered at the villa earlier?'

He looked at me with frightened eyes and gave a doubtful nod. 'You mean in the orchard? Before you left me at the vineyard?' His voice was quivering.

'I promised then that I would find the men that killed Pauvrissimus,' I took his hands gently in my own. 'I've got an even stronger reason to try and find them now. You asked if somebody important had died. Well, I'm afraid that's true. Two important people have been killed. One of them is the Emperor Pertinax himself . . .' I squeezed his fingers as I heard him gasp, but he did not interrupt, '. . . which probably explains the soldiers in the streets just now. And the other is someone that the town won't care about, but is very important indeed to you and me . . .'

I felt the shuddering breath that shook the little frame. 'Not . . . Maximus . . .?' he whispered, and I had to signal that it was.

'This patrician citizen has been very good,' I said, nodding at our dark-clad visitor and wondering again about his motives for all this. 'He's brought the finest funeral herbs that can be had, and arranged for a priest to come and purify the shop – and even a wise woman to bring talismans and cleanse the corpse.'

At the word 'corpse' the sobs and tears began. I forgot convention and simply held him close and let him cry.

It was a most unRoman thing for me to do, of

course, and I was aware of an awkward little pause. Then Vesperion gave a cough and murmured, 'Citizen?' as if to signal that it was time to show a little more propriety.

I glanced around the room, fearing that my behaviour might have caused my visitor offence, but Alfredus Allius seemed a little misty-eyed himself, while Junio had turned away and was deliberately busying himself with setting a new candle on the spike.

'This old one was guttering,' he said, defensively, disproving this by using it to light the other wick. 'And we'll be needing better light. I think the priest and wise woman are here – did you not hear the knock?'

I hadn't. I had been too concerned with Minimus, I suppose.

'I tried to draw your attention to it, citizen,' Vesperion supplied, and I realised that had been the reason for the cough. 'And there it is again. Would you like me to go and answer it?'

'Thank you, steward, I would be glad of that,' I said. It should have been Minimus's job to go, of course, now that he was here. But he was clearly in no condition to deal with visitors.

Nonetheless I let go of the boy, who gave his wet cheeks a surreptitious wipe and made a visible effort to control his tears. He came and stood behind me deferentially just as Vesperion ushered in not the little party we were expecting but a woman on her own.

That would have been astonishing enough – respectable women do not generally roam the streets alone – but even more astounding was the way she looked. She was huge, quite the most enormous female I had ever seen. She was not only fairly tall, she was immensely wide, dressed in a long grey Grecian robe that bulged at every seam. Added to that, her feet were sandal-less and her straggling grey hair hung loose down to her waist (or what would have been her waist if she had been less vast). The effect was quite shocking, even when one remembered who she was – only a lunatic or a soothsayer would appear in public dressed like that. She carried a large pail of something in one pudgy hand and smelt strongly – though not unpleasantly – of aniseed and bay.

Her presence seemed to fill my little outer room, which was small and narrow at the best of times. 'Councillor Alfredus!' Her voice was as big as she was. And she had not waited to be addressed by him, as any normal matron would have done with someone of his rank. 'I hear you summoned me.'

'Ah,' Alfredus Allius said, in his flat, nasal voice. 'I see you found the place. Did my servant not come with you? Or has he gone to fetch the priest? I asked him to accompany you to show you where to come. I rather supposed that he would bring you both at once.' It was a veiled apology, I thought, for having allowed her to walk here on her own.

But the woman simply snorted. 'A wise woman has no need of slaves to guide her, citizen. I know the citizen Libertus by repute. It would not be difficult to ask my way. Besides, there are piles of cut stone outside the shop – it isn't hard to work out where the pavement-maker works.' She turned and looked full into my eyes – something else no other unfamiliar female would do. Her own were disconcerting: they were bluer than the summer sky, but shrewd and sharp with the suggestion of a knowing twinkle in their depths. 'I imagine you're the client I'm supposed to help?' She did not wait for me to answer, but went on, in ringing tones, 'I'll give you some rue to chew for protection later on, and find you an amulet to wear to ward off more bad luck. In the meantime there is work to do. Where's this corpse of yours?'

At the mention of a corpse I sensed Minimus stiffen at my back, and realised that he was close to tears again, but all the same there was something in her brisk enquiry which made me feel that we were now in skilled and able hands. 'Through here,' I told her, and went to lead the way into the inner room.

She shook her head. 'Not you. I'll take the younger citizen and the old slave with me. You'll have another visitor – and very soon – and it's bad luck for us to be disturbed before the corpse is fully cleansed. Besides, it is forbidden for a priest to see the body of the dead.'

'Maximus has been washed and wrapped already,' Junio ventured, in a tone that was unusually meek. The woman's forcefulness was clearly starting to affect him too.

'Only with water from the well, though, I presume?' she said, dismissively. 'That's a useful start, but I've brought running water from the spring.' She reached into her pail and produced a little stoppered jug. 'Much more efficacious in a case like this. I've picked fresh herbs as well, as you can see, to ward off any curse. And here's a little bag of earth to sprinkle on him afterwards to give him the ritual symbol of a burial. It's a lot of ceremony for a simple slave, I know, but that's what is required to give a murder victim rest.'

I boggled at her. 'How did you know that this was murder?'

She withered me with those deep blue eyes of hers. 'Citizen, I am a wise woman and noted for my skills – did you not expect that I would know? Now, you and you . . .' She gestured at Vesperion and my son. 'Come rub these bay leaves on your hands . . .' She shook the pail at them, and they sheepishly obeyed. 'That will keep the victim's spirit from pursuing you and demanding that you avenge this death. So follow me and you can help me with the ritual. And you . . .' she turned to Minimus '. . . can guard the door. Don't let anybody come in while we're at work – just wait out here for us. It won't take very long, and when we've finished and the body's wrapped again the priest can come and purify the room.'

And without a further glance at Alfredus or myself, she led the way into the inner room and shut the door.

Alfredus gazed after her with admiring eyes. 'Isn't she a wonder? She thinks of everything. You notice that she even goes barefoot, so that there is no knot around her person where evil ghosts might lurk? You're in safe hands with her. She'll purify the corpse and make sure the spirit of your slave can rest.'

261

I nodded. It was a good deal more than Marcus's household slaves were going to get, even with the services of the Funeral Guild.

'And she has psychic powers,' the councillor went on. 'See how she found her way here without assistance from my slave – and knew that this was murder without a word from you.'

'I expect she met the woman from the tannery next door, who told her so,' I said, remembering that I'd seen my neighbour hovering in the street. 'She knew the truth and she would love to spread a little gossip of that kind.'

But Alfredus was not to be convinced. 'I tell you, the wise woman is a wonder, citizen,' he said, in that peculiar monotone of his. 'She cleansed my warehouse perfectly. I'd had the priest, of course – the same one who is coming here today – but nothing went right until she took a hand. I've started consulting her every day or so. I'm sure that's why the business is now prospering. And everything she'd told me has turned out to be true. She even predicted there'd be a death today.'

I looked at him with dawning realisation. 'She told you to come here?'

'Not directly, citizen, of course. She simply told me that if I heard about a death today – of any person and of any rank – I must avert ill fortune by engaging her at once. That could not apply to Publius or the Emperor, of course, so I knew it had to be your slave.'

So that explained his presence at my shop and the unnatural generosity towards my slave! I smiled, amused by the shrewd simplicity of

262

the woman's stratagem and offered a mental apology to my visitor for having doubted his sincerity.

Alfredus saw the smile. 'I wonder you don't ask her who it was that killed your slave. It may be she could cast the stones for you, as well, if you have an aureus or two to spare.'

An aureus is a lot of money, even for a wealthy citizen like the councillor. For somebody like me, it is an awesome sum – and not one I am likely to expend on doubtful sorcery. 'You think the stones will tell her, too, who robbed my patron and murdered all his slaves?' I said, trying to keep derision from my tone. 'I hardly think so, councillor. Anyone who could genuinely offer knowledge of that kind would be regularly called upon to testify in court, and would be very lucky to survive once guilty people got to hear about her skills.'

Alfredus looked at me indulgently. 'You don't believe her powers? Wait until you get your talisman and see.'

I did not press the point. I was glad to have the woman's services in laying out poor little Maximus. It's acknowledged that the process is best done by female hands, and I did not doubt the woman's skill with herbs and cleansing rituals. And her presence was welcome for another reason, too. If the tanner's wife had seen her coming here, as I surmised, the news would swiftly spread – so much the better for the reputation of the shop. Potential customers would have no fear of coming here again once it was generally known that a proper herb woman had attended to the corpse and there was no risk of meeting any vengeful ghosts.

So I smiled at the councillor and was saying, 'I'm quite sure she . . .' when there was another tapping at the outside door.

'There you are,' Alfredus said, triumphantly. 'She said there'd be another visitor, and so there is.'

I desisted from reminding him that he himself had told her that the priest was on the way. Instead I ordered Minimus to go and let him in.

It was indeed the priest. He seemed to be an acolyte of Mars or Mercury, an aging man with skin as white as marble and as dry as bark-paper, framed by a fringe of thin white hair and eyebrows of a terrifying size. One of those supported by the temple, I presumed – too old and frail to officiate at public rites again for fear of making errors in the proper rituals, but still available for hire for private rites. He was accompanied by the little slave I'd seen with Alfredus Allius on the street.

The boy seemed ready to come into the room, but Alfredus ordered him to wait outside. 'There are too many people in here as it is,' he said, 'And until the rite is over, this is a house of death.'

The boy turned pale and hurried out again.

The priest inclined his head. 'I hope you will be good enough to spare him later on to guide me to the villa that I'm to deal with next.' His voice was high and piping like a child's, but he exuded a certain dignity.

'Of course!'

'I'll need his help to carry extra items for that ritual, as well. It will require more than the simple consecrated elements that I'm using here – salt and spelt and water – to pacify the *cultus geniali* after what happened at that unhappy house. The spirits of the family won't be pacified with less than the full ritual with oil, scent and smoke and the sacrifice of several doves, at least.' He pulled up his toga folds to form a hood. 'So there is much to do, and not much time to do it in. I believe you have the herbs that we require?'

'People are dealing with the body as we speak,' I said, fetching down the casket from its safe place on the shelf. I was in the act of handing it to him when the woman surprised us all by coming in again – alone – her bucket of equipment in her hand.

She saw the priest and gave an awkward bob, setting her rolls of flesh aquiver as she moved. 'I've finished with the body. You can get on with the room,' she boomed, without ado. 'I've left a slave and a young citizen in there – if you've got roast spelt and salt to purify the place, the citizen can help you scatter it, and the slave will help to sweep the floor clean afterwards. There's a broom of tied twigs hanging up behind the fire.' She turned to me. 'Your son has moved your chippings into neater piles, and put the ladder back where it belongs, so the ceremony should not disturb your working place too much.'

The priest looked quite shocked at the effrontery of this. Women were not expected to know how rituals were performed. But Alfredus Allius gave me a glance that said, 'What did I tell you? She thinks of everything!' as clearly as if he'd spoken the sentiment aloud.

I nodded. I was secretly impressed by her thoroughness, myself.

She turned to me. 'Your slave was not registered with the Slave Guild, I assume. Otherwise you would not have called on me. Which means that you are arranging the funeral yourself. If you wish to move the body, you may safely do so now. Where do you hope to take it?'

'To my roundhouse,' I told her. 'It is some miles away, but we have a mule outside. We'll carry him on that.' Maximus had ridden on Arlina many times – it seemed fitting that she should carry him on his last journey home.

She nodded. 'I see that you have wooden racks – to carry your pattern pieces on, your son declares. One of them would make a fitting bier – the body isn't large, and it would fit on your donkey easily enough.'

It was a good suggestion, though I hadn't thought of it – much better than having the poor boy dangling, as he would otherwise have done. 'Thank you,' I acknowledged.

She met my eyes again. 'And don't forget that you require a cleansing ritual too. Put out your hands and I'll pour water over them.' She lifted out the jug and suited the action to the words, murmuring some incantation which I could not hear. 'And then you can have a spring of rue to eat – that will cleanse you from the inside out. Open!' she said, as a mother feeds her child, and put the bitter-smelling herb into my mouth.

I chewed on it obediently, though it tasted sour and sharp.

'And don't forget your talisman. I've chosen this for you.' She reached into the inner recesses of her Grecian robe and pulled from somewhere between her massive breasts a thin plaited leather cord on which was suspended a crude miniature marble carving of an arm.

I could see no evidence of there being any 'choice' but since Alfredus Allius was providing this for me, it would have been bad-mannered to refuse. I took it from her with my still-dripping hands.

'Put it round your neck,' she boomed, imperious as a centurion rallying his men. 'And do not take it off until the slave is laid to rest.'

I did as she instructed, though I felt ridiculous. As I tucked it in my tunic, though, I glanced at the clenched fingers of the modelled hand – and realised why it counted as a talisman. 'Ah, that's clever,' I said, with admiring surprise. 'The edge of the fingers make the profile of a face.' It was crude, but quite effective. 'Is it Jove or Mars – or does it represent some local Celtic god?'

'It is whoever you expect to see,' she said unhelpfully. 'And may it guide you safely through the next few hours.'

This conversation was interrupted by the priest, who was clearly impatient of these rival rituals. 'Well, if you are going to move the body, citizen, I suggest you do it now – as soon as possible. I can't pretend that it won't make my job a great deal easier.'

'And if you're going into the town I'll come

267

with you, citizen,' the councillor chimed in. 'I'll pay the celebrants and after that I won't be needed here. It's time that I got back to my warehouse, anyway. I'll take Vesperion to accompany me, and leave my young attendant here to guide the priest. But won't you need to wait until the shop's been purified, so that you can lock it after you?'

I had thought of that. 'I'll leave my son,' I said. 'He has an errand to the east gate that he's going to run for me. He'll wait until rites are finished here and then he'll follow me. My living slave can help me, and I'll take my dead one home.'

Twenty-Four

It was no simple matter to arrange the bier, in the event, but with the aid of Minimus and Vesperion (who was released from his vigil to assist) I managed it. Minimus was almost overcome again at dealing with the body of his friend, but he put a brave expression on his little face and did his best to help, while the old steward's knowledge of transporting packages made him a very useful assistant in the task. So a little later we had Maximus arranged, decently swaddled in my toga winding-cloth and securely lying on the frame along Arlina's back.

I sent in for Alfredus Allius (who had by this time paid the celebrants their promised fees) and together we four set off towards the town, leaving the priest and Junio to complete the cleansing rites. As we were leaving, the herb woman waddled out, still carrying her pail.

I half expected her to want to walk with us – the Egidius house lay in our direction anyway and she would have had an escort for the best part of the way – but she'd obviously decided to accept the pageboy as a guide this time. She waved her bucket at us in farewell, lowered her enormous bulk onto my stockpiled stones, and began to ply him with stories of successful prophesies and ghosts she'd laid to rest. When I looked back from the corner of the road, she'd drawn a little audience of passers-by, including Festus and the tanner's wife, both of whom were listening open-mouthed.

I nodded, satisfied. The future of my shop was in no danger now – these tales of her expertise would spread across the town and do more to restore the confidence of potential customers than any cleansing rituals by the priest. I turned my attention to dealing with the mule.

Arlina did not seem to mind the strange contraption on her back. Indeed she moved quite willingly, without the need for me to use my switch at all. 'Almost as if she senses what she is carrying,' Minimus said, wistfully – though privately I suspected that this unusual obedience had more to do with her being accustomed to bearing panniers: her previous owner used to fit her with a pair to carry crops into the town for him to sell.

'I hope the soldier on watch will let us through the gate,' I said, as our little party plodded through the muddy streets towards the northern entrance to the town. 'And we're not delayed by a lot of questioning. The shadows are already lengthening. I want to be sure that we are home by dusk, and I don't want to take the long way round the outside of the walls.'

Alfredus Allius, who was picking up his feet and carefully lifting his mourning toga clear of mire, looked up anxiously. 'But I hope we're not caught up in the proclamation crowds. There may be a disturbance when the news about the Emperor is read, and the army won't be gentle if they have to curb the mob.'

270

But we need not have worried on either count, it seemed. It was clear that rumours of all kinds had been spreading faster than the plague through the suburb where the workshop was, and people were pouring out of every shop and alleyway and surging through the gate in the hope of getting to the forum to hear what this promised proclamation was about. There was no question of the soldier stopping them.

If we had not had Alfredus with us, in fact, we might have been caught up by the throng and simply swept along like sticks in the Sabrina when the tide-race runs. The councillor was not wearing his curial stripe, of course, but even his dark *toga pulla* was a distinctive one, marking him out as an important man, and people did their utmost not to jostle us. So with myself and Alfredus flanking Arlina at the front and our two servants doing the same thing at the back, we managed to transport Maximus with a little dignity.

Once beyond the forum, though, the problem was much eased. The crowd was thinner here in any case – there are not so many houses on this side of town – and now that we were moving against the human tide, people saw us coming and could step aside. A route through the back streets speeded us still more and it wasn't long before we found ourselves beside the garrison, close to the mansio and the south gate of the town – where I'd last parted company with Maximus, alive.

'I'll see you safely through the gate, and then I'll take my leave. Farewell, citizen. May your little servant rest in peace,' Alfredus murmured as we approached the gate.

I was about to thank the kindly councillor once more for his generosity, but a voice from the soldier at the gate interrupted my farewells. 'Citizen Libertus! So we meet again.'

I glanced towards the speaker, half expecting to see the bored sentry who had admitted us at noon, and who had been so amused by my descent from Arlina. But obviously the watch had changed and he had been long since relieved. The man on duty now was of a different build and as he stepped out of the shadows of the arch I realised who it was: none other than Villosus, of the hairy legs.

That was a relief. Villosus knew me and there would be no need for awkward questioning. In fact he'd been ordered to assist me if he could. I smiled at Alfredus. 'Thank you for being willing to speak up for me, but I know that soldier. There'll be no problem now.'

But I'd spoken prematurely. As I watched, another figure moved into the arch, and there, resplendent in his distinctive sideways crest, was the centurion I'd nicknamed Cerberus. He had a squad of half a dozen other soldiers with him too. They could be seen drawn up beyond the gate as if they'd just returned from some expedition under his command. He was uglier than ever. And he had clearly spotted me. He was talking to Villosus now and gesturing towards me with his baton as he spoke.

Alfredus Allius had been about to leave, but seeing what was happening he came back to me. 'There seems to be some difficulty, citizen.'

'There may be,' I murmured urgently. 'I've met that centurion before, as well, and he doesn't care for me. I think he might make trouble if he sees a chance. Perhaps, after all, you could come and speak to him. It may need your authority to make him let me through.'

At the prospect of a confrontation with an armed centurion, Alfredus looked unhappy – as anybody might – but he nodded pleasantly enough. 'If it involves the safe passage of your slave, of course I will. I wouldn't flout the wise woman's advice.' He touched his amulets.

So he was still hoping to avert bad luck by offering his help? I could only hope it worked. Things weren't looking very promising. Cerberus had stopped talking to Villosus by this time and stood to meet us, hands upon his hips.

Then, as we approached the gateway with the mule, he deliberately moved into the arch to block the way, his features wreathed in an unpleasant smile. 'Well, if it isn't that pesky so-called citizen. You turn up everywhere. What are you up to this time? Content to be in tradesman mode again, I see.'

I did not draw attention to where the toga was. If he saw how I had used it, I could expect a swingeing fine. I gritted my teeth into the semblance of a smile, and said, with what politeness I could summon up, 'Greetings, officer. Could you let us through? I have completed my business for the day in town and – as you see – I'm returning to my roundhouse with my slave.'

Cerberus gave Minimus a quick, incurious

273

glance. 'Ah, the little fellow who didn't get into the garrison with you!'

Minimus seemed about to answer, but I shook my head at him. I didn't want to correct the man's mistake about the slave. I didn't want him asking where the other one had gone and taking too much interest in the cargo on the cart. I tried to look as meek as possible and made no response at all.

Cerberus had clearly not expected that. Perhaps he'd hoped to goad me into some unwise retort. 'Well, I suppose we'd better let you pass – again! You're clearly on good terms with the current commandant. But don't expect such privilege to last. Things are going to be quite different around here very soon.'

Despite his words, he did not move a thumb's breadth from our path, and the threat – it clearly was one – was still hanging in the air. I was just debating what I was to do – we clearly could not stand there face-to-face for evermore – when Villosus left his post and came scurrying across.

'Greetings, citizen. I hope you succeeded with your business in the town.'

I had to think for a moment what he meant. 'Ah, the warehouse steward! That's him over there. And this citizen's his master. Thank you for your enquiry. I did get the information that I'd been looking for. Though it was not entirely conclusive, I'm afraid. All the same, please convey my thanks to your commander when you can.' This last was aimed at the centurion of course, who was openly listening to the interchange. I flashed Villosus a friendly, conspiratorial smile. 'And now I want to hurry home before the trouble starts.'

He looked from me to Cerberus as if considering if he ought to speak or not, but all at once he smiled and took a chance on it. 'Well, be very careful, citizen, that's all I can say. There has been a lot of trouble on this road today – rebels on the rampage by the look of it. They must have learned somehow that there'd been tragic news from Rome—'

'Soldier!' the centurion gave a warning bark. 'None of this information has been made public yet.'

'Oh, the citizen knows all about the Emperor, sir,' Hairy-Knees replied. 'The commander made that clear to me when I was ordered to assist.'

'Knows all about it, does he? I rather thought he did. It wouldn't surprise me if he knew a great deal else, as well.' Cerberus came forward and – rudely ignoring Alfredus Allius – stuck his chin an inch from mine. 'We've suddenly got rebel raids on travellers again today – quite a coincidence, wouldn't you agree? You'd almost think that someone had warned them that the troops were likely to be off the roads, and that the commander had other problems on his mind. Or perhaps it isn't a coincidence at all. What do you think, citizen? You come from this direction, you – and only you – appear to know the news from Rome, and you're a Celt yourself. You wouldn't know anything about this Druid raid, I suppose?'

'Druids?' Beside me, Alfredus Allius drew in a sharp breath. 'I thought the Silurians had finally been quelled.'

There had been trouble a year or two ago when bands of dissident Silurians – still resisting the presence of the Romans in the land – had roamed the neighbourhood, mounting raids on army transport and harrying patrols, though lately these attacks had largely ceased. The rebels had been driven back into their secret hideaways in dense areas of forest where there are wolves and bears and where ordinary people do not go – even woodcutters and charcoal burners rarely venture there.

'Not these rebels, citizen,' the centurion replied. 'And as to being Druids, there's no doubt of that. We've had a report of a brand-new sacred grove . . . stumbled on by children collecting kindling. There were none of the usual patrols today and the commander wasn't seeing visitors, so it took a little time for the news to reach us at the fort. But, of course, whatever problems there might be overseas, the army could not ignore a rebel raid. I was told to take a party and investigate at once.'

'And you discovered . . . what?' the councillor demanded. 'You have found the culprits?'

The centurion shook his head. 'No trace of them, I fear – though we'll catch them in the end. But the evidence is there. There's been a massacre. Killed the whole family, by the look of it – the males at any rate. Children too, it made no difference.' He squared up to me again. 'Doesn't it make you proud to be a Celt?'

I didn't answer him.

'No doubt we'll find another oak tree some-where else with all the female heads displayed

276

on it – unless they took the women off as slaves. We haven't found out who the family were, or what they were doing on the road, as yet, so we don't know how many people were involved. So if you've any information, tradesman-citizen, we'd be glad of it.' He was standing dangerously close to me again.

I should have stood my ground, but instead I took a few steps back and stared at him. 'A sacred grove? That means decapitated heads.'

'Perceptive of you, citizen,' he sneered.

But I was no longer listening. Heads. Of course! I hadn't looked for them. Dear gods! I must be getting old.

'How many heads?' I asked him. Why had I not asked myself that question earlier?

Cerberus looked astonished. 'About a dozen so far, I suppose. What difference does it make?' He turned to stare at me. 'You know something about this. I can see it in you face!' He seized me roughly by the arm. 'I knew that there was something about you which I didn't trust. Let's see what a little questioning—'

'Centurion! What are you thinking of? Release the citizen!' Alfredus Allius's monotone had taken on an unexpected ring. 'Whatever's happened, he is not involved in it. He's been in my company or my warehouse all the afternoon.'

Cerberus shook his head and gave his horrid grin, but he did release his grip. 'I'm sorry, councillor. That's no defence at all. No one suggested that the raid took place this afternoon. This morning, possibly. Certainly not very long ago.

277

I've seen a few dead people in my time, and these heads were fairly fresh. None of them had even started to decay.'

I think he hoped to shock me, but he did not succeed – after all, I'd seen the victims of the atrocity.

'I'm almost sure it happened yesterday,' I said. 'And I think that I can tell you where the matching bodies are . . .' I trailed off. *Matching bodies?* I was an idiot. There was only one reason for removing heads. What was it the wise woman had said? 'It is whatever you expect to see.' And I'd fallen straight into the trap!

Cerberus was smiling at me nastily. 'Perhaps you'd like to accompany me to the commander, then – and you can tell him who the victims are.'

I shook my head. 'He already knows. This is the very crime I came to warn him of – though at the time I didn't know about the heads. Ask him when you go in to report.'

The councillor was frowning at me, doubt-fully. 'You think the heads are from the villa slaves? I suppose it's possible. But why on earth remove them and hang them in a grove? To make it look like rebels . . .?' he broke off suddenly. 'By all the powers of Dis,' he cried. 'Perhaps it was the rebels! They would have seen Marcus as a special enemy – a wealthy Roman, friendly with the Emperor . . .' He put his hand up to his throat and clutched his amulets. 'And I'm a friend and dining-intimate of Marcus.' He stared at me, his toneless voice full of emotion, suddenly. 'Great gods, citizen – you think I might be next?'

I shook my head again. 'I don't think that these killers will strike round here again. I believe they have accomplished what they meant to do.' I turned to Cerberus. 'I didn't kill these people, officer, but I think I know who did – though I don't see how to prove it, even if I'm quick enough to find the murderers. So I daren't make accusations – I'll find myself in court, facing serious charges of *injuria*. But for the sake of my dead servant, I shall do my best – if you will permit me to be on my way. You can put that into your report as well. And earn yourself a commendation, too. Assure the commandant that no Celtic rebels are involved.'

Twenty-Five

For a fleeting moment Cerberus looked nonplussed. Then he gave a snorting laugh. 'You really expect that I will simply let you go, when by your own admission you know something of these deaths? You must be moon-struck, citizen. What do you think my superiors would say?'

Villosus cleared his throat. 'I don't think you should hold him, sir. My orders were quite clear. I was to assist him in any way I could, and I was to tell the other soldiers just the same. My understanding was that it applied to all of us, including – if you'll pardon me for saying so, sir – officers like yourself. I should not like to think that because I didn't speak, you'd accidently disobeyed the commandant.'

'I don't recall that I gave you leave to speak, Auxiliary!' Cerberus snapped, clearly furious, but unable to contest the truth of this. 'I'll have you on a charge as soon as you get back – insubordination to a senior officer. That should be a flogging at the least. And you . . .' he turned to face me '. . . you have leave to go, this time. But next time that I find you meddling . . .!' He left the threat unfinished 'Now, stand aside. You're blocking the road. Don't you know that it's illegal to impede the army on the march?'

It was totally unjust. The soldiers were not moving and if anyone was blocking the roadway, it was the centurion himself. But his little outburst had improved his self-esteem. He tucked his baton underneath his arm and swaggered off to organise his men.

I waited dutifully until they shuffled into line and marched with ringing hobnails through the gate and disappeared into the garrison. When they had gone, Villosus turned to me.

'Did I hear you say your slave was dead?' He was staring at Minimus as though the boy might somehow be a ghost. Indeed, I realised with a smile, that's what he was half ready to believe.

'Not that slave. There's a dead one, on the mule,' I said. 'I'm not sure how and why he died, but I suspect it is connected to these other deaths and he thought he was protecting me. So my first duty has to be to him. Much as I would like to go into the town and try and find the truth about these murderers, I must see he's taken home with dignity. If I had a faster carriage . . .'

'Do you wish me to hire a cart for you and speed the trip?' Alfredus was still standing at my side. 'Or Vesperion could take the mule for you, perhaps.'

I shook my head. 'It's getting far too late. By the time he reached the roundhouse it would be getting dark, and he's far too old to be benighted in the wood. And there's nowhere we could offer him hospitality. Maximus will lie in the slave hut overnight, and the other slaves will have to sleep in the main roundhouse with us, as it is. Besides, I wouldn't like a stranger to turn up at my door and have to tell my poor wife what had happened to the slave. I couldn't ask Minimus, he is far

281

too young – I'll simply have to take the body back myself.'

'You could leave it in my warehouse,' the councillor suggested.

It was a kind offer – and I did not turn it down at once. It would call for additional and expensive cleansing rituals, no doubt, given his current superstitious attitudes. Maximus would lie alone in a strange warehouse overnight, and the whole transport problem would arise again next day, but it would allow me to travel on the mule and have time for enquiries in town. So it offered a solution, of a kind.

I was still debating what to do when I heard a distant *tuba* sound. 'Great Mars,' I said. 'They'll be reading the proclamation in the forum very soon. I'll have to do some—'

'Father?' I was interrupted by a cheerful cry and looked up to see my son hurrying towards me down the main street of the town. 'What are you doing here?' he said, as he came up to us. He sounded out of breath. 'I thought you'd be halfway to the roundhouse by this time. I know the cleansing rituals did not take very long – especially after you two citizens had left – but I didn't expect to catch you up so easily.'

'I had a brush with that centurion again,' I said. 'He wouldn't let me through. But there have been developments. The army's found a dozen severed heads. They supposed it was rebels, but I'm certain that it's not.'

Junio thought about it. 'Marcus's slaves? Of course!' He frowned. 'But why on earth . . .?'

'It took me a moment to work that out myself,'

282

I said. 'Tomorrow we'll get Georgicus to collect the heads, and see. But I'm certain that we'll find that one of them's the missing gatekeeper.'

He stared at me. 'I'd forgotten about him. But . . .?'

'He was among the bodies all the time – though I didn't realise it,' I said. 'Funnily enough, it was the wise woman who gave me the idea. "It is whatever you expect to see" – that was the talisman.'

'I didn't see either gatekeeper.' Minimus had been listening to all this with interest.

Junio exchanged a glance with me. 'That's because we didn't let you look,' he said, and then to me, 'the front gatekeeper was hanging in his cell. Why was he killed by such a different method, do you think?'

'I have a theory about that,' I said. 'But there are other things I need to check on first. And fairly urgently – supposing that it's not too late by now. Would you be willing to take Arlina home, and tell your mother about Maximus for me? I would be happy leaving that with you and I'll try to be home myself as soon as possible, though if it gets too dark, I'll have to stay in Glevum.'

Junio pressed my arm. 'Of course I will – if you're sure there's nothing else that I can do in town.'

'Did you manage to get round to the gates and ask if they'd seen Cacus and his master leaving?' I enquired.

He shook his head. 'I didn't need to ask. I saw him for myself when I was on my way to ask

283

them at the Isca gate. It was difficult to hurry – everyone was pushing to the forum by that time – so I tried to take the shortcut by the docks. And there was Cacus, with his back to me, going into that taverna – you know the one I mean? One of the girls who works there sidled up to me, wanting to know if I was thirsty – though that wasn't what she meant. I said I wouldn't enter the premises tonight for all the world, because I'd just seen a giant walking in and she laughed and said, "His master's in there, too," so I gave her a quadrans and came to tell you. So there's your answer, Father. Commemoratus hasn't gone to Isca after all.'

'The docks, you say? So they intend to leave by water after all – in that empty little boat, no doubt. The captain said he'd lost a fare that he expected yesterday. I'm sure that was Commemoratus and his party only – because I happened to pass him on the road and thereby forced him to produce his alibi – they didn't leave as quickly as they'd intended to. Did Cacus see you?'

Junio shook his head. 'I don't think so, Father – and certainly Commemoratus can't have done.'

Alfredus Allius touched my tunic sleeve. 'Who's this Commemoratus, citizen? I've not heard of him. And what is this about? Is this connected with those murders we've been hearing of? If something's happening at the docks, perhaps I ought to know.'

'But surely you know Commemoratus, councillor?' Junio was surprised. 'He was at your warehouse just this afternoon, arranging to buy wine from you, I understand. Or perhaps you didn't meet him – Vesperion spoke to him.' He looked at the steward, who was standing at a respectful distance by the arch, still helping Minimus to hold the mule. 'Or so my father says.'

Vesperion saw that he was needed and shuffled up to us.

'I hear we had an enquiry for wine this afternoon,' his master said, severely. 'You didn't mention it.'

The steward looked contrite. 'I didn't want to bother you with time-wasters, master, when you were so concerned about this citizen's dead slave,' he said. 'But it's true there was a visitor – though nothing came of it. Wealthy fellow with a fancy cloak. I thought we'd get a handsome contract out of him, but he wasn't really interested in buying wine at all. He was very rude, saying one minute that he wouldn't do business with an underling, and then complaining when I wasn't at his beck and call. Then his servant came to get him and he went away without a word except to say he didn't like our wine, though we'd given him some of the best Rhenish we had in. I don't imagine he will call again – though I suppose he may come back and talk to you.'

'Then that must be the man you're looking for,' Alfredus said to me. 'And he's called Commemoratus, did you say? Funny sort of cognomen – I wonder where he's from.'

Vesperion frowned. 'That's not the name he gave me!' he exclaimed. 'I can't recall exactly. I didn't really bother in the end, when he obviously wasn't a proper customer, but I'm sure it wasn't that. It's some name I think I've vaguely heard before . . . Honorius Flavius . . . something?'

'Egidius?' I prompted.

The steward stared at me – and so did Junio. Then Vesperion spoke. 'Of course it was,' he murmured, sheepishly. 'Same name as the villa that Scipio man has bought – perhaps this chap's distantly related to the family. I should have noticed that. He rattled off his full three names, of course, and a couple of nicknames for good measure, too – though Commemoratus wasn't one of them. Perhaps that's why I didn't make the connection at the time. I'm sorry, master, if I should have taken better note.'

Alfredus was fingering his amulets again, but it was Junio who spoke. 'Commemoratus is Egidius?' he said. 'That isn't possible. The man's in lifetime exile, forbidden fire and water anywhere within the Roman Empire and liable to death if he is found within its bounds. He would not dare to come here and announce himself by name.'

'Unless he has a pardon, as I believe he has. In fact I heard his servant saying so. He produced that scroll that I was talking of, and said "your pardon, master". I thought it was an apology for interrupting us, but I now believe he meant exactly what he said. That was the pardon, under Imperial seal. The commandant told me that Pertinax had issued lots of them, even some that were not really justified.'

Junio was still looking unconvinced. 'But why would Egidius tell you he was called something else? If he'd been pardoned, surely, he has nothing more to fear?'

'He wanted to avoid me knowing who he was – though he'd already told Vesperion by that time, it seems. In fact, I think he came on purpose to identify himself. He wanted a witness who could prove that he was there. And then I came and spoiled all his plans. I noticed when I asked him for his name, he sent the steward out before he answered me. He gave me the nickname he'd adopted for himself: "the remembered one". It was a message to Marcus, which he knew I would pass on. In fact, he made a specific point of asking me to do so.'

Junio shook his head despairingly. 'But why? Even if everything you say is true, there can't be a connection with the murders and the theft. You said yourself that he had alibis. Egidius was not in Glevum till sunset yesterday. He had no opportunity to arrange the carts and guards, and didn't have the knowledge to make that inventory – and there are lots of witnesses to every part of that. And he was in the warehouse at the docks with you when Maximus was killed. He can't have been responsible for any of the crimes.'

'I know,' I assented. 'It's clever, isn't it? The ultimate vengeance on a magistrate. The man who hated Marcus for what he'd done to him – the ruin of his family and the loss of all he had, and years of miserable exile on an island in the sea – has witnesses to prove that he was somewhere else throughout. As of course, he genuinely was.'

'So it was not Egidius who did it?'

'Not that Egidius,' I said. 'He was an obvious suspect – that's why he took such pains to make

287

sure that his alibis were unshakeable. It was the other Egidius, of course. The younger brother that Marcus was employing as a scribe.'

'But we saw the body of the scribe . . .' Junio began, then tailed off in dismay. 'You mean it wasn't him at all?'

'He changed clothes with the dead back-gatekeeper, and I think he simply got into his brother's travelling coach and was driving off when I encountered them – leaving a headless body which seemed to be the scribe. It was clever, No one would look for the amanuensis after that, and once in town, he put a toga on. A simple but effective method of disguise, especially with lots of strangers in Glevum for the will.'

'But wasn't that a risk? Suppose that someone recognised his face?' Alfredus Allius asked.

I shook my head. 'That brother sold himself when he was very young – no one was likely to recognise him now. I was the only person likely to connect him with the house. I'd briefly glimpsed him there when he was copying the text. That's why they wanted to be rid of me.'

'What about Marcus's land-slaves? They would have seen him while he was working there.'

'They never leave the property, except Georgicus perhaps, and even he would not have known the amanuensis well. Besides, they thought that he was dead. If they were looking for anyone, it would be the gatekeeper! It isn't easy to persuade a witness that someone isn't dead when they are convinced they've seen the corpse. And I think that is why the other household slaves were massacred as well. One body without a head does not attract attention where there are a dozen others in the pile. But I'm sure we'll find the brothers are together now. So, if we've finished talking, it is time for you to take Maximus back home and I'll go and see if I can find our suspects before the gates are shut.'

But even as I spoke there was a clamour from the town.

Twenty-Six

As Junio turned to leave us, Alfredus tugged my sleeve again. 'Citizen,' he said, 'do you hear what I can hear? There's disturbance in the town. If you wish to catch these people you must go at once – and your son must have a proper cart to take the servant in so you can have the mule to ride home afterwards. Don't shake your head like that. I have an interest in solving this affair as well.' His flat tone made the statement a more surprising one. 'I've agreed today to underwrite a loan to Scipio for the purchase of the household items that I told you of. You know the law: "the buyer must beware". If, for some reason, the purchase of the Egidius house was not what it appears, he stands to lose a lot of money – some of which is mine. If I had not helped you with the transport of your slave, I could only blame my ill-luck on myself for not obeying what the wise-woman advised. Accept my offer and let me do this to propitiate the Fates.'

Put like that, I could not well refuse. 'In that case, thank you councillor,' I said.

'Vesperion!' Alfredus Allius was decisive now. 'Go to the hiring stables over there and arrange a cart. Have them bring it to the gateway here. The fastest one they've got. And a driver with it, as soon as possible. Tell them I will pay them twice the normal rate – double if they get it here before the tuba sounds again. Tell them to send help to load the bier onto the cart, and for good measure, they can take care of the mule until its owner comes to call for it.'

Vesperion looked startled, 'But the stable-owner—'

'Will do as he is asked for a curial magistrate,' Alfredus told him, flatly. 'And he will not try to cheat by asking an unreasonable sum. I can rely on my amulets for that.' He touched them as he spoke.

I only wished I had his confidence, though, truth to tell, my own had sparked a useful train of thought. 'Councillor, I can't express my thanks for what you've done. I won't forget it – but now I'll have to go. You can still hear the noises from the town. If this goes on, they'll put the soldiers in the street, and I won't be able to find the men that I am looking for.' I turned to Minimus. 'You'd better come with me. I know you'd rather ride with Maximus, but I may have need of you.'

Minimus abandoned the mule to Junio and came trotting obediently to my side, then calling a farewell to Villosus – who was at his post again – I began to hurry back towards the city and the docks.

'Don't go without me, citizen!' I turned to find Alfredus Allius hastening after me, rearranging his sombre toga into neater folds. 'Vesperion will catch us – he knows where we're going. He would be returning to the warehouse anyway.' He fell into step beside me as he spoke.

'You will accompany me?'

Alfredus looked surprised. 'Naturally, I'll come

291

with you, citizen. You may need witnesses and as a councillor I can call out the town watch if they're required. Anyway, as I say, I have an interest. And I am intrigued by what you say. I'd heard that you were clever, but I never dreamed of this. What made you so certain that the caller was Egidius?'

I made a rueful face. 'I didn't work it out until I'd heard about the heads – but looking back there were a lot of things which I should have noticed at the time. For one thing, there was the colour of his skin. I noticed it was reddened, but I did not think of sunshine as a cause for this. But if he was exiled on an island in the Inland Roman Sea, of course that would explain it perfectly. And he as good as told me that he had. He said he'd bought his servant as a boy "in one of the poorest islands of our sea". I thought he meant the waters round Britannia, but I should have realised. *Mare Nostra* – our sea – is what the Romans call it, and that's where Commodus always sent his exiles. No wonder Cacus has such golden skin.'

Alfredus nodded, not looking much impressed. 'This is the best way to the docks from here.' He led the way around the corner to the street which offered the most salubrious route down to the river quay. It was virtually deserted, the shops were closed and shuttered, entry doors were shut, and even the tavernas had no lamps alight inside. Our footsteps on the cobbles seemed unnaturally loud. It was positively eerie, the more so since – from the direction of the forum not very far away – there was now the muted but unmistakable roar of angry crowds. I glanced at Alfredus Allius but he seemed unconcerned.

'So it was Egidius himself who sold the villa, after all? I suppose it would have been restored to him when he was pardoned, since it had not been sold before.' I nodded 'And he shrewdly turned it into gold and silver straight away. I saw the bracelets on his arm.'

'I don't suppose he cared to live in the old house himself. But it's a legal sale.' He sounded much relieved.

'He wouldn't have the money to repair it anyway,' I said. 'He only gets the part of his fortune which remains, and there was not much of that. It was all forfeited to the Emperor. That's why one brother sold himself to slavery. And, of course, they blamed Marcus, who found against them in the courts.' I shook my head. 'I can't imagine why I didn't wonder more about the gatekeeper who wasn't there. But now I understand. They dressed him in the distinctive tunic the amanuensis wore – and you see what you expect to see, as your wise-woman said.'

The mention of the wise-woman caught his interest. 'And the fact that the amanuensis had access to the house . . .?'

'Of course, it made it easy for him to make the list. And he had constant access to Marcus's writing desk. No doubt he stole the seal-ring – or had a copy made – and he, of all people, could construct the messages purporting to instruct the staff to load the goods. And I'm sure we'll find he took the message to the land-slaves too – telling them to construct that useless woodpile and keeping them busy a long way from the house. Another forged letter which he could produce. Of course, they would believe that it was genuine.'

'And you think he killed the slaves?'

'Not personally, perhaps. He'd hired the thugs and carters – they may have done the job. It would not even be a very serious crime, if they thought they were working for the owner of the place. No doubt the carters thought the house was his – they don't ask questions, provided they get paid, and some of Marcus's treasure would have seen to that. He had a space under the pavement in his office-room, where he kept a money-box, and there was nothing in it when I was there today.'

We had reached the corner of the docks by now, and were about to turn onto the quay when the clatter of following footsteps stopped me in my tracks. In the unnatural silence of the empty streets the sound was ominous. I had not forgotten that my quarry was a murderer, and I pulled Minimus into the shadows of a portico with me.

Alfredus had more courage – or less imagination. He simply turned to face the follower. 'Vesperion!' I heard him cry. 'You almost frightened us. Did you manage the business with the cart?'

The poor old steward was completely out of breath, but he managed to convey that the arrangements had been made, the mule was in a stall, and Maximus was safely on his way. He mentioned a sum which took my breath away.

Alfredus merely nodded. 'I will see that it is done.' He turned to me. 'One more thing, citizen.

What happened to the treasure and the furniture the brothers stole?'

'I've been thinking about that. There's no sign of it in Glevum, so it didn't come this way. I fear that you may discover you've paid for it,' I said. 'I think you'll find it is the furniture that Scipio thinks he's bought – the things that were alleged to have been stored elsewhere – which I suppose, in a peculiar way, is true. I'm almost sure you'll find an elaborate travelling carriage in the stables too. They must have put it somewhere, and that's the likely place. And of course Egidius senior wanted me to think that he was going to drive away in it, though he didn't actually mention carriages. I think he takes a strange delight in saying things which are nothing but the truth – but which give the wrong impression to the listener. Look, here's the tavern – you can judge that for yourself.' And without waiting for an answer I led the way inside.

I don't care much for wine shops, and this one less than most. The floor was filthy and the wine vats, set into the counter, were rimed with sediment. One or two customers perched on wooden seats looked up blearily as we came in, but to my dismay there was no sign of anyone I recognised. But it was too late to escape. The owner, a toothless ancient with an aimless grim, came lurching over to accost us instantly.

'Can I assist you, gentlemen?'

'I was looking for a customer,' Alfredus rescued me. 'I missed him earlier. I believe he came in here. This citizen has seen him, and can describe him properly.'

'Fellow in a patrician toga, with an enormous slave,' I supplied, without much hope.

The owner drooped one rheumy eye into a wink. 'Busy at the moment upstairs, citizen. Which one were you after? The young one or the older gentleman?'

'They're both here?' I exclaimed. 'I was not expecting that.'

'Been here all the afternoon – young one first and then the other one. Hope they're going to pay the poor girls properly!'

I turned to Alfredus and Vesperion. 'You realise what this means? I knew that Cacus had been looking out of your warehouse window-space, but I didn't realise what he was looking for. Of course, they were waiting for the young one to get back – and no doubt he's the one that Junio saw with Cacus on the dock. That explains one mystery. I was sure that Commemoratus was the one who called at our workshop when Junio was there, but he insisted that he didn't recognise the man. Of course he didn't – it was the younger brother he glimpsed the second time.'

The taverna owner paid no attention to my words. 'Now, gentlemen, what can I offer you? It's been quite a day for us. We don't have a lot of patrician visitors, but suddenly today we've had a run of them. Watered wine, or ale, or our own special brew . . .?' He waved a hand at his disgusting wares.

Alfredus turned to me. 'I think that if the other men have gone upstairs, we ought to go ourselves. We don't want them realising that we're here, and dropping out of windows while we're loitering downstairs.'

'Upstairs, gentlemen?' The owner gave us a delighted leer. 'I'm not sure if there's space. Most of the rooms and girls are occupied. There's only Livia . . .' He put his fingers to his lips and gave a piercing whistle. There was a flurry on the staircase and Livia appeared – the plump and aging prostitute I'd noticed earlier. She'd taken off the toga and was wearing a stained tunic which did not enhance her charms. 'You've got a vacant cubicle?' he barked.

She was chewing on a stringy chicken bone, but she removed it from her mouth sufficiently to say, 'Only the small one this end left.'

'That will do nicely. We two will go upstairs and we'll leave the slaves down here to guard the door,' I told the astonished owner of the shop.

'Here!' he said loudly. 'Two of you at once? There's extra charge for that.'

'It's the room we're after, not your mangy girls,' I said. 'We'll go up there now. If there's any problem, call the watch at once.'

'Don' need the watch,' Livia said indistinctly, through a lump of chicken skin. She looked animated suddenly. 'I got my soldier up there, though he's half asleep. What's this all about?'

'We've come to get those purple-stripers who are here – they're thieves and murderers.'

She stuffed the nibbled chicken inside her tunic top. 'Blinking incomers – they think they own the place. Keep the proper customers away and won't give a girl a quadrans for her time. What's it worth to help you, citizen?'

I glanced at Alfredus Allius, who was looking dazed. 'A sestertius says you get me in the room with them, another sestertius if we get them under guard.'

'Done!' She spat on her two palms and offered them to me. I realised this was a kind of contract, so I did the same with mine. She squeezed my fingers briefly and then leaned forward as if we were the only people in the room, saying softly, 'It won't be difficult. They're in the big rooms round the corner at the back. They've sent the girls away into a single cubicle, and they're sitting together in the other one, whispering, while the big slave's standing in the doorway keeping watch. They think they can't be heard but . . . come with me.' She placed a chubby finger to her lips and led the way upstairs.

I was glad I'd not brought Minimus up here. It was a frowsty place, a row of little cubicles with ill-fitting doors with graphic illustration of the 'skills' available, and – judging by the one that Livia showed us to – nothing but a scruffy mattress and a bench within. Alfredus Allius had followed dutifully, but he was looking very uncomfortable indeed.

'The others are just like this – round the other side. But put your ear here . . .' Livia leant over against the wooden inner wall, as if to demonstrate.

I did as I was told. I could hear a muffled mumbling, but that was all. Any hopes of trapping the Egidius brothers in this way disappeared as quickly as they'd come. Alfredus Allius came to take my place, and then disaster struck. The

298

bench-bed buckled and he tumbled to the floor, taking the outer door with him. He landed in the narrow passageway with a crash and an oath that rang across the dock.

The result was instant. I rushed out to help him, but he'd disturbed the house. There were shrieks and cries, and frightened faces peered from every door. The owner was already charging up the stairs and round the far corner came an enormous form. Cacus was standing on the landing watching me.

'Great Dis,' I heard him murmur. 'It's that citizen again.'

'What is it, Cacus?' It was Commemoratus, in his fancy cloak – utterly incongruous in this shabby place.

'It's Libertus, master. He must have followed us.'

'Nonsense, Cacus. We saw him leave the quay.' Commemoratus pushed the slave aside. 'Dear Mercury, you're right! It *is* the citizen. What are you doing here?'

'Looking for the Egidius brothers,' I said, evenly. 'To accuse them of theft and of murdering several slaves they did not own. I've brought a curial magistrate to witness it.' I gestured to the shadows at my feet, where Alfredus Allius was picking himself slowly from the floor.

Behind Commemoratus another man appeared. In this light it was difficult to see, but he was clearly younger – and as Festus had declared – his skin was pasty white. And he was burly – almost big enough to be a gatekeeper. But the wise woman was right – in his striped toga and elaborate cloak I would never have recognised the hunched amanuensis that I'd seen at work.

'Citizen Libertus!' His voice was dangerous. 'I told my brother we should have killed you straight away. I've heard so much about you from your patron that I knew at once that you were dangerous. If we'd only run you over when we met you on the lane . . . But my brother wasn't sure that it was you at all.'

'And you did not want to draw attention to yourselves by leaving corpses on the road,' I said. 'Your intention was to disappear. No one was ever going to look for you – you were supposed to be among the dead. And you almost got away with it. If I hadn't happened by, it would have been tonight, at least, before the bodies of the slaves were found. And no one would make a connection with a Druid grove.' I saw a flicker of surprise. 'Of course, you did not know that some children found your so-called sacred oak while they were collecting firewood today. Unfortunate for you. You must have hoped that by the time the heads were found they would be so decayed that nobody would recognise the features anyway. As it is . . .'

'I told you we should have burnt those stupid heads.' Commemoratus turned on his brother angrily.

'And I told you to bring Libertus back out to our own villa where we could dispose of him. I knew he would bring trouble if we let him live.'

'I did my best. I couldn't help it if he wasn't at his workshop when I called. And you did no better – you went to find him afterwards, and all you did was kill a slave!'

I felt myself go pale. 'It was you who killed him! And now I've proof of it! Your brother has admitted it in front of witnesses.'

The huge form of Cacus detached itself from the surrounding shadows. 'What witnesses are these? Who do you think is going to live to tell the tale? Don't stop me, master – this is the only way. It was such a perfect plan. By the time the deeds were known you would be far away – and we made sure you had an alibi for every incident. Whatever people thought, there was not the slightest proof. And no one knew your brother was involved – the amanuensis was dead, apparently. You had got the gold and we would all have got away – even selling Marcus's own treasures with the house. It was perfect vengeance for what they did to you.'

'No vengeance is enough. Justice would never bring my other brother back,' his owner said.

'So you devised a symbolic vengeance of your own – by hanging that poor gatekeeper?' I said. 'Hanging, as your brother had once hanged, in the front entrance to your own house – is that right?'

'You may be clever,' the younger brother cried. 'But that won't save you now. Let me have this one, Cacus – you can kill the rest – but I'll slit his throat with that same knife his servant tried to use on me. On me!!! Because I asked him what his master knew – and then he wouldn't tell me, though I shook him till his teeth were rattling in his silly little head. Even then he got away and went up the ladder like the fool he was – and after that it wasn't difficult.' He laughed, a crazy laugh that made my blood run cold. 'And now we'll see his master follow him.'

He made a lunge towards me and I saw the knife blade gleam. He was a big man, big enough to change clothes with a gatekeeper – far too big for me to stand a chance. I closed my eyes and tried, as a last resort, to decide which way to jump. There was a sudden rushing from between my legs, and I sat down heavily just in time to see a small form hurtle at my assailant's knees. They buckled under him, and the man came tumbling down on top of me. I just had time to grasp his arm and force the knife away – and realise that the blood that covered me was not my own at all.

I rolled aside and let the body tumble down the stairs. It made a dreadful noise and a still more dreadful mess. I heard the taverna owner shrieking in the street, 'Send for the town watch! The army! Anyone!'

I looked up, expecting to find an angry Cacus bearing down on me. But to my surprise the slave was backing off. The scruffy-looking soldier that I'd seen on the quay was holding Commemoratus in a practised lock with a drawn dagger pointed at his throat.

'One move from you and the patrician's dead,' he snarled. Cacus looked uncertain. It seemed ridiculous. He could have smashed the soldier with a single blow – but his master would have died, and some ancient loyalty prevented him.

'Take that, you horrible great man!' That was

Livia, furnished with the plank of broken wood. She raised it high and brought it down with force – not on the giant's head, but on his crotch. Cacus doubled up and moaned in pain.

After that, things seemed to happen all at once. Several of the customers who had been watching this – not certain what was happening, but happy to join in – overpowered Cacus and bound him with a chain. Then, summoned by the shrieking, the town watch arrived, and shortly afterwards two soldiers hurried in, demanding to know what the disturbance was.

Alfredus Allius – who had hobbled to safety in the cubicle – reappeared and ordered the arrest of the Egidius brothers and their slave. He would personally bring a case against them in the courts, citing the crimes of theft and unlawful servicide – for both of which there were substantial fines – and wearing a patrician toga without entitlement. The amanuensis, as he afterwards explained to me, had sold himself to slavery and not bought his freedom back – obviously, since he was apparently a corpse – and therefore had forfeited the right to Roman dress. For a slave to wear a toga was a capital offence.

It wasn't important. The erstwhile amenuensis slave was dead and the knife that had killed him was my patron's own. It had been stolen from my workshop after Maximus was killed – for wielding that same knife in my defence. I had the concrete proof that I'd been looking for that the younger brother had been the killer of my slave. Between them, the watch and soldiers took the body off, and marched the others off to custody,

When they had gone, the girls came creeping down – including Livia. I slipped her the coins I had promised her. 'It's thanks to you I found them here at all. You told my son that Cacus and his master were inside.'

She shook her head. 'I said, "You'll find Cacus and his masters in there" – meaning both of them. Your son misunderstood. But everybody in the house knows what has happened now, and several of the "customers" will bear witness to the facts if you've a few more spare sesterces to encourage them!'

I nodded. 'That could be arranged. And here's another coin for you if you'll take a message for me to an apartment in the town. It's over the wine shop near the public baths – the biggest apartment, anyone will know it. Tell the slaves their mistress will be returning soon, and I'll send a more detailed message later on.'

She tried the coin with her teeth and, satisfied, she hurried off with it and the taverna owner and his slaves began to clear up the blood. Alfredus was still talking to a member of the watch, who had stopped to take a statement and preferred the councillor. He was talking animatedly about the trouble in the town and how the soldiers subdued the crowd and were guarding every street.

I sighed. I clearly wasn't needed here. I called to Minimus, who was winded but otherwise unhurt, and with the aid of old Vesperion I got him to the gate, put him on the mule in front of me again, and took him slowly home through the encroaching dark.

Epilogue

We cremated little Maximus next day, and I gave him a simple funeral, burying his ashes by the enclosure fence. It was a small affair compared to the enormous pyre which Georgicus had made next door for the Funeral Guild to use and which filled the air with acrid smoke for several hours. I did succeed in sending word to him in time and the heads were added to the fire before it died, so Marcus's household had as good a funeral as could have been arranged.

I did not attend the trial of Egidius, though I was willing to – Alfredus, as a curial magistrate, was a more impressive witness than I could have been, and he had a financial stake in the affair. The outcome was predictable, of course. Egidius was exiled again for having planned my death and arranged the robbery, and his goods were confiscated to pay the fines and compensation that he owed. I don't know what became of Cacus – he would have had a less official trial. The tanner's wife tells me that they sent him to the mines instead of executing him, on the grounds that he was following his master's orders all the time.

A little of the fine-money should have come to me in compensation for the loss of Maximus, but Julia – who had received my courier in time – offered to provide another slave instead, and leave

305

it to Marcus to meet the bill for it when he returns (which won't be very long: he's sent word that he's already on his way). It was the least that she could do to repay me for my help, she told me warmly when she and her children did arrive in town. Marcus would want to reward me much more handsomely, she thought (though I was less convinced) but in the meantime I could have the choice of any slave available.

Naturally I selected Tenuis. He knew nothing of the duties of a household slave, but he is young enough to learn and pathetically grateful that I've chosen him. He's only been with me half a moon or so, but he's already filling out now that he is getting sufficient food to eat, and he's promising to be a sturdy little chap and helpful with the chores. Soon I'll have to teach him how to help me dress. Minimus liked him from the start, and Gwellia – though she grumbles at his childish carelessness – is growing fond of him.

But soon I may be able to buy her another slave as well – for her own personal use. My peculiar talisman may have brought me luck. Alfredus Allius is convinced of it. I had a meeting with him and Scipio only yesterday. The court held that the purchase of the Egidius house was still a valid one. The formal contract that Egidius had sworn so publicly could not be overturned, and though the furniture and Marcus's effects were returned to their rightful owner without recompense, the house (together with the travelling carriage) is Scipio's.

He's had the wise woman and the priest to cleanse the villa of its ghosts and offered me a contract to replace the floors. The fee will keep my little family for a year or more, so – despite the troubles which rocked the Empire on that fateful day – I, at least, have some small cause to celebrate.